STZ

STZ

Andrew Nienaber

POST MORTEM PRESS
CINCINNATI

Post Mortem Press Cincinnati, OH

www.postmortem-press.com

.

FIRST EDITION

Printed in the United States of America

ISBN: 9780692021866

Library of Congress Control Number: 2014906680

For Liam Roche, who came to me one day and said
"I want to make a movie called *STZ: Sexually Transmitted
Zombism.* Write that for me."

This right here? This is your fault, my man.

"They say sex will keep you young and make you older at the same time.
They say sex will have left you aged normally.
And so I guess it's sorta like smoking and walking at the same time,
In that it will have left you aged normally."

-WHY? "Into the Shadows of My Embrace"

Prologue - Cassie Yearwood

Cassie's vacation was marvelous.

Barbados was every bit as beautiful as she'd heard. The food was exotic and delicious—she'd only eaten at McDonald's twice, and after discovering that the local food would neither kill her nor give her diarrhea she put the thought of cheeseburgers behind her for the rest of the trip—and the clothing-optional beaches afforded her an opportunity that she had never had back in Idaho to rid herself of tan lines.

And the men…dear god, the men.

Cassie was what she and the rest of middle America considered a "good girl" at home, but her friend Joanne had encouraged her to loosen up a bit on vacation. Joanne's advice was rarely good—she was notoriously easy, and while Cassie certainly wasn't as prudish as the rest of their small hometown, she didn't always approve of Joanne's choices. On the other hand, she figured, what happened in the Caribbean…

Her first afternoon was spent wandering the touristy areas, buying trinkets made from seashells and drinking fruity cocktails with umbrellas. That evening, after having three high-test beverages served in coconut shells, she found herself back in her hotel room with the bartender. She liked his accent, and his huge hands. She was nervous and awkward, but he was so confident and—and she never, *ever* thought this would turn her on— domineering that she melted in his arms, doing things for a stranger that she had never done for any of her long-term boyfriends. When she woke up the next morning, she felt reborn, a phoenix consumed in the flames of a raucous night of raunchy anonymous sex and reconstituted in the light of dawn.

After that, her sex life on the island was active and varied. Lacking the money for one of the posh all-inclusive resorts, she spent the bulk of her time on the public beaches of Bridgetown, her blonde hair and not-yet-fully-recovered-from-the-Idaho-winter pale skin making her stand out from the crowd. She couldn't spend an afternoon sunning herself without ten different locals catcalling her and inviting her back to their sumptuous beach houses, thoroughly average apartments, or tiny one-room fishing shacks. And she had no compunction about taking them up on their offers. She was not shy about her looks; back home she was everyone's sweetheart, but they knew her as little Cassie who went to the reservations on missions for the Methodist Council of Idaho, or the girl who was too busy with her studies to really take an interest in boys, which was all more or less true. Though she had not come to Barbados a virgin, she had always been extremely selective with her sexuality.

But here in this tropical wonderland, with the sun baking her usually porcelain-pale skin to a slightly less pale taupe and drinks with rum and fruit juice in them everywhere she looked, Cassie Yearwood had turned into a voracious humping machine. There was something about the atmosphere here that got her motor revving and she had no reason not to drive it full throttle.

Aside from the persistent itch of the bug bite on her lower thigh (she thought she had gotten it on one of her romps—maybe the guy with the enormous hands and the Sunsplash poster on his wall...Jacques, was it?) that would not go away, she had had the best week of her life. She felt a slight twinge of guilt about letting her libido run wild on a trip her father had paid for as a gift to honor her graduation from Harrison Community College--Daddy would definitely NOT have approved of her behavior, especially with *negroes*—but she was a grown woman now, tasting everything the world had to offer. Aside from a class trip to Boise when she was in high school band, she'd never been outside rural Idaho, and now she never wanted to go back.

But, sadly, her time here was at an end. As she sat in the airport waiting for her row to be called to board, absently scratching at the small welt on her thigh and reading a two-month-old issue of *Cosmopolitan*, she began to formulate her escape plan. She had majored in French thinking that it might help her get away from Idaho—maybe she would be a translator for the United Nations, or perhaps she could teach English in a school somewhere in Provence—and this trip was the final stitch in her resolve. As soon as she got home, she would put in an application for graduate school somewhere exotic like Minneapolis or, why not, Chicago. The world—or at least the Midwest—was her oyster.

The flight to Miami was uneventful. There was a screaming baby somewhere in the back that fell asleep an hour and a half in then woke up every twenty minutes for the rest of the trip, but Cassie never minded that. Chastising a baby for crying, she figured, was like chastising the ocean for being moist. She read her magazine (clucking her tongue at the article about a bitchy reality star who supposedly found a missing, abused child and paying special attention to the half-dozen articles about new things to try in bed, now that she was so *liberated*), occasionally napped, and stared longingly out the window at the Caribbean.

Her layover in Miami was brief, and she would have given anything to get outside that nightmarish airport and see the city. Flying over all those palm trees, swimming pools and pastel-hued buildings that she could only assume were hip, sexy nightclubs full of people dancing to the latest computer-generated music, sweating profusely in the stifling heat and humidity, and dry-humping each other in public, she longed to be a part of such a magical metropolis. As she boarded the flight to Spokane, she fantasized about driving a Mustang convertible through the streets of South Beach, the salty wind tossing her blonde hair and the nice sodomites holding hands on the sidewalk waving at her.

She had to get out of Fulton Flats by any means necessary.

After the long flight to Spokane, there was a small commuter hop to Moscow, where her parents met her at the airport for the four-hour drive back home. They cooed over her tan and asked endless questions about her adventures. She gave them the answers that they wanted to hear: that she had been hiking and swimming, tasting the local cuisine and snorkeling in the crystal blue waters of the Caribbean. She left out the two dozen or so men she'd slept with, some two at a time. Mother and Father, good Methodists and small town folk that they were, wouldn't understand the effect an island vacation can have on a young woman.

For their part, her parents updated her on all of the happenings in town since she'd left, which, even for a flyspeck town like

Fulton, was admittedly not much. Shelly Macavoy had finally had her baby, which was due three weeks ago, and it was, like its father, a huge, round, pink, mewling mass of blubber. The elementary school musical had been a huge success. Most people who attended said that they had never seen a better version of *The House at Pooh Corner.* Most exciting, though, was the fire. A few days ago, a forest fire had broken out in the hills west of town and, because of a dry winter and the windy conditions that had made Cassie's landing in Moscow such a white-knuckle affair, was beginning to burn out of control. Authorities thought it might have been a campfire that wasn't adequately extinguished, but since the area around where the fire started was currently a blazing inferno, they hadn't yet had a chance to fully investigate. The timber farms to the north weren't threatened yet, but since the forestry service was saying the blaze was only about five percent controlled at the moment, everyone was living on pins and burning pine needles.

A heavy, choking sense of despair overcame Cassie as they passed the sign welcoming whomever might be lost enough to stumble this far away from civilization to Fulton Flats. She felt the weight of the town and its nine hundred residents like a bear sitting on her chest.

That night, as she settled in to bed, the calamine lotion flaking off her bug bite like a gentle pink snow shower, she began coughing for the first time.

It started as an irritating, persistent tickle in her throat, but throughout the sleepless night it worked its way into a full-blown rattling cacophony. She could barely catch her breath by morning, and to make matters worse she was developing a pretty serious fever. Soaked in sweat and racked with an ever-worsening cough, she called Doctor Jeritt to set up an appointment.

Doctor Jeritt was the town's only physician, and also served as pharmacist, midwife, and occasional psychiatrist in the absence of any other such medical professional. There wasn't an opening until the following morning, so Cassie settled in on the couch in her parents' den and dozed on and off while the television droned out endless daytime court shows, punctuated with by-the-minute fire reports, her laptop open to the admissions pages of several of the Midwest's finest mid-grade graduate schools.

She awoke to her mother shaking her. Evening had fallen, and the den was dark. Mother had a worried look on her face and urged Cassie to sit up and take some Robitussin. Cassie hacked for a few minutes, then used the lull between coughs to choke down the foul-tasting medicine. The Vicks Corporation claimed that the swill was cherry-flavored. The Vicks Corporation were goddamned liars, but she figured that "Floor Cleaner Infused With Elephant's Asshole" flavor wouldn't sell many bottles.

Mother put a thermometer in her mouth and when she withdrew it, both women were startled by the reading. 127 degrees could not possibly be right. They set the device aside and waited for it to zero out so they could try again.

After the third attempt came back with the same reading, Mother called Doctor Jeritt and told him it was an emergency. The office was closed, of course, it being after nine in the evening, but Doctor Jeritt was always available for house calls in dire situations such as this.

As Cassie waited for the doctor, she tried to drink down the glass of water Mother had brought her. She felt as though she was being burned from the inside out, and no amount of ice held to her temple could cool her off. She felt hot in an entirely separate way too, a way she was not eager to explain to her mother. Every time Mom left the room, Cassie's hand wandered down between her thighs. She could not get the images of all the men she'd known on vacation out of her mind. Their bodies, their smell, the big, dangling slabs that hung between their legs – she would blush if she weren't already scarlet from the fever. To use a word that good, Methodist, bookish Cassie Yearwood would never have uttered a week ago, she was horny. Extremely horny. In fact, she thought, she was extremely *fucking* horny. No sooner did the f-word cross her mind but she immediately sought the Lord's forgiveness. What was wrong with her?

Doctor Jeritt arrived around nine-thirty, and by then Cassie was a complete mess. Her pajama shirt was soaked through with sweat and the bottoms were soaked through as well, though she alone knew that had nothing to do with the heat. The Doctor helped Cassie up and walked her into her bedroom. The touch of his arm around the back of her shoulder was driving her insane.

She'd never noticed before how attractive the octogenarian doctor was. He had a thick shock of grey hair and a neatly trimmed beard, and the wrinkles around his eyes and cheeks made him look extremely distinguished.

She took a deep breath to steady herself and her knees buckled as she caught a whiff of him, English Leather cologne and a slight sour note of the day's sweat. It made her mouth water. As he was helping her lay down on the bed, she intentionally shifted her weight so that his hand dragged over her breast, his fingers accidentally raking over her diamond-hard nipple. She moaned loudly. The doctor apologized profusely and when Mother came to see what the problem was he explained that he had handled her harder than he intended to. Cassie wondered if that was a Freudian slip.

Doctor Jeritt took her pulse and her blood pressure, looked in her ears and eyes, then put an old-style mercury thermometer in her mouth. Cassie looked up into his eyes as she ran her tongue over the tip of the gauge, but he didn't seem to notice at all. When he withdrew it, it confirmed yet again that her temperature was over a hundred and twenty-five degrees.

"That's not possible," the doctor said, staring at the thermometer with his eyebrows furrowed. "That kind of fever should have killed you."

Cassie shrugged. "I can't help it, Doc. You make me hot." She immediately clamped her mouth shut and looked away, praying that he hadn't heard. She absolutely could not believe she had just said that.

"Cassie, I think you're delirious. Can you tell me where you are?"

"I'm right where I want to be. In bed with an older man." Objectively, she knew she should be ashamed of such a frank outburst. But she didn't care anymore. She wanted him. Wanted his tough, experienced hands on her. Wanted his cock inside her dripping—

…Wait, did I just think the word "cock"? That's new.

Jeritt looked worried now. "Cassie, tell me about your trip. Did you eat anything strange? Did you drink the water? Any insect bites?"

"I never drank the water, but I ate all sorts of strange things. *All sorts.* Oh, and I got this bug bite." She looked into his eyes and slowly peeled down her sodden pajama pants, exposing the smooth, shiny skin of her cleanly waxed mound to the doctor, then rolled over on her side to give him a look at her bug bite and, incidentally, a clear view of her naked rear.

"Do you mind if I touch it?" the doctor said cautiously.

"God, I wish you would," Cassie replied.

When she looked down at his hands gingerly reaching toward her thigh, she noticed that the bug bite had swelled to an enormous size, nearly as big as her fist. It was a livid, angry red and almost looked to be pulsing.

"Good lord, what did this to you?"

"I don't know, I got it during one of my…" Cassie breathed slowly. "…workouts."

Doctor Jeritt fished in his black doctor's bag and pulled out a small scalpel and a wad of cotton. "I'm going to try to lance this to relieve the pressure. You might feel a slight pinch." He put the tip of the scalpel to the inflamed skin on her thigh and pushed it gently in.

Cassie groaned. The pain was—and she could think of no other word for it no matter how hard she tried—delicious. She squeezed her thighs together as he cut, and as pus began to gush from the bite, other fluids began to gush from between her legs. Her moans brought her mother to the door in a tizzy, but the doctor, mopping up the mess on her leg with the cotton, assured her that he was just opening an infected bug bite. Mother, satisfied but still visibly worried, went back to the kitchen and whatever mundane, meaningless task she had been working on. Father, in typical fashion, had not shown his face at all during Cassie's ordeal.

When the cyst had completely wept out, Doctor Jeritt wrapped it in gauze. His hands on her thigh sent Cassie whirling into another involuntary orgasm. She buried her face in the pillow to mask her whimpers, but the doctor didn't even seem to notice. He rolled her gently onto her back and pulled a chair up next to the bed.

"Cassie, this bite was very seriously infected. Are you sure you don't know where you got it?"

The room was spinning around her. She worried that the heat coming off of her skin would ignite the bed linens at any second. She looked up into Doctor Jeritt's wrinkled, leathery face. "I got it fucking an island boy in his tin shack near the beach."

She had not intended this much candor, but she found that she couldn't stop her mouth, anymore.

"I beg your pardon?"

"Lean in…please…I have something I must tell you, but I don't want Mother to hear." He leaned down. "Closer…I need to whisper it in your ear." The doctor looked slightly put out, but he bent down and put his ear by her mouth. She could feel his breath on the burning skin of her chest. "Doctor," she whispered in his ear, "I want your big, throbbing co-"

Cassie coughed. Hard. Flecks of mucous and blood spattered the side of Doctor Jeritt's face as he pulled away. And she kept coughing, her body shaking violently with the force of it. Her eyes opened wide as she gasped for air. Her sheets were spatter-painted with blood.

The doctor, in the relaxed panic of those skilled in his profession, tried to hold her to the bed to stop the convulsions. His hands on her were driving her crazy with lust, even though she couldn't breathe. She never dreamed she could be so turned on by being choked, especially by her own phlegm. A new world of sexual possibilities opened to her, and the seismic orgasm building inside her—who would have thought she could come so many times in quick succession?—produced moans and screams of pleasure that fought through her rapidly closing throat and escaped as burbles and squeaks.

No longer caring what Dr. Jerrit or her mother or anyone else in this stifling little town thought of her, she slipped her fingers inside herself, clawing at the swollen patch on the front of her uterine wall like a riled tiger fighting to escape its cage. She was literally drowning in her ecstasy, her vision blurring then slowly blacking out as she bucked her hips.

She tasted blood in her mouth, realized that she'd bitten her tongue in her excitement, and was flooded with the hunger she'd felt before. She was just turning her head to look for any piece of warm meat she could sink her teeth into, when the climax hit. She tried to draw a breath, but her throat was entirely blocked now, not even allowing the coughing that had sent her into this spiral in the first place. She closed her eyes and let the orgasm wash over her, her fingernails pulling away shreds of soft flesh as they raged inside her.

This was everything she'd never known sex could be: urgent, violent, bloodthirsty. She would never be the same. Good, studious, bookish Cassie Yearwood was burned away in the conflagration that was consuming her body. She would never be confined to quiet, whimpering missionary sex again. From now on, she was going to let her body be torn apart, let her appetites rule her, let—

Her limbs began to flail wildly as she seized. Mother came rushing to her bedside, tears streaming down her face, and the sight of her pink, liver-spotted hands made Cassie hungry. She gnashed her teeth as her body began to shut down. Just another inch and she would have the loose skin of mother's arm in her mouth. Just another inch…

Cassie's entire body gave one last enormous, heaving spasm and then she was still. As she faded from consciousness she was dimly aware of her mother's sobs and Doctor Jeritt's pleas for her to hold on a little longer. And, of course, of her burning need to really get bent over and fucked good.

The Corner Diner

The Corner Diner was an institution in Fulton Flats. It was, in fact, the only diner in town. Sure, there were a handful of fast food restaurants by the interstate if you were willing to drive the half hour to Denville, and The Rusty Bucket Saloon served burgers and fries, but you had to be 21 to get in there, and they were relatively strict about checking IDs for a small-town bar. So for families looking for a night out and teenagers escaping from home for a few hours, The Corner Diner was pretty much the only option.

It was a small, ten-table sort of place with black-vinyl-upholstered stools bolted into the floor at the counter and those big glass sugar containers in each booth. The waitresses (and they were, of course, all women—no self-respecting man in Fulton Flats would stoop to working in foodservice when there were farms and timber lots to be run) all wore their hair in nets and sported pink aprons. There was a machine for making milkshakes, and the wallpaper was stained yellow with nicotine – the smoking bans the rest of the country were so hot about had not yet reached northeastern Idaho. You never wanted to order fish on the weekends, but the patty melt was always good and they cooked their French fries in lard like God intended. There were pies sitting in a glass case that would make Paula Deen weep butter tears with envy.

Clayton Barre and Jerry Stone sat in one of the booths, listlessly pushing bits of those heavenly pies around their plates with their forks.

"Ok, it's gonna sound weird, but her eyes," Jerry said as a shaving of chocolate fell off of the immaculately sculpted whipped cream that topped his chocolate silk pie and plopped to the table. He licked his fingertip and picked it up, then stared at it for a moment as if he'd never seen chocolate before in his life.

"Oh bullshit," Clayton said. "Whaddaya mean, 'her eyes'?"

"Well, she had these…her eyes was so big and blue. Every

time I tried to talk to her, I just stuttered like a goddamned fool."
He sucked the chocolate off of his finger and went back to fiddling
with his food.

"You're a goddamned—" Clayton accentuated with his fork.
"Are you gonna sit here and look me in the face and tell me your
favorite part of Cassie Yearwood was her *eyes*? Son, you are either
lying to me or you're queer as a three-dollar bill."

"Fuck you, Clay." Jerry began mashing a bit of piecrust into
dust with his fork. "What was your favorite part, then?"

"Not even a question: her belly. Did you see, when she'd go
joggin', how her belly was all flat n' perfect? You could bounce a
goddamned quarter off her abs. And not all muscley and gross like
a bodybuilder, just…I don't know…*tight*."

"Her belly? You're giving me shit for liking her eyes and
you're all bonered up for her *belly*?"

Clayton leaned in closer. "Plus, if you was staring at her belly,
it wasn't far to go to get an eyeful of them gorgeous tits of hers."
Both boys laughed.

"You're dead right on that one," Jerry said. "Nobody in this
town has tits like Cassie's. Just perfect and bouncy and—"

"Not too big, but not too little, either. Like two squishy,
beautiful grapefruits. God, how I'd a loved to—" He cut short as
his mother Myrna walked up to the booth. She glared at the two,
then leaned in and half-whispered with a stern, steely look on her
face.

"You boys ought to have a little more respect," she said,
adjusting her bun and tugging her pink apron straight. "That girl
was an angel sent down from heaven, and it's a fright how she
passed. Let that be a lesson to us all: God does not want us going
to those heathen islands. He wants us to stay right here in his
chosen nation."

She jabbed a finger at each in turn. "And you best watch that
language, too. This is a family establishment. Now are you gonna
finish up those desserts? There are starving children on some
heathen island somewhere that would kill for a slice of our pie."

"Sorry, Mom." Both boys forked pie into their mouths, which

earned them a satisfied nod from Myrna.

"We were just reminiscing, is all," said Jerry, specks of crust spraying from his lips. "Cassie was our friend and we miss her something awful."

"Well, I know how sweet you all were on her. I could have sworn she would have made one of you boys a fine wife some day." Myrna ruffled both men's hair. "Clay, honey, how's that work search coming?"

"I'm lookin', ma. Not much around here at the moment. I might have to go put in an application at the Arby's over by the freeway."

Myrna gave him a withering look. "No son of mine is going to sling rubbery roast beef to out-of-towners when there's good honest farm work to be had. Go talk to Mr. Neumann tomorrow. He was in here this morning telling me he needs hands on the ranch. You like cows, you'd be happy there."

Clay groaned. "Why is it ok to work with the cows while they're alive, but not after they're cooked?" Myrna gave him a glare that could have flash-frozen lava. "You work in a restaurant."

"Because food service is a woman's dominion, boy, how many times I got to tell you that?" She jabbed a red-nailed finger in his face. "You go to the Neumann place tomorrow after the funeral and tell him I sent you, or you can find yourself somewhere else to live. You hear me?"

Clay nodded sheepishly. Myrna spun with a "hmph" and strode back to the kitchen.

"Your mom's pretty heated about getting you on a farm," Jerry said, scraping the last of his chocolate silk off of the plate. "You gonna go over to Neumann's tomorrow?"

"Not if I can help it. Anyway, we've got the funeral to go to tomorrow."

Jerry sighed. "I don't know if I can handle it. I mean, seeing her all laid out in a box, it's just…it's too weird. Wasn't three weeks ago we was all sitting in the parking lot behind the hardware store drinking Natty Lights and listening to her talk about all the adventures she was set to have. And look where those adventures got her. Some kinda fu—" He looked over his shoulder to make sure Myrna wasn't within hearing distance, then dropped his voice to a whisper. "Some kind of fucking leg herpes or something, from the way the guys over at the Bucket tell it. Tim Worth, the bowlegged dude who works in Doctor Jeritt's office sometimes, he said the doctor said she was all wild just before she went. Grabbing at him and saying all kinds of weird shit." He leaned in to Clayton. "I think it's that hoodoo. I hear tell they do the hoodoo in Barbados, like it's their religion or whatever. I bet she pissed off some hoodoo witch and got a curse put on her."

Clayton stared intently into Jerry's face for a moment then, quick as lightning, gave him a playful slap. "You're damned fool, you know that, Jerry? Can you even picture Cassie pissing someone off? That girl was the sweetest creature that ever walked this earth and you and I both know it."

Jerry sat back up, his pride nicked. "You don't know what kind of shit would get a hoodoo witch's dander up, do you? I'm just sayin', is all. Weird how she's all perfectly healthy one minute, then boom—" He pounded his fist on the table for emphasis. "Dead of leg herpes."

"People get all kinds of weird diseases in the tropics, you nitwit. They got all sorts of shit down there that'll kill you, and it all ends with an 'a'. Cholera, malaria, diphtheria…"

"Diarrhea."

There was a moment of silence, then they both burst out laughing, slapping the table and drawing looks from the families scattered around the diner finishing up their Saturday night chicken-fried steaks and mashed potatoes. There were a number of disapproving head-shakes from all corners of the room.

Every town, no matter how small, has its outcasts, and in Fulton Flats those outcasts were Clayton Little and Jerry Stone. The boys grew up next door to each other and had been best friends since before they could talk. They'd never been particularly focused kids, and their need for adventure got them in constant trouble. Everyone had been stunned when, in junior high, they had become close with Cassie, the town paragon. It was general knowledge that she was far too good to be hanging out with them, and most people assumed it was some sort of long-term, altruistic project on Cassie's part aimed at improving the boys' characters. Cassie had seen them, though, not as a charity case but as people who understood what it was like to be separate from the rest of town. Though everyone had loved her—and once puberty set in, every man wanted her—Cassie was the perfect, untouchable queen of Fulton Flats and she had been, as she would frequently and emphatically say, sick to *daggoned* death of it. With Clay and Jerry she could just be herself. And the boys had had a genuine affection for her that went beyond their early, rejected attempts to get their hands under her bra. Though she could be a bit priggish and she strongly disapproved of their potty mouths, she understood their hatred for the tiny little wasteland they lived in better than anyone else. The difference, of course, was that she was poised to get out while they had more or less accepted that they were stuck there forever.

And gotten out she had.

When he could breathe again, Jerry leaned in over the table. "How 'bout that ass? Man, Cassie had an ass like…like a…" He floundered for a simile. The produce allusions were starting to wear thin. "Well, it was just a fine, fine ass."

"No question about that," Clay said wistfully. "No question about that."

The Morgue

Fulton Flats did not have its own hospital, but it did have a morgue. With the number of farm machinery and timber-cutting accidents in the fall and freezing deaths in the winter, it would have been impractical not to.

The morgue was set up in the basement of the Lutz and Sons funeral home, the only establishment of its kind in the county. It was, by morgue standards, a relatively cheery place. Martin Lutz—one of the eponymous Sons—enjoyed his work and looked on it as a natural part of the cycle of life. Martin was the county coroner as well as one of the morticians at the home, along with his two older brothers. Reginald Lutz, his father, had retired some five years ago, when Martin came on full time. Martin's light-hearted decoration scheme, with its cheerful yellow walls and serene landscape paintings protected from splatter by plastic covers, had not sat well with his brothers at first. But over time, they came around to his way of seeing things.

It certainly lightened the mood during long, late-night preparations and the infrequent but often wrenching autopsies. Dr. Jeritt was also a big fan of the décor, often telling Martin that had this room been set up in the same sterile, fluorescent-lit manner as most morgues, his job of cutting open friends to find out what killed them would have been unbearable. Everyone knew everyone in Fulton Flats, which made both the doctor's and the coroner's jobs trying at times.

Today was a particularly trying one for Martin. Cassie Yearwood lie nude on the stainless steel table in front of him. Her skin was beginning to turn the blue of skim milk, and aside from the enormous wound on her thigh, she was also sporting a y-incision down the center of her chest, the arms of the cut reaching toward her shoulder blades. Doctor Jeritt did the majority of the work on the autopsies, being the only true medical professional in town, but Martin was always around to assist—usually in the company of one of his brothers—and was the one to write the findings up and sign the death certificate. Cassie's autopsy was particularly challenging to all involved, as she was so beloved and had died so young under such terrible circumstances. Martin specifically had a hard time performing his duties, as he had always harbored an enormous crush on her. When Dr. Jeritt sliced away her pajamas to begin excavating the chest cavity, Martin had instinctively turned away to keep from looking at her nude form. He was accustomed to the human body, having dressed and prepared so many in the last five years, but this was the first time he'd ever had to work on someone he would have actually very much liked to have seen naked when she was alive. After a moment, and feeling rather foolish and unprofessional, he turned back to the table and assisted the doctor in his work.

They lifted her major organs out one by one and examined them closely. The heart, lungs and liver showed no sign of inflammation or, for that matter, anything out of the ordinary at all. The site of the bug bite that Doctor Jeritt had lanced was still discolored, but had turned from the livid red it was in her last moments to a dark, waxy purple as the blood beneath the skin cooled and coagulated.

The two decided to end the autopsy and were gently placing her innards back inside her when Martin noticed something awry. As he was replacing her liver, the back of his hand brushed against something under the skin that he couldn't see, something that shouldn't have been there.

He brought it to Doctor Jeritt's attention, and they cleaned out the cavity to have a look. Jeritt extended the incision down below Cassie's pelvis and when they peeled back the layers of skin and muscle they found something extremely odd and wholly out of either man's experience. Her uterus and ovaries had swollen to enormous size, entirely filling her pelvic basin and pushing up into the chest cavity, almost as though she were several months pregnant.

With a great sense of trepidation and foreboding, Doctor Jeritt made a cut into the lining of the uterus, steeling himself for what he might find inside. The womb opened with an audible sigh, as though a bladder of pent-up gasses had been breached. Pulling back the edges, the men found no baby within, but the walls of the organ were decayed far beyond where they should have been only two days after death. The uterus itself was swollen and engorged, and there were a number of what the doctor could only guess were cysts covering the lining.

The two men conferred for some time, and decided that given the strange circumstances of Cassie's demise, they would prefer not to bring the Centers for Disease Control in on the matter. The CDC would likely perform endless tests on the poor girl, and neither she nor her grieving family nor, to be honest, the town itself needed that. From the looks of her lady parts, Jeritt was prepared to call this death by uterine cancer, exacerbated by a malaria-like fever acquired in Barbados. Martin wrote the report and got to work sewing the poor girl back up. Jerrit went home to his wife.

As he spread the cream-based foundation over her face to hide the bluing skin, Martin sighed. Even in death, Cassie was stunning.

Her face was round but not fat, her cheekbones striking and focusing attention to her ocean-blue eyes. Her lips were perfectly shaped and, though now purple, had once been a glorious, rosy red. She'd rarely needed to wear makeup of any sort, and Martin felt somewhat ashamed of the fact that he would need to apply in death what she'd so often spurned in life. It was a bit like finger painting over a Renoir, he thought as he applied just the slightest hint of blush.

He opted to use the subtlest shade of eye shadow he had, as anything more ostentatious simply wouldn't have looked like Cassie.

Martin was extremely good at his job, by far the most talented of his brothers and, if the stories he heard were true, the best makeup artist in his family since his great grandfather Job Lutz had founded the funeral home in 1894. When he first returned from mortuary school, the guys in town had made relentless fun of him for having spent so much time in cosmetology classes (they, of course, did not use the word "cosmetology", but instead a rather unflattering array of euphemisms that, more often than not, involved either the word "faggot" or "bitch" in conjunction with "hairdo school"), but Martin had quickly proven his talents and won the entire town over. Nobody mocked his skill with makeup and hairbrush now, because they all wanted him to make them look beautiful when they passed away.

Blotting the lipstick that nearly matched her natural living color, Martin's hand began to tremble.

He'd never had an issue performing his duties before, but this was by far the most personal project he'd ever undertaken. Martin knew that every man in town harbored at least a small crush on the girl, but he had been wildly in love with her for some time. She was just entering the Junior High when he was a senior, and even then he knew she was something special. She was six years younger than him, and he knew he couldn't approach her, but he had become a friend as she grew older and even a bit of a confidante as she entered college. He knew she only saw him as the older brother she'd never had, but he refused to let go of the hope that someday her affection for him would turn into something more. He watched how easy she was with those two chuckleheads from Elkwood St., Clay and Jerry, and envied the relationship they seemed to have. He had decided that when she got back from her graduation trip he would make his feelings known, but of course by then it was too late.

Suddenly struck by his reminiscing, he stood up and walked over to the counter where his supplies lie spread out in meticulous order. He set down the cloth he used to blot and took a deep breath. He was a professional, and he was not going to let this get to him.

He picked up the mascara.

For the first time he took a moment to really look at Cassie's body lying naked on the table. The y-incision, flawlessly stitched and nearly invisible, ran directly between her perfect, round breasts. He guessed her a c-cup, but although he was more proficient at applying makeup than most women, bra sizes were certainly not something he was expert at. Her nipples were roughly the size of quarters and, though turning a deep blue now, were still engorged and hard. Her belly had been flat and sculpted but was now slightly puckered from the stitches, and her hips, though slight, had the shape of a perfectly-formed flower bud just on the verge of blooming. He noticed for the first time that her pubic hair had been cleaned entirely away – her own work, not his.

Without even noticing he was moving, he found himself standing by the table, his hand on its surface, just barely brushing the top of her arm.

"Goddammit, Cassie, why did you have to go so far away on vacation? Why couldn't you have gone to Seattle or Denver? You'd still be alive, and I could have told you—"

He stopped. He was a professional, and fully versed on the biology of death. He was also somewhat of an agnostic, a very rare condition in these parts, so he had serious doubts that she could hear him, wherever she happened to be. He shook his head. This wasn't like him. He'd never spoken to a corpse before.

He leaned over and began applying the mascara, looking down into those cold blue eyes. He hadn't been able to bring himself to shut her lids, because that would mean that she was gone. He was not prepared to let go of her just yet, his first real love. He'd conducted the autopsy, he knew how sick she'd been, but he wanted to hang on to the flawless, sweet young woman who'd had him so head over heels for so long.

With a snap, Martin came out of his reverie and discovered himself face-to-face with Cassie, his warm, trembling lips pressed against hers, cold and wax-like.

He stood up in shock and backed away from the table, stumbling into a cart on which the autopsy tools were laid. Scalpels, bone saws and the heavy chest spreader all fell clattering to the floor. In the dim back recesses of his mind, Martin thought that he would have to go through the process of autoclaving them all again, but that idea was quickly shouted over by the realization that he had just caught himself kissing a dead woman. He steadied himself against the counter and looked back at her.

"I'm sorry, Cassie, god, I…I've never…I would *never*…"

She simply stared at the ceiling, unblinking, her lipstick now slightly awry.

"It's just…well, I never told you this before, but Cassie,

I…I've been in love with you for a long time. I was gonna let you know how I felt, but then you went off and-"

Martin found himself stroking her cheek. He didn't even remember walking back to the table.

"What in the hell is wrong with me?" he said, shaking his head to try to clear it and stumbling to the morgue's door. He went out into the hallway for a breath of air and looked both directions. The hall was empty, as was the whole funeral home at this hour. Nobody would be back here until eight the following morning to set up for the wake. He took a deep breath, went back inside, and locked the door behind him.

"I can do this. I've done dozens and dozens of these preparations before. You're no different, just because you're so special to me. God, Cass, you're so beautiful. I know everyone tells you that, but I mean it from the heart: you're the most beautiful woman I've ever seen. Even when I was in school out in Spokane—those big-city girls couldn't hold a candle to you. You were all I ever thought about. Can I…can I tell you a secret? Something I've never told anyone before?" He leaned in to her ear and whispered. "The night I lost my virginity—it was with this girl named Heather, real knockout—but the whole time I was only thinking of you, wishing you were the one I was with." He nibbled her earlobe gently. "Mmm…you like that, sweetheart?"

Martin dimly realized that he was cupping her cold, stiff breast in his hand, running his thumb over her nipple. It was a fantasy come true: at last he was going to be with the girl of his dreams. He couldn't believe his luck. He'd waited his whole adult life for this moment. She smiled at him and pursed her lips. Taking the invitation, he kissed her deeply, felt her tongue in his mouth for the first time. Her lips were heaven. She tasted like vanilla beans. He was getting hard.

"My love, you have no idea how I've longed for this." He climbed up on the table with her, draping his body over hers. He stopped kissing her long enough to pull off his shirt and admire the smooth, sweet-smelling skin of her chest. "God, Cass, you're absolutely flawless." He lowered his mouth to her nipple and kissed. Feeling her strain against him, he took a gentle, experimental bite. She responded by pressing her hips against his. "I want you, Cassie Yearwood. I want you more than I've ever wanted another woman in my entire life." She smiled up at him again and motioned toward his belt.

Martin peeled back his belt and unzipped and unbuttoned his pants, kicking them off. She looked at him with an arched eyebrow as if to say, "you're stopping there?" so he stripped off his boxers as well. He was proud of how stiff he was for her, showing her the depth of his longing. She seemed impressed, and angled her hips, opening herself up to him. He arranged himself between her legs, looked deep into her ocean-blue eyes, and pushed himself inside her.

It was magical. It was like a dream. She was so warm and soft, and her body moved in perfect synch with his. He watched her breasts heave as he thrust, her head turning to the side, her eyes rolling up. It was everything he'd ever wanted, and he could tell it was the same for her. As he felt the pressure build in his pelvis he gently reached up and turned her face back toward his.

"Cassie, my darling…I'm going to…"

She smiled, and he knew she wanted him to come inside her. Laying his full weight on top of her, he wrapped her in his arms and pounded away. She rocked her hips against him until the moment he erupted, filling her with his love. Then he lay spent, clutching her in his arms, wrapped in her limbs like a knot. He buried his face in her neck and breathed in her scent. He'd thought before it was vanilla, but there was a definite undertone of formaldehyde.

When he finally came back to himself he awkwardly climbed off of the table, put his clothes back on, fixed her smeared lipstick and began dressing Cassie's corpse.

Lutz and Sons Funeral Home

It was a beautiful wake, everyone agreed on that. The flowers were first-class. A girl who played harp in the Garfield High School band over in Harrington was brought in, and though she only knew how to play *Pachelbel's Canon* and did so nonstop for three hours, all who heard it declared it moving.

Tears were shed, hugs were given, and an endless stream of "God took her too soon"s were declared to the grieving parents. Cassie's mother was a royal mess, her makeup melting down her face like a festive ice cream cake left out in the hot June sun before she even entered the funeral home. Her father, as always, was quiet and seemingly utterly unconcerned except to occasionally mutter about the filthy living conditions in those "brown places" that had killed his precious little girl.

But most of all, the entire town—and make no mistake, the entire town of Fulton Flats had shown up for this monumental occasion—agreed that Cassie looked absolutely, crushingly radiant. Martin, who stood quietly and respectfully in the corner as was his wont at such events, received more compliments on his work that day than he ever had before. And he couldn't keep his eyes off of the dead girl himself. She was the most beautiful woman in the room by far, and he was already regretting the fact that she would shortly be locked into her tastefully carved mahogany box with chrome accents and lowered into the ground, forever inaccessible to the world.

He never regretted the temporary nature of his work; in fact, in his more introspective moments he found the transient quality of the funerary arts to be part of their beauty. He applied his skill to a sallow and disintegrating lump of flesh in order to bring some solace and closure to its family, and then his artwork was hidden away forever. Not only was it never to be seen again, but in point of fact most people tried to put it out of their minds entirely. But there was always death, and so Martin Lutz would always have a canvas to work his magic on.

For the first time, though, looking at Cassie's flawlessly subtle makeup and expertly coiffed hair, he didn't want one of his creations to be buried. He wasn't positive if that was because of the exquisite nature of his work—by far the best he'd ever done—or the depth of his feelings for this particular corpse. To be honest, Martin wasn't entirely sure of a lot of things lately. He found his thoughts to be extremely muddled since last night and all he could really concentrate on was ogling the body, and the women in their flattering black dresses that paraded in and out of the room the entire day.

In his more lucid moments, he felt a twinge of guilt at acting like a pubescent boy at such a difficult and emotional time. But damn, Kaci Johansson looked good. She must have known that dress would show off her tits. He suddenly realized he had slipped his hand into his pocket and was fumbling around with his half-erect penis. He did a quick adjustment to hide his arousal and folded his hands respectfully in front of him.

Clay and Jerry arrived at the service around noon. They had spent the morning getting plastered on the swing set in Little Park down the street in memory of Cassie, watching the fire in the west and north belch smoke into the sky like the apocalypse, slowly lumbering toward them. They considered it an Irish wake, though as far as they knew nobody in the town was Irish and the only thing they actually knew about Irish wakes was that they almost certainly involved getting as drunk as you can.

The boys attempted, with little to no success, to cover the fact that they needed each other's support to stand by pretending to be so overcome with emotion that they were inseparable. As was the case with pretty much everything they ever did, their efforts were met with much clicking of tongue and withering of look. It took a full half hour in line to get to the casket to pay their respects, and as they approached they were both increasingly overcome with actual, genuine grief.

"I don't think I can do this," said Jerry. "Seriously, Clay, I can't handle it. Let's go back to the swings and have more Irish shit. I don't wanna look at no dead body."

"That ain't just some dead body, that's our dead friend. If you went to Barbados and died of leg herpes, Cassie woulda come and looked at your corpse. Show some fucking respect."

Reverend Barnes, head of Futon's First Methodist Church and Cassie's pastor (and, theoretically, also Clay and Jerry's had they bothered to ever go to church like their families told them to) turned and glared at the boys.

"It is simply shameful that you would disgrace little Cassie like this, you hooligans," he spat quietly. "She was a gift from God, and you come in here reeking like the devil's breath and using that sort of sailor talk? You should be ashamed of yourselves."

Jerry stood upright for the first time in several hours. "How dare you, Reverend? She was my best friend in this whole world."

He shot a look at Clay.

"Well, definitely my second-best friend in this whole world. And what Cassie woulda wanted was for us to remember her and hold her in our hearts and love her and not judge me because I was drunk by ten on a Thursday morning 'cause I miss her so much and she was so nice to me all the time while you people just think I'm a worthless shit because I don't have a job and I hate this town and the only good thing that ever come out of this shithole was me and Clay and mostly Cassie but she was gonna leave this place behind and go away to Chicago and be a translator for the United Nations Negro College Fund and now she's dead. *She's dead!*"

Jerry took a breath and looked around. Every eye in the place was on him, except for Reverend Barnes, who had turned away after the mention of being drunk at ten in the morning. Even Clay was starting at him slack-jawed.

"Well, it's true. I loved Cassie as much as any of you people, and a hell of a lot more than most of you, and I don't hafta stand here and listen to you talk dirt about me. C'mon, Clay, let's get out of here." He turned toward the door and stumbled. Clay caught him and dragged him back to a more-or-less standing position.

"Um, hey buddy. It's cool. Nobody was talking any dirt 'bout you until you started carrying on. Let's just go pay our respects, then we can get lunch. Does that sound good?"

"Can we go to the Corner Diner and get some pie? I want pie today. Sad days are better with pie."

"Pie's on me, pal."

"Ok." Jerry was silent until they made it to the casket. For the rest of his life, Reverend Barnes gave the credit for that silence to the prayer he said after he turned away from the raving heathen.

When they reached the head of the line, both Jerry and Clayton were stunned.

"Holy shit, Jer...she looks..."

"She's perfect. Beautiful."

"God, so beautiful. Like, even hotter than she was when she was still alive." Jerry gave Clay a bit of side-eye. "I know it's weird to use the word 'hot' to describe a dead body, but damn...look at her!"

Jerry couldn't argue. "Martin has really outdone himself this time." He kissed his fingertips and pressed them to Cassie's forehead. Then, without entirely understanding what he was doing, he caressed her cheek. "I'll always miss you, Cassie Yearwood. I love you." He leaned in awkwardly and planted his lips on hers to audible gasps from the rest of the people in the funeral home. "I hope there is a heaven for you, baby. And I hope when I get there you're looking this good. Damn." He stumbled away, leaving Clayton alone.

"Um, hi Cass. I just wanted to say that I miss you, too, and...wow, Jerry totally just kissed your dead body, didn't he? That's a little fucked up but I totally understand 'cause you look real good right now, girl. Like, I want to make out with you pretty hard right now. Even though I know you're dead. And you wouldn't make out with me if you were still alive, and I always respected that but I wish you'd just let me feel you up once because now you're dead and I'll never get the chance."

He stopped and looked her over, taking a moment to contemplate his options, his hands hovering over the rim of the coffin. The entire room breathed a sigh of relief when he patted her hands, folded neatly over her pelvis, and staggered over to Jerry, wiping the snot from his nose with the sleeve of the jacket he'd bought at Goodwill two years before for a cousin's wedding. The pair sought out Martin in his corner. He had a strained look on his face, but not the same barely-contained outrage that everyone else who had witnessed their emotional outpourings wore. Clay grabbed his hand and shook it roughly.

"Martin, man, this is definitely the best you ever done. She's the prettiest dead girl I ever seen in my life. You're a wizard, man. You're a fucking wizard. A corpse wizard."

Through gritted teeth, Martin thanked him. Clay patted him a little too hard on the back and Martin winced, looking for all the world like he was trying not to fart. Then Clay headed out into the incongruously bright June sun.

"Thanks for making her look so good, Martin," said Jerry. "I know you was her friend, too. It must have been seriously fucked up having to work on her dead body." He shook Martin's hand and followed Clay out.

Martin swallowed hard. The semi-chub he'd been sporting all day was now a full-fledged raging erection, but all thoughts of Kaci Johansson's perfectly supported and outlined sweater melons had been replaced by a burning need to tear into Clayton Barre and Jerry Stone's tender face meat with his teeth. He was hungry, he realized. He shook his head to try to clear it.

When he opened his eyes, Joanne Hallstrom was standing in front of him.

Joanne had been Cassie's best friend, though she had never approved of Cassie's relationship with Clayton and Jerry. Martin's first thought, after the mild shock, was how perfectly Joanne's little black dress outlined her considerable curves.

"Martin…hey, I just wanted to say…well, thank you. Thanks so much for doing such an incredible job with Cassie…" Joanne faltered momentarily. Her face was a mixture of grief and a strange sort of puzzlement. "She looks just like she did when she was—" She made a half-cough-half-yelp noise, then quickly and expertly pulled a tissue from her formidable cleavage, wiped her nose with it, and put it back into the valley whence it came. "It really means a lot to me, and to everyone who loved her. I know that she meant a lot to you too, and I'm sorry for your loss and I wish she could have been here today to see how beautiful she looked and…"

As the words faded out, the grief in Joanne's face morphed into a look of appraisal. A gleam appeared in her eye, but she blinked and it was gone.

"Thank you, Joanne. I'm glad I got to be the one to work on her," Martin managed. He was growing increasingly distracted by Joanne's body.

Joanne opened her mouth as if to say something more, but instead shuffled awkwardly forward and wrapped her arms around him, hugging him a touch more tightly than perhaps the situation called for. With her enormous breasts pressed against him and her breath warm on his neck, Martin's erection went from full-mast to painfully bulldozing against the constraints of his pants.

"Mmm…you smell so good, Martin," Joanne breathed into his ear.

"I, uh…well, thanks I guess? I don't really wear cologne, so…"

"It's funny," she whispered, her voice trembling slightly, "but I am having the strangest urge right now."

"What urge is that?" Martin whispered back.

She flicked her tongue against his earlobe then blew on it. The warm moisture of her saliva went instantly cold, sending yet another surge through Martin's cock.

"The urge to drag you to a secluded corner of this funeral home and fuck your face clean off of your body."

Martin swallowed hard. Somewhere deep in the recesses of his mind he was shocked that this was happening. Cassie had been far out of his league, but she was the friendly type, the kind that you always thought you might have a chance with, if only out of pity or compassion. Joanne was a stone-cold bitch with a body to kill for, and she absolutely knew it. She was the cheerleader who continued to fuck the quarterback even after high school. She had even rejected him in his most heated dreams.

"That's pretty typical," he stuttered. "People are reminded of their mortality at funerals, so they feel the need to celebrate life by copu—"

"Take me to a janitor's closet now or lose this opportunity forever," she whispered back, and to accentuate her point she pressed her pelvis against his. "I can feel that you're already good to go." She dropped the hug then and pulled away from him.

Martin cleared his throat and hoped that nobody could see the aching bulge in his pants.

"Well, Miss Hallstrom, I certainly understand your grief. I am distraught, too," he said, loud enough for anyone nearby to hear. "Let me walk you to the office, I'm sure I can find what you're looking for." It took all of the willpower he could muster to contain his strides to a normal, respectful slow walk. When he was out of the room he looked back and, to his complete disbelief, she was following him. He turned a corner out of sight of the collected mourners then grabbed her and pushed her against the wall, kissing her roughly.

"There's somewhere I've always wanted to have sex, but never found anyone willing," he said when the kiss broke. "You game?"

She smiled and took his hand. "Lead on, baby."

Little Park

Clay pushed himself listlessly on the swing, his foot planted in the pile of empty Natural Light cans on the ground beneath him. The wind had picked up and the sun shining through the new patina of haze hanging over town looked like a smear of orange jam on heavily buttered toast.

Neither he nor Jerry had said a word to each other since leaving the funeral home, but something was nagging him and ignoring it like he usually would with such persistent and inconvenient thoughts was doing him no good.

"Jer, did you notice anything weird goin' on at the wake?"

Jerry lifted his head with a start. Clayton realized he had been dozing on his own swing. How he managed to do so in his current state of inebriation without falling on his face was the sort of mystery that scientists decline to investigate and true believers the world over would attribute to ley lines or the influence of Saturn.

"Huh?"

"The wake. The funeral thing we was just at. Where we was paying our respects to Cassie. Did you notice anything weird goin' on? Like, did you feel weird?"

"Well, it was the first time I ever actually wanted to kick a holy man in the balls, does that count?"

"No, I mean…well, I watched you kiss Cassie. It was…it wasn't really the way people normally do at funerals, was it?"

Jerry threw the empty beer can he found in his hand at Clay's head. "Fuck you, man, I was grieving. Don't you go judgin' me too!"

"No, I'm not judging or nothing it's just…did you feel weird when you did it?"

"I don't know, I wasn't really thinking." He scratched his stomach and burped. "I mean, I remember thinkin' how good Cass looked…like, really fucking good. Seriously, I think I was sportin' a semi when I saw her, and then…oh fuck."

"Right? Dude, I felt the same way. People always talk about how natural someone looks at their funeral, but I never heard anybody say the dead person looked hot. Jerry—Cassie looked fucking *hot*. Like, I thought for a minute about honkin' her titties right there in front of everyone. That just don't seem normal to me."

Jerry was pensive for a moment. "You know, you're right. But maybe it ain't so weird as that. I mean, they say people get horny at funerals. Pretty sure I read that somewhere, maybe in *Penthouse Letters*. We was both so close to Cass and, let's face it, we both wanted to slip it to her while she was still alive. Martin did a great job making her look pretty, so I guess it's not so strange that I was entertaining some pretty serious thoughts about climbin' in that coffin and givin' her the business."

Clayton looked at him, slack-jawed. "No, man, that's definitely strange. And I'd call you a severely fucked up pervert if I wasn't entertainin' the same thoughts. And Martin, there's another thing. He was acting really weird, don't you think?"

"I mean, I guess we were bein' kinda drunk idiots in there. He had every right to be mad at us for disrespecting him and his brothers' place of business."

"But Jerry, I didn't think he looked mad. I thought he looked…shit, I don't know, something else. Like…well, it's weird, but I think he looked kinda like he wanted to hurt us. Not in an angry way, in a psycho killer way."

"You think?"

"Yeah, I mean…well, he had that look I get when I get out of bed all hung over and find mom puttin' a fresh plate of biscuits and gravy with hash browns on the kitchen table. Like, that 'I am about to devour the fuck out of this' look."

Jerry closed his eyes to conjure up a vision of Martin at the funeral and nearly fell backward off of his swing.

"Yeah, I guess I can see that," he said once he had righted his balance. "I mean, let's be honest, my memories ain't been so good today since we got shitfaced earlier than we even wake up most days, but I do see what you mean. I wonder why that was."

"I guess he's pretty tore up, too. I know he had a huge crush on Cassie, maybe even bigger than anyone else in town. Like you said, it musta really fucked him in the head to have to cut her open with Doc Jeritt and then sew her back up and do her makeup and everything. That's gotta be tough, 'specially when you're workin' on someone you was so sweet on."

A wave of consternation passed over Jerry's face. "Damn, Clay, I just thought—Martin finally got to see Cass naked. Neither one of us got that privilege. Shit, my grandma was right all along: I shoulda got myself a profession."

"You'd want to look at her naked, even if she was dead and cut open?"

"I mean, either before she got cut up or after he put her back together. I bet they didn't slice up her boobs none. After Martin did her makeup and everything she was definitely lookin' real nice again." He thought for a moment. "Sure, I wouldn't have minded gettin' an eyeful of that. I'd rather she was alive when I did, but you know what they say about beggars and choosers."

Clay nodded gravely, fished the last two cans out of the second twelve-pack at his feet, tossed one to Jerry and held his aloft.

"To Cassandra Yearwood's magnificent hooters. May they remain as glorious in death as they were in life."

The boys toasted and drank.

The Morgue

The heavy wooden door to the basement room flew open and Martin and Joanne, awkwardly entangled in each other's arms and in a constant struggle against gravity, bumbled their way through it.

Without disengaging his mouth from hers, Martin kicked the door closed and managed to throw the deadbolt with one hand while unzipping Joanne's dress with the other. He wasn't particularly worried about anyone wandering in—the morgue was beneath the viewing rooms and on the other side of the building and virtually soundproof between the concrete walls and the thick door—but some tiny part of his mind insisted that he lock the door, anyway. He wasn't entirely sure, in his compromised state, whether the intention was to keep stragglers out or to keep Joanne in. She wriggled her dress to the floor then immediately went to work on his belt. With his pants successfully on the linoleum, she dropped to her knees in front of him, but he grabbed a handful of her hair and pulled her back up.

"No time for foreplay."

Her hair still in his hands—and her moaning loudly, surprised at how much the rough treatment was turning her on—he guided her over to the stainless steel examining table and pushed her down. Bent over the table that Cassie had been autopsied on less than twenty-four hours earlier, she looked over her shoulder at him and made her best pouty "come fuck me" face. Martin pulled out his cock, pushed her neon pink panties (which, of course, matched her bra—Joanne was never without matching underwear "just in case", even at a funeral) and thrust inside her. She grunted loudly and nearly asked him to slow down, but then thought better of it; he was, in fact, hurting her, but she found that though she had never really been turned on by any sort of pain before and, to be sure, was generally in charge of any sort of sexual encounter she participated in, Martin's complete domination of her was driving her wild. She did manage to wonder at this for a brief half of a second before all thought was completely drowned out by the flood of dopamine that her orgasm released on her brain.

I just came in a matter of seconds, and from pure penetration, she thought through the post-orgasmic haze. *Why have I never wanted to fuck Martin before?*

For his part, Martin was well beyond any sort of thought. Standing behind Joanne, his hands gripping her waist, nails digging into the soft, tan flesh of her hips, his black suit coat flapping behind him with each savage thrust, all that was going through his mind was images of naked female bodies and meat. He thought about Cassie, how sweet and tender their lovemaking had been, how she had coaxed him on. He thought about her perfect body, lither than Joanne's but made all the sexier by the fact that she didn't show it off the way other girls did. Without even thinking he reached forward and grabbed Joanne's bra strap, tugging it toward himself. She curled her torso up and looked over her shoulder into his eyes.

"Yes…fuck me harder, daddy. Make me come again!"

He couldn't hear her. He didn't care. He gave one more solid tug and her bra split in half, falling away from her bouncing breasts. She groaned as the fabric tore, surprised at his strength. He casually tossed the shredded undergarment over his shoulder and fondled her, pinching and groping and bruising her soft beige skin. Even Idaho's bitter winters couldn't keep Joanne from her flawless, line-free tan.

In his admittedly few previous sexual relationships, Martin had always been a gentle, generous lover. Once, with a girl named Kate he had fucked a few times in college, he had tried to be in control, but he found it awkward and, to be honest, they were both completely turned off by it. And he was always a firm believer that a man owed a woman oral sex every single time they were together. In his opinion, it was way harder for a woman to get off and, since the sex was usually over once a guy came, it was only fair to make sure she climaxed at least once or twice before he got his.

But now, with Joanne bent over his examining table, he could give less than half a fuck about her needs or, frankly, her physical safety. And she was screaming like a banshee.

Joanne was holding on to the far edge of the table for dear life. The table was on wheels, and they had managed to fuck their way slowly across the room until it caught itself up against the wall. Her fingers were being crushed, but for reasons beyond her comprehension this was turning her on even more. She wanted him to hurt her, to scratch wounds in the thin skin of her back, to leave her tits mangled and sore. She wanted him to savage her, and he was doing a damned good job of accommodating her. She put her head down on the tabletop and screamed as her fourth orgasm washed over her.

The images in Martin's head were becoming increasingly dominated by food now, and it was becoming difficult for him to distinguish between the meat and bodies. He grabbed a fistful of Joanne's dyed-black hair and pulled her head back toward him, then buried his face in her neck. She whimpered as he kissed her then, experimentally, nipped at her shoulder. She seemed to like it, so he did it again. She seemed to like it more, so he bit harder.

"Fuck…yes…bite me…fucking bite me, daddy. God, I love how you hurt me…"

But he wasn't as excited by the biting as he thought he'd be. It wasn't right. She was not what he wanted to bite. He did it a few more times half-heartedly because he liked the noises she made when he did, then he concentrated in earnest on fucking her as hard as he could. He wanted to drive his cock so far into her that it came out the other side. He wanted to pound her into dust. He had never felt this way before, but the animal violence of it excited him no end.

He could feel his orgasm building, the tingle spreading over his skin more like a fire than the warm blanket he usually found it to be. And then, before he entirely realized what was happening, he grabbed her around the waist and held her tight against him, her ass pressed to his pelvis, while he spurted what felt like half a gallon of semen inside her. She yelped and he knew she had come again herself.

He held them like that for several more minutes, finally letting go and walking away on shaking legs. As the fever of orgasm receded, it slowly dawned on him exactly what was going on here. He looked at Joanne's nude body slumped over the dressing table. He had prepared dozens of corpses on that table, had helped Doctor Jeritt cut many of them open and examine their insides there, and most recently had done both to the great love of his life. There on that table. The table where he had just fucked the ever-loving hell out of her best friend.

He found his cock coming back to life.

Joanne, sore and exhausted, stood up and got her first real glimpse of Martin since they'd gotten into the room. He was puny and pale and looked ridiculous, still sporting a suit coat, tie and white oxford shirt but completely nude below the waist. He was dorky and pathetic. He was not even remotely her type.

She wanted him more than anything on earth.

She walked over to him, nuzzled her head against his chest and looked up into his eyes with her best disarming little girl gaze.

"Is there time for foreplay now, daddy?" she whimpered, batting her eyelashes. Then she dropped to her knees.

The Lutz Funeral Home

Tara Sokoloff had never met Cassie Yearwood, but she decided that morning to put on a modest gray dress (she had not owned any black clothing since she sloughed off her goth college persona upon graduation, stopped calling herself "Lilith Wolfsong", took the piercing studs out of her cheeks and got a goddamned job) and go pay her respects, nevertheless. The entire town was going to show up for this shindig, and if she hoped to ever be accepted here she would have to put some effort into fitting in.

Tara was an abomination in this town for more reasons than she could count. First and foremost, nobody ever moved *to* Fulton Flats. Though everybody here was a good protestant with the requisite 2.3 children, the population never grew because as soon as that three tenths of a child reached the age of eighteen they fucked off right out of town, never looking back. But that was precisely the kind of atmosphere Tara was looking for, somewhere that never changed. She had spent her whole life—up until three months ago when she moved to Idaho—in San Francisco, a city that changed so often and so drastically that you got whiplash just walking out your door in the morning.

It wasn't that Tara disliked San Fran—far from it, in fact—but she was desperate to find a life somewhere where she could be absolutely positive that when she woke up in the morning, she'd be waking up in precisely the same town she went to sleep in last night, and the night before, and so on back to, by her estimation, the pioneer days.

It had been an eye-opening move, to be sure. She figured out early that she was required to at least pay lip service to either the town's one Methodist church or its one non-denominational Brethren in Christ church, and did so begrudgingly. There were dozens upon dozens of things about her life and lifestyle that those places would never approve of, but she figured if she kept as much hidden as she could the people here would regard her as a suspicious eccentric rather than an abomination before the lord. She could deal with suspicious eccentric. In fact, she rather liked the sound of it. She thought fondly of the Log Lady on *Twin Peaks* and rather hoped that she could develop some extremely flamboyant personal quirk as she grew older that would make her the town oddity. Something other than coming from Sodom on the Pacific, that is. After the first dozen times people who had never been to San Francisco scolded her about what a vile, wicked place it was she started telling strangers she was from Omaha.

Tara's job writing and editing copy for technical manuals meant she could work from home and live anywhere she damn well pleased. Her laptop was her office, and even though the internet was damnably slow here in the northern hinterlands, she was perfectly capable of getting done what she needed done. Most folks in town that she talked to didn't really understand the concept of working from home and assumed that meant she was a housewife. The lack of a man or children in the small ranch-style house she purchased on Taylor Street hadn't seemed to dissuade them from this idea, so she decided she wasn't going to bother trying to do so, either.

She knew that relocating to a small, insular town like this was going to be the last nail in the coffin of her dating life, but she'd been single for so long she didn't really care, anymore. It was no small relief when the visitation line moved forward enough to get her out of the hot sun and vaguely campfireish smell into the near arctic air conditioning of the funeral home. She wondered if the home were kept so cold to aid the preservation of the body laid out in the other room, or if it was just the preference of mankind to divorce themselves from nature as much as they possibly could. Looking around at the silk flowers and faux wood paneling, she decided on the latter.

She'd kept deliberately quiet in the line, not wishing to disturb anyone in their grief and also to not out herself as an outsider any more than she had to, but after twenty minutes of standing silently the short, stern-faced woman with steel-gray hair in front of her turned and engaged her.

"Were you a friend of Cassie's, dear?"

Tara was momentarily lost for a reply. Though she knew she would face some scrutiny here, she was not quite prepared for such an all-out assault on her anonymity.

"No, sadly I didn't have a chance to get to know her. But everyone spoke so highly of her, I wanted to come pay my respects. I know she was well loved."

Inside, she smiled. Flawless dodge.

"Oh," the matron said, recognition dawning on her face, "you're that girl from Nebraska, aren't you? I should have known—I didn't recognize your face. We don't get many outsiders here."

Fuck. A riposte.

"Yeah, I just got here a few months ago. It's a lovely town and I hope I can fit in here."

Parry.

"Well, we don't generally cotton on to big-city types here, but you've done good by coming to see Cassie off. She was an angel, and everyone in Fulton knows it. God called her back far too soon, but she brought it on herself, going to vacation on that nigger island."

Tara's eyes grew big as dessert plates. It was her first face-to-face encounter with such bald, open racism. The woman completely misinterpreted her expression, however, as people so firm in their wrong convictions are wont to do.

"Oh, you didn't know? She went to Barbados for her graduation trip. I know, it was a baffling choice with so many beautiful beaches in Texas, but she made her mistake and was punished for it. I think it's a little much, taking her home like he did, but who am I to question the Lord? Nevertheless, that one indiscretion aside, she was an absolute peach. I'd hoped that some day she would have married my good-for-nothing grandson Jerry. They were real close. I kept hoping she'd rub off on him, but now she's gone and he's got no positive influence left in his life. It's a double loss, in my books."

Tara was completely gobsmacked. "I'm uh...I'm so sorry for

your loss?"

"That's ok, dearie. I pray for that boy every single day. Sooner or later Jesus has got to hear me, right?" She tittered in that high-pitched old lady way that was either ovary-shatteringly adorable or like dragging a metal rake across a chalkboard, depending on the disposition of the person hearing it. Tara was firmly in the chalkboard camp. "What's your name, sweetheart?"

"Tara. Sokoloff."

She woman extended her hand, palm down as though she were the Queen of England. "Trudy Polaski. Nice to have another Pollack in town. We're few and far between here."

Tara took her hand awkwardly, not sure whether she was supposed to shake or kiss it, and opted for a dainty shake.

"My dad came straight from Krakow. Moved to Sa—" She caught herself just in time. "Moved to Omaha just a few years before I was born. My mom's family are from Lodz, but had to flee during the Holocaust."

And then the sinking feeling in her gut began, and by the look on Trudy's face she knew she had not caught herself nearly fast enough this time.

"So, you're a..."

"Well, my mom's Jewish. I'm not. I've never been very interested in…Judaism…" *Why is my mouth still moving?*

"Well, dear, it takes all kinds, I guess. But I'm glad you came to the light. I wouldn't rightly know how you could have worshipped here if you were a member of your mother's tribe. I don't think there's a synagogue within five hundred miles of Fulton."

"Yeah, well…um, God provides, am I right?"

That seemed to put the older woman at ease.

"He does at that, dear. He most certainly does. Oh, look at me here gabbing your ear off, and the line's already moved up. Guess it's my turn, then." She turned and strode to the open casket with the purpose and command of a woman half her age. Bowing her head, she said a silent prayer over Cassie's body that Tara could only assume included a stern word or two about judgment and "nigger islands", then gazed down into the coffin for a long moment before turning back to Tara.

"Well, it was lovely meeting you, my dear. One of these days I'll have to introduce you to my Jerry. He's lived with me ever since his parents passed. He was still just a little one, then. Car accident. They were laid out in this very funeral home, matter of fact. He's a good boy deep down, I'm sure. Just doesn't show it often. But for the right woman, I bet he'd turn right as rain."

Tara nodded wordlessly, wishing for something—anything— to happen that would break off the intensely awkward conversation before Grandma Trudy officially offered her grandson's hand in marriage.

Trudy offered a pained grimace that Tara thought was as close to a smile as the old battleaxe was capable of and patted her gently on the shoulder with a withered, wrinkled hand. "Hopefully I'll see you at church. Welcome to Fulton Flats." She turned briskly and rode her exceptional stride right out of the home.

It was Tara's turn now, and she was beginning to panic. She hadn't been to a funeral as an adult, and never to a stranger's funeral, so she was entirely unclear on precisely what was expected of her. She stepped cautiously forward to the casket and lowered her eyes respectfully.

She was shocked. She had heard unceasingly the past few days of Cassie's beauty, but she was not expecting this. The girl in the coffin was absolutely radiant, the very picture of middle-American perfection. She was a WASP pinup, with flowing blonde hair, delicate features and just enough curves to be sexy but not voluptuous. For the first time, Tara felt a pang of regret for the loss of this creature. That everyone said she was the smartest person in town and as kind as she was attractive only added to the feeling. This was the mythology of small-town America brought to life, then struck down cruelly in the flower of her youth.

She realized she was gawking and bowed her head to give the impression of a prayer.

After what she considered to be an appropriately long moment of silence, she opened her eyes to get one last glance at Cassie's mortal shell, then turned and headed slowly for the door, lost in thought. She actually regretted not getting to know this girl.

As she passed out of the viewing room and into the hallway, another woman wheeled around the corner and almost ran directly into her. She was as dark-haired as Cassie was blonde, but much curvier and, Tara thought, nowhere near as sweet-looking. If Cassie was the embodiment of the farm girl fantasy, this woman was more in line with a softcore porn model, more the sultry trashiness of *Penthouse* than the glamour of *Playboy*, the kind of woman one would expect to find on a beach at one of the discount tourist towns north of Miami, desperately baking the Midwestern pallor off of her skin. And she very much piqued Tara's interest.

The woman was disheveled, her form-fitting black dress askew and bunched in odd places, and it was abundantly obvious that she was not wearing a bra, as her nipples were clearly visible through the bodice. Tara caught herself staring and forced her eyes up to the woman's face. She was leering at her, licking her lips in the sort of slow circuit that one sees in skin flicks and commercials for canned pasta meals starring children. Suddenly, Tara felt a stirring that she had thought dead for some time.

"Excuse me," the woman said. "I was just…I didn't see you there." Her eyes were focused like lasers on Tara's neck, and a tiny fleck of spit sparkled in the corner of her mouth. She thrust her hand out and Tara's heart leapt, but she stopped just short of touching her. Slowly, Tara realized she was offering a handshake. "Joanne Hallstrom. I'm Cassie's best friend. Was her best friend."

Tara took her hand. It was warm and, she thought incongruously, slightly sticky. "Tara Sokoloff. I just moved to town. I'm sorry for your loss. Everyone tells me what wonderful woman Cassie was."

Joanne looked strangely disconnected. Tara chalked it up to grief.

"Oh, you know…shit happens, I guess. I'm getting over it. If you'll excuse me, it's been a long day, and I just got seriously fu—" She affected the fakest cough Tara had ever heard. "I just got seriously flustered. Because of the funeral and all that. I should get home and get my shit together."

"Of course," Tara said. "If there's anything I can do for you…"

"Oh, I'm good. I'm *way* good." She shook her head and took a deep breath, then seemed to actually see Tara for the first time. "But I'll tell you what, if you're feeling frisky tonight some of the girls and I are going down to the Rusty Bucket to have a few in memory of Cass. You're more than welcome. I'm sure it'll be nice to meet some women your age."

"That would be nice. I'll make it a point to drop by."

Joanne gave her a last look that Tara could only describe as famished. "Please do." She licked her lips again. "See you tonight."

As she watched Joanne saunter away, Tara began to believe, for the first time in years, that her celibacy might soon be coming to an end.

Martin's House

Martin woke up in a cold sweat. His bedroom was the cool blue of late summer evening, just after the sun has finished setting. His work required early hours, and he had always been a morning person, anyway, so he tended to be in bed by nine most nights. It was a bit more challenging to keep that routine up in the summer, when the sun was so long in going down, but the emotional weight of the day followed by the frankly exhausting sexual exercise he had taken part in that afternoon, conspired to put him down shortly after eight. Though he didn't notice it at all, the clock on his bed table said 9:23pm.

Truth be told, he didn't notice much of anything but the gnawing, grumbling hunger in his gut. He had dreamt, though he did not remember, of eating. Nothing too specific; in that strange way dreams had of communicating with us, he had not dreamt specifically of eating cheeseburgers or dandelions or Now n' Laters, he had simply dreamt of eating. He fell out of bed more than he stood up and, once he had regained his balance to the extent that he could move, staggered down the stairs into the kitchen.

He had never been much of a cook. Like most men who were raised in Fulton Flats, Martin had always assumed he would survive on ramen noodles, grilled cheese and pizza deliveries until he managed to lock down a wife who would, from that point and in perpetuity, be in charge of the preparation of food and of the cleaning up after food had been consumed. He had always hoped that sooner or later he would have Cassie to cook for him—and true to her status as the Eisenhower-era American wet dream, Cassie was a superb cook—so he had never really made any sort of effort to learn to take care of himself in that regard. So were he in any way cognizant of what was going on at that particular moment, it would not have come as a huge surprise to him when he opened his fridge that there was very little in it to slake his hunger.

He picked up a closed jar of mostly pickle juice with a few small, round slices floating in the brine, sniffed it momentarily, made a face not unlike he had just detected a stranger's hangover flatulence, and immediately tossed it over his shoulder, paying no mind when it shattered against a countertop and sprayed its contents all over the empty bread box and spice rack filled with mostly full and sealed jars of dried herbs he never had any clue what to do with in the first place.

Next he pulled out a bag of saggy, browning celery that he'd bought when he remembered that he had liked filling the concave stalks with peanut butter when he was a child and decided that it might make a better snack than the candy bars he was constantly buying from the machine at work. The celery—no doubt not really edible by any first-world standards anyway—also did not meet his needs, and joined the shattered pickle jar on the floor.

Next out was half a pound of raw bacon, sealed in plastic wrap. Bacon was something Martin could always deal with: it was fatty and delicious and all he had to do was heat up a pan and make sure not to burn it too badly. He sniffed the bundle in front of him appraisingly then, deciding that it might be what he wanted, took an experimental bite.

He recoiled at the unexpected blandness of plastic and examined the bacon closer. Tugging at an end of the wrapper, he managed to free the meat inside. His second bite was more satisfactory, but he found that the peppered edges made him sneeze, so after another few tentative nibbles the bacon joined the growing pile of discarded food in the corner.

At last, after rifling through the drawers of the refrigerator, he lighted upon a large porterhouse steak, arranged beautifully on its Styrofoam tray and shrink-wrapped to seal in the freshness. Having learned his lesson with the bacon, Martin poked at the wrapper until he made a small hole, then a strange instinct took over and compelled him to get as many of his fingers as possible inside, shredding the plastic wrap in a wholly unnecessarily violent fashion. With the red, bleeding meat exposed he began to salivate, licking his fingers and sizing up his kill. A shrinking voice in the back of his head warned against the dangers of eating raw beef, but he no longer cared. He was famished. His guts growled like an ancient printing press, all grinding gears and groaning machinery. He devoured the steak in a few savage bites then cleaned his hands with his tongue.

It was good, but it wasn't what he wanted. The cogs in his stomach still screamed. He wanted something very specific, but he wasn't entirely sure what exactly it was. Meat, definitely meat, but the cow was not sufficient.

He shambled toward the door, leaving the fridge hanging open, and headed out onto Harrison Street, no concern whatsoever for the fact that he was bare-ass naked, and public nudity was not the kind of thing that a God-fearing town like Fulton looked kindly on.

With no destination—or, really, much of anything else—in mind, he moved forward into the road and toward the block-long concentration of businesses that was called "downtown" by people who had never even seen a gathering of people large enough to be called a town. Streetlights were few and far between, and the city's one traffic signal blinked incessantly, filling the intersection with an intermittent blood-red glow, then plunging it into darkness. The streets of the tiny hamlet were typically entirely deserted between the ten o'clock period when most people were settled into their beds and two in the morning when the drunks were driving home from the Bucket.

Martin stumbled along, the growling in his torso propelling him onward.

He stood transfixed under the blinking red light at Main and Harrison, staring up at the signal as though it were pulsing out a message to him in Morse code, filling him in on the vague details of what he craved. He jumped when a car horn sounded behind him.

"Hey, man, you alright?"

Martin turned and immediately snapped to attention, gaining a focus he had not had since some time earlier in the day.

A young man was leaning out of the window of one of those goddamned Prius cars that people in California wanted the rest of the world to drive because they hated America and oil.

He began to move toward the man, who got his first clear look at Martin and put the car into park.

"Dude, you should really have some clothes on. I mean, I don't know how you do here in this little pigfuck town, but I'm pretty sure you're not supposed to be walking around with your junk flapping in the breeze." The man waited for a response but got none.

Martin kept walking closer, his hunger drowning out the man's speech.

"Do you want me to call a doctor or something for you? I'm not from around here, just driving through to visit my cousin in Denniston down the road a ways, but if you tell me who to call I'll make sure you get the help you…"

Martin was at the window now, staring down at the man who was, for his part, staring back up with visibly increasing discomfort.

"Look, I gotta be honest, you're spooking me a little right now, so I'm just gonna go ahead and roll up my window and get the fuck out of this shitho—"

Martin reached through the window and grabbed him by the throat. The man made a gurgling noise and looked up at him in disbelief. Squeezing tighter, he began to pull. The man struggled to get a seatbelt around himself, but it was entirely too late for that. Martin had him halfway out the window before he could get a decent hold on the belt.

He began to scream—or try, at any rate; it came out more like a moaning quack through the tiny opening Martin's vice-like grasp left in his trachea—and impotently scratched at his assailant's arms. Martin seemed entirely impervious to his attempts at defense and, having drug him entirely out of the still-idling car, pushed him roughly down on the ground, pinning him with one knee on his chest. Then he leaned in and took a bite out of the man's cheek.

The gurgle-squeaks became more frantic and desperate as Martin chewed on the soft flesh of the man's face, never letting the grip on his throat slacken. Shock and suffocation were taking their toll, and the man's flailing slowed as Martin sunk his teeth into the opposite cheek, tearing the skin and thin muscle away in strands. His blood was warm and salty, and Martin realized that this was precisely what he was looking for. He bit down on the nose and felt the gamy crunch of cartilage as the man slipped into unconsciousness.

With no more need to struggle, Martin could concentrate on his meal. He dug his finger into the corner of one eye and pried, popping the eyeball out with only a little difficulty and watching it drop to the ground beside the man's head. He picked up the freed sphere and brought it to his mouth, but was surprised when it jerked free of his hand and landed on the man's chin just before he could consume it.

With a chuckle that sounded for all the world like a car slipping gears, he realized that the ocular nerve was still attached. He bent close to the man's face and put the entire eye into his mouth, biting down hard to sever the nerve. The man's body spasmed, but he did not wake up. Martin rolled the eye around his mouth for a moment, looking for a way to chew it; it was too large to get his teeth around, and he was having trouble spitting it back out.

At last, through a series of manipulations with his tongue and cheek, he managed to get it far enough off center in his mouth to pin it between his molars and bite down. It popped like a grape, filling his mouth with a cooling, tangy jelly that he swallowed the way he'd swallowed dozens of oysters at the bar he'd frequented during his time at Boise State. He went after the other eye and repeated the experience, this time being careful to bite the nerve free without putting the eye in his mouth then taking two bites to eat it. When he examined the man to decide which delicacy to try next, his victim began to move.

"Whaassh ghoongh ahn," he croaked, his crushed vocal chords and lack of cheeks making word formation very difficult.

"Whaayooh gho? Whaasat sah daahk?"

Martin looked down at him and frowned. Nobody—I mean nobody—wants their meal to talk to them. The man began to writhe and moan as the shock started to wear off and waves of pain washed over him.

Martin watched for a moment, puzzling out what to do with this wriggling, bleeding mess, then instinctively balled his fist and punched the man in the chest as hard as he could. His fist sunk into the man's torso with the loud spaghetti snap of breaking ribs. Shocked and delighted by his own strength, he worked his hand back out—a task made more difficult by the contraction of the man's pectoral muscles around the wound—and punched again, directly over his left lung. The man jerked as Martin's fist crushed his heart messily against the back of his ribcage. Martin let off another gear-grinding chuckle and opened the hole in the man's chest the way he and Doctor Jeritt had done in so many autopsies but, lacking a chest-spreader, he used his bare fingers. And this time, after giving each organ a cursory examination, he devoured it.

After half an hour spent feasting on the man in the middle of the deserted intersection of Harrison and Main, the corpse was picked clean of all of its most delicious bits, but Martin was still hungry. He stood and walked away, leaving the barely recognizable pile that had been the stranger beside his softly humming car and trailing footprints of blood and gore behind him.

The Corner Diner

It had been a long day for Myrna. She was on the schedule to work a double today, but managed to cut a deal with the Diner's other full-time waitresses to sneak out for an hour midday to attend the wake. She missed the funeral itself, but she'd never really been one for the hair-tearing and hand-wringing, and watching them put poor Cassie into the ground would have been far more than she could handle. So she waited in line to pay her respects, stopped to thank Martin, who had been visibly addled, for the superb job he'd done, and then hurried back to work. She didn't even notice until she was back at the Diner that she'd forgotten to take her apron off.

She loved her job, no question, but double shifts like this one were beginning to take their toll on her. Myrna was not a young woman; she and her husband Ralph had had trouble getting pregnant, and Clay didn't come until she was in her early forties. She often wondered if that was the cause of his generally lazy demeanor—he took so long getting conceived, why wouldn't he take his time doing everything else? She'd read an article in *Good Housekeeping* or *Redbook* or one of the other magazines she enjoyed so much, that said that scientists were becoming more convinced that the older a woman was when she got pregnant, the more likely their child was to be gay. She had never put much stock in science to begin with—the Good Lord was all the science she'd ever needed—and she was pretty sure that being gay was a choice, anyway, but just in case she kept a close eye on Clayton as he was growing up.

If the collection of magazines she'd found under his bed before she quit cleaning his room for him were any indication, either the scientists were full of it or their family had definitely dodged a bullet.

She finished mopping behind the counter, turned off the dining room lights and tiptoed over the wet floor to lock the front door for the night. Her routine was set when she closed: input her tips, close out the register, finish the cleaning, turn off the lights, then lock the door and leave through the back. The younger waitresses always locked the door first, but in a town the size of Fulton Flats there was little to no fear of crime, and everyone in town knew that the Diner stopped serving at ten, so nobody ever showed up after then, anyway.

She pulled the door closed tightly and unlocked the crash bar, then turned the deadbolt and pulled down the shades, taking a quick peek out the window first. As always at this hour, it was dark and deserted. Though she couldn't see the town's solitary traffic signal at the other end of the block, it persistently painted the police station across the street a vivid red, then left it its natural wood hue, then splashed it red again.

One of the things that Myrna loved best about her hometown was that she never, ever felt nervous walking home from work alone. Nothing stirred in the street, not even a speck of litter to blow around. She nodded, satisfied, and turned to go out the back door.

That's when she saw Martin standing just outside of the kitchen, the swinging doors oscillating behind him. There was something strange about him, but in the half-light of the kitchen fluorescents behind him, it was hard for her to quantify precisely what.

"Martin, good lord, you startled me."

He didn't react; he just stood there, staring at her.

"Well, dear, are you ok? Do you need something?"

No reaction.

She slowly sidled over to him, not exactly scared but not entirely at her ease, either. It was highly unusual for anyone who didn't work at the Diner to come in the back, especially after closing. But Martin was Martin, she'd known him since he was a pup, and she knew there was no gentler or kinder man in town, despite his creepy (but necessary) profession. As she got closer she could start to make out more of his appearance in the dark, and became increasingly nervous.

"Hon, you're naked. Did you know you was naked? Are you feeling alright?"

Silence.

She moved closer. "You're also covered in blood. Martin, has there been an accident?"

He simply stared at her. His face was covered in red, radiating out from his mouth, like a toddler who has just finished a plate of spaghetti.

"Oh mercy, Martin, here. Let me help you."

She pulled a handkerchief from her sleeve, looped a corner of it over her index finger, licked it, and set to work cleaning off his face. He was remarkably still, but she found that instead of being more frightened, she was getting comfortable with the clearly strange situation.

As she wiped off his cheek she looked into his eyes and saw the cold, iron gaze he fixed on her. Her pulse shot up. Her Ralph was a stoic, steely farm man and she'd always gone in for those men—the quiet, sure John Wayne type who walked tall and never talked about their feelings or hers. The kind who would always be there at your back with a shotgun when you needed one and didn't give a fuck about bringing you flowers. The kind who would give you a good solid smack when you needed one.

She saw all of this in Martin's eyes, and she had to admit, it was making her a little weak in the knees despite having watched him learn to crawl.

"Martin, honey," she cooed, "is there anything I can do for you? Are you in some kind of trouble?" Cooed? *What's gotten into me?* She noticed that her hands, entirely of their own will of course, had made their way from Martin's face to his chest. He was not a burly man like Ralph, but she found that his wiry frame was just as big a turn-on as her husband's barrel-chestedness.

Martin's stare had not altered whatsoever.

"Come back into the kitchen, sweetheart, and let's see if we can't get you cleaned up a bit."

She applied the slightest pressure to his chest, but he didn't move. Solid. Reliable. Her heart fluttered.

"Come on now, mama's gonna take good care of you."

She took him by the hand and led this time, instead of trying to push him around. He followed, letting her bring him to the dishwashing station. She turned on the water, checking it to make sure that she got the heat down from the typically scalding levels it was kept at by health department standards, then brought him over to stand on top of one of the many small drains in the kitchen's floor.

"Let me know if this is too hot, sweetie." She turned the flexible hose that hung above the sink on him and pressed the trigger. Water rushed over him, the blood running down his chest and his bird-like thighs in rivers of red. She stole a glance between his legs and saw that he was enjoying his shower as much as she was. Myrna had only been with two men before Ralph, and that had been forty years ago. She was flattered and more than a little excited to see that she could still have such an effect on a young man like Martin.

When he was clean he still stood there, in all his glory, not even shivering from the cooling water on his skin. She picked up a dish towel—woefully inadequate for drying off a body—and went to him, pressing herself against him as she pretended to care about toweling off his back. Her apron was soaking through, but she didn't even notice. He smelled good. So very, very good.

And then she was kissing him. She didn't even realize it was happening until his tongue pushed into her mouth. And she couldn't have stopped him if she'd wanted to. He was overpowering her, not with his body but with his raw, animal attraction. Myrna was used to getting a little tingle in the nethers from younger men—she was a devoted fan of *Days of Our Lives*, after all—but this was wholly different.

She was in thrall to him, incapable of resisting. She wanted him inside her. She was a married woman, and she and Ralph had always had a regular if not particularly varied sex life, which they thought admirable for a couple that had been together as long as they had, but for the first time in more than forty years she was in heat. She was so intoxicated that she didn't even notice she was being undressed until the sagging skin of her bosom was pressed against his sunken chest. He cupped her breast and fondled it, lifting it up to a height it hadn't seen on its own power since the Reagan administration. She felt young again, the pain in her hip and her feet from being on the move all day melting away in a flood of shameless passion.

"Take me, sugar. Take me now."

She grabbed his member and led him, as she had by the hand moments ago, to the lunch counter. She was suddenly glad she always pulled the blinds.

The Rusty Bucket Saloon

The night was not going at all the way Tara wanted it to.

She'd shown up hoping to spend some time with Joanne, but quickly realized that she had completely misinterpreted the other woman's intentions. Joanne had given her a warm, somewhat lingering hug when Tara first arrived at the bar, which had given her an initial burst of hope, but had barely spared a glance for her after introducing her to the table full of strangers she'd sat at for the next hour and a half. The rest of the girls had all been part of Joanne's high school clique, and were every bit as bitchy and shallow as Tara would have expected from small-town Methodist cheerleaders.

It was more *Mean Girls* than *Caged Heat*, and every moment it became more evident that she was simply not supposed to be here. The girls were at first guardedly polite and asked Tara questions about her job and what it was like growing up in a thriving metropolis like Omaha, but they swiftly lost interest in her when it became obvious that she was smarter than them and had little to no interest in the town's gossip or what three-years-out-of-style shoes were available at absurdly low prices at the outlet mall seventy miles away in Bannon.

Joanne, for her part, had been an utter gadfly, flitting about from table full of men to table full of men all night, periodically disappearing for a while and coming back looking progressively more rumpled. At the moment, for instance, she had been in the ladies' room for twenty minutes with a chubby, pockmarked guy she'd apparently met moments before over by the pool table in the corner. Tara certainly wasn't the type to judge anyone else's choices—especially where their sex life was concerned—but Joanne's grieving seemed to be spiraling into a nosedive of self-destruction. She wondered how many cases of the clap one woman could pick up in a single night.

By the look of most of the guys in this bar, Joanne should be a walking Petri dish by now.

The Rusty Bucket was not the shittiest bar she'd ever been in, but it was by far the shittiest bar she'd ever gone to on purpose. It was a small, wood-framed building on Main Street (which, this far out, was called Rural Route 1455) set far enough away from anything else that they never needed to worry about how noisy the patrons got, or whether they decided to go shoot their guns in the air Yosemite Sam-style after a few dozen rounds of Steel Reserve.

It also, ironically, ensured a nearly nightly epidemic of drunk driving, but Fulton's lone police officer didn't seem to have much concern for that, since the streets were always deserted by the time the drunks got out of the Bucket, anyway.

Inside, the wood-paneling walls were covered with thousands upon thousands of bottle caps, meticulously attached with tack nails. Tara thought this might have been the work of some sort of OCD savant or the desperate attempt of a bar owner to both cut down on the trash he sent out and fill an aesthetic void in his tavern at the same time. The place was lit by strings of Christmas lights run across the ceiling, the seemingly indiscriminate mix of white and colored lights reflecting off of the gold, silver and green-speckled walls making it virtually impossible to see anything inside with any clarity. That the bartenders in this place were not all subject to crippling migraines seemed a minor miracle.

As Tara contemplated leaving, the door to the ladies' swung open and Joanne emerged, blotting her lipstick on a length of paper towel from the roller dispenser, then using the same rough brown paper to wipe a glob of something Tara was sure she didn't want to know the provenance of off of her cheek. She strolled over to the table, and just as she pulled out her chair to sit, the door swung open again and the doughy, sloppy man she'd gone away with popped his head out, peered around and, clearly realizing he wasn't going to make a clean escape, gingerly walked out of the restroom, tucking in his shirt and skittering back to the pool table corner. He got five steps from the door, made a face, stopped, picked something out from between his teeth, examined it, then rubbed his hand clean on the thigh of his jeans. There was no evidence of lipstick on his face or neck. Tara shuddered. The thought of penises themselves had always been distasteful to her to begin with, but the thought of one attached to such a scumball...

"Don't you think so, Tara?" Joanne was saying. Tara started, realizing she'd been completely tuned out of the conversation.

"Sorry, I didn't catch that," she said, turning back and getting lost for a moment in Joanne's eyes. She was a gorgeous creature, to be sure, but definitely not Tara's type, insomuch as she could be said to have a type.

"I said we should all do a round of tequila shots in Cassie's honor."

Her eyes had that same yearning in them Tara had noticed at the funeral home. All the hooking up she had apparently done in the last hour and a half, and she was still horny for something? Tara felt that faint flutter again, even though she knew she shouldn't. *It's not me. It can't be. The best I can hope for is a sloppy, drunken makeout with her at the bar to procure ourselves a few free rounds.*

Nevertheless, here she was, still hanging on. It made her feel like she was in high school again, following her crushes around like a puppy dog, hoping for them to come to their senses and realize that she was the one they had always wanted. Even though it had been virtually impossible for a girl who knew she didn't care for boys to find a date at that age.

She blinked. *Focus, Tara. It's time to get out of here.*

"Sure," she heard herself saying. "I'd totally do a shot for Cassie!"

Goddammit!

Joanne sidled up to the bar, flitted her eyelashes at the bartender (who was nearly as foul-looking as the man she'd just sixty-nined in the bathroom), and came back with a tray filled with shot glasses. The urine-yellow hue of the liquor was not promising to Tara, who had never been a huge drinker to begin with and could most definitely not swing with tequila, especially the piss-poor brand they looked to be shooting.

"Well," Joanne said with a leer, "it came out of the well, but it was free." She distributed the tiny glasses to the girls then took a seat. Raising her glass she said, "Here's to Cassie—everyone in town who didn't want to fuck her stupid wanted to marry her. She was my best friend, and this dead-end, no-horse shithole of an ass-backward pioneer re-enactment village will never see her like again."

They clinked glasses to a murmur of agreement from the girls who, apparently, were utterly lost after the word "shit", then they slugged down the shots. Tara winced as the tequila hit her tongue then teared up as it burned its way down her esophagus and into her already roiling stomach.

"Hey Jo, check it out –Jimmy Barber's over there at the bar," said one of the ladies—Donna, maybe? "Don't be too obvious when you look, but he's staring at you pretty hard."

Joanne, completely lacking anything approximating subtlety, turned a hundred and eighty degrees in her chair and waved at the sad-sack boy sitting at the bar in a mesh trucker hat that Tara assumed he sported without a hint of irony. He quickly looked away, but Joanne waved emphatically with her entire arm.

"Jimmy! I didn't think you were old enough to get in here!" She stood and walked over to him. He seemed to shrink into his chair with every step she took. She leaned in to him, pressing her breasts against his back, and Tara couldn't hear what she said over the ancient vinyl jukebox crooning Lynyrd Skynyrd, but little Jimmy—who honestly did look to be about fifteen years old—suddenly sat up straight in his chair and nodded. Joanne dragged a finger across his shoulder as she sauntered away, and the boy stood up, downed the rest of his beer, tossed a five dollar bill on the bar, and walked out the door.

Tara decided that she had reached the end of her desire to be here. The tequila was not playing nice with the two Jack and Cokes that were already crowding her stomach, and she wasn't sure she'd want to sleep with Joanne now, even if she had the opportunity and a Hazmat suit.

She stood up to leave as Joanne got to the table and opened her mouth to say goodbye, but before she could get the words out, Joanne wriggled her hips, ran her hands down over her legs, then bent over and stood up with a pair of neon pink underwear in her hands, which she placed in the palm Tara had outstretched, expecting a goodbye handshake.

"Hang on to these for me, dear," she said with a slight growl and a significant slur. "You can put them back on me in a little bit, if you'd like." Then she turned and walked out the door.

Tara decided to stay a few more minutes.

Myrna's House

Clayton had opted not to go meet everyone else at the Bucket. Despite what the entire town might think, he was not used to being drunk at ten in the morning, and he was tired.

As he slowly sobered up over the course of the day he found himself more and more depressed. He'd superficially accepted Cassie's death days ago, and he would never show it to anyone else—especially not Jerry—but he was not ready to let go of her just yet. It all struck him as supremely unfair: Cassie was supposed to be the one who had a glorious life, reaching escape velocity and rocketing out of Fulton Flats, hopefully dragging Jerry and himself behind her. She was the promise of a somewhat less shitty future, and now she was gone. It was like those scores of pretty blonde American girls you always saw on *Nancy Grace*, who went exploring on some Caribbean island and disappeared while the primetime newsmagazine shows went apoplectic.

Except Cassie wasn't missing. He knew precisely where she was right now: she was six feet beneath a gaudy marble angel that the whole town had pitched in to place in All Souls Cemetery to commemorate their favorite daughter.

So instead of going to get even more shitfaced with Jerry and a passel of people he could barely stand, he had opted to stay home and drown his sorrows in late-night b-movies about small American towns being overrun and devoured by various horrors. He never wondered for a moment why these movies always took place in backwaters like the one he lived in; there was a very real and righteous pleasure in watching this particular way of life being terrorized time and again. He wished daily for a werewolf or an enormous irradiated ant to wipe out this idiot town and all of its idiot inhabitants.

He was beginning to nod off in the recliner when the front door banged open, waking him with a start. His mom walked in with a purposeful stride and headed straight for the stairs.

"Hey, Ma," he said, trying to get his racing heart under control. He looked at the clock. "You're late getting home. Last-minute customer show up?"

She stopped in her tracks and swiveled her head to look at him, her body remaining poised mid-stride. There was a strange look in her eye, one that struck him as vaguely familiar, but he couldn't precisely place where he had seen it before.

She squinted at him for a moment, apparently evaluating, and then continued up the stairs. Clayton shrugged and went back to watching what appeared to be a swarm of alien-infected people devour their neighbors.

When Myrna reached the bedroom she dropped her purse to the floor with a clatter, spilling loose pennies, rolls of Chapstick and about a dozen paper tissues. She shrugged out of the drab pink dress that was the uniform at the Corner Diner and pounced on Ralph, who was snoring contentedly on the bed. He tried to scream as he was startled from slumber, but her mouth was already locked over his. Wide-eyed, he recognized her and stopped struggling, giving in to her insistent tongue. When the kiss broke he sat up.

"Well, damn. Welcome home, baby. Good day at work?"

She tore the covers off of him without a word and went to work.

Downstairs, Clayton was awakened by what he at first thought was some sort of violent confrontation going on in his parents' bedroom. He'd never known them to fight, much less get physical, and was in the process of bounding to his feet when he heard his father's voice very distinctly yell "Yeah, woman, ride it hard!" and promptly quit listening. He settled back down in the chair and did his best to ignore the crescendo of groans and screaming bedsprings coming from the top of the stairs.

His head was pounding now, and all he wanted was some peace and quiet and to go to sleep, but his bedroom was across the hall from theirs, and he was definitely not going to get any closer until whatever was going on up there (his brain steadfastly refused to form any sort of opinion on what precisely it was) was well and truly finished. They were an elderly married couple, how long could it possibly last? He picked up the remote, turned the volume on the television up to its maximum, and watched his movie with a laser-like focus.

The Rusty Bucket

That's it, I am really, certainly, definitely leaving now.

It had been half an hour, and Tara was sick of waiting. She ran her fingers through the satin of Joanne's panties, which she hid under the table. No lay was worth this torture, no matter how long she'd been celibate. Things were definitely getting weird in the bar, and the cheerleader klatch that she'd been foisted on had made it abundantly clear that they were in no way interested in her. She sighed and looked around one last time.

Whatever was driving Joanne's libido (and, to be honest, her own—she'd not been this compelled to sleep with a woman since Betsy and she...but that was not something she wanted to dredge up just at that moment) was apparently extremely contagious. In every dimly-lit corner and dark booth a couple was making out, pawing each other openly and without regard to the very public nature of their surroundings. Tara had been in sex clubs in the Castro that were more restrained than what was going on here. It was hard to tell in the glow of the string lights, but she was pretty sure the man and woman over by the jukebox were actually having intercourse on a tall bar stool. It seemed like a dangerous proposition to her, if not an outright physical impossibility.

Though some part of her was secretly delighted to have every salacious rumor about small-town America confirmed before her very eyes, she had never been an overtly sexual person; she was proud of who she was and not cowed by her sexual preference, but it had never been something she felt the need to wear on her sleeve, even in a city as open as the one she grew up in. She was, frankly, growing quite uncomfortable.

Three of the girls from the group she had been sitting with had been pulled away from the table already: one was stuffed into a booth with a man in full cowboy regalia, her hand pretty obviously down his pants; the other two had disappeared out the door into the parking lot with the skeevy-looking guy Joanne had blown in the bathroom. Tara knew she wasn't the most attractive woman in the room, but she was really not prepared to fend off the advances of some drunk, horny Idaho farmhand tonight. She looked over to the bar to see what she would have to contend with when she went to pay her tab and saw the bartender leaning on the back bar, his pants around his ankles.

Hairy man-ass. Yup, I'm out of here. I'll come back to get my credit card tomorrow.

She stood, but once again the moment she got to her feet the door burst open and Joanne strode in. It was like she knew every time Tara was about to depart and conspired to keep her where she was. Joanne's eyes no longer held the look of conflict they had before—now they looked purely ravenous. She had obviously dressed in a hurry. Her dress was on backwards and her bra was missing. Her right breast was hanging fully exposed out of the immodestly plunging back, covered in livid red hickeys and bite marks.

She headed straight for the table and, without a word, crooked her elbow around the tiny blonde sitting across from Tara—*I'm pretty sure she said her name was Maureen?*—pulled her over backward, toppling her out of her chair, and clamped her teeth down on the girl's neck. Before anyone knew what was happening, Maureen was screaming and Joanne had a hunk of skin in her mouth.

Tara was dumbstruck. She stared in horror, not entirely sure what she was supposed to do in this sort of situation. There were catchy phrases for nearly every emergency that she had been taught as a child—stop drop and roll; duck and cover; get in the doorway—but nobody ever told you how to deal with a situation in which a girl you barely know but want to have sex with attacks her friend in a cannibalistic rage.

She looked around desperately, hoping someone else knew what to do. The first thing she noticed was that those who were already engaged in sexual activities throughout the bar were completely oblivious to the violence going on and, if anything, were going at it with even more gusto. The rest appeared just as at sea as she was, desperately looking to each other to make the first move. Finally, a huge man in biker's leather—he must have weighed three hundred and fifty pounds and was five feet across if he was an inch—walked over and grabbed Joanne's shoulder, trying to pry her off of the writhing, bleeding Maureen. No sooner had his fingers brushed her skin, though, than the front door flew open again and Jimmy Barber came running in, made a beeline for Joanne and the biker, and latched himself onto the man's wrist, biting through the tendon before the behemoth could even react.

The man yelled and took a swing with his other arm, but Jimmy had already severed the hand entirely with two more bites and the biker's swing went wide as he swooned with shock.

Joanne, her hair now matted to her head with the man's blood, paid no notice as she continued to gnaw through Maureen's throat, barely taking time to chew her flesh before swallowing.

The other girls at the table had scrambled away screaming once they recovered their ability to move, and were now cowering in a corner, huddled together for safety. Tara inched slowly toward them, doing her best not to draw Joanne's attention. Backing along, she ran into a tall man in jeans and a Nirvana t-shirt who instinctively wrapped his arm protectively around her.

Without thinking, she shrugged him off and stepped back toward the chair she'd been sitting in, bumping it and making it squeal as it skidded across the linoleum floor. Joanne, seemingly aware of her surroundings for the first time since re-entering the bar, looked up, her mouth and chin a mess of blood and scraps of torn muscle tissue.

Tara froze in place.

Joanne seemed to stare right through her as though she weren't there at all. There was no spark of recognition in her eyes, nothing even remotely human; only the hunger and a slight but palpable confusion.

Tara inched her way back toward the group of girls, not really knowing if she was going to them for safety in numbers or because there was a greater chance for her to get away if there were more potential victims around. When she dared to shoot a glance over her shoulder, she noticed that the man in the Nirvana shirt who she had fled a moment ago now had his arms around two of the girls and was surreptitiously fondling their breasts. The girls he was groping seemed to have lost their concern over the fact that one of their friends was devouring another and instead were pressing themselves against him.

Tara was completely befuddled. She looked back at Joanne, who had resumed her butchery. She had torn Maureen's blouse open and bitten off a fair portion of her right breast. The blonde girl's nipple flapped luridly back and forth, connected to the rest of her now by only a shred of skin, as her body convulsed.

Behind Joanne's back, Jimmy was punching the pulpy remains of the biker's head then licking his fist clean before punching him again.

Tara looked from the massacre over to the door. She would have to go right past the two monsters if she wanted to get out, but there was really no other clear exit. She could try for the kitchen, but it was much farther and she didn't care to go past all of the couples now openly fornicating around the room.

She looked back at Joanne, made a snap decision, and ran for the door as fast as she could.

Joanne looked up from her meal as Tara passed, gave the same bewildered look, then went back to finish off Maureen's tits.

Tara slammed the door open, ran outside, and smacked directly into a young man, throwing them both to the ground.

Her nose throbbed from the collision with his chest and her knees were skinned from the fall. She scrambled to pull herself off of him.

"What the fuck, lady? Watch where you're going! Where's the fucking fire?"

"It's…inside, it's terrible. Eating. They're eating each other," she panted. "And…and also fucking. They're fucking and eating each other. Need the police. Help me. *Help me!*" She managed to get to her feet and help him up.

"What are you babblin' about? Are you drunk?" He gave her a light but insistent shove. "Get the fuck away from me, nutso. I have had an epically shitty day." He moved toward the door, limping slightly. "I just wanna go have a few beers with my friends. Well, a few *more* beers, with people who don't really like me that much." He reached for the doorknob.

"*Don't go in there!* Mister, look…mister…"

He turned. "Jerry. Don't call me 'Mister', you sound like Dennis the fuckin' Menace."

"Jerry, please, don't open that door. It's hell in there. Like, real, actual hell. And I say this as an atheist."

"Lady, you are tap dancing on the one ragged nerve I got left. What the sam hell is wrong with you?"

"We need to get help. Everyone's gone crazy in there. My friend Joanne…well, not really my friend, just someone I met today…she's…god, she's eating another girl in there."

His eyes grew wide. "Joanne Hallstrom?" Tara nodded eagerly. "Is eating another girl?" She nodded again. "And you think I *don't* wanna see that?" He turned the knob and opened the door. "I always knew that girl was a freak."

Jerry turned his head and looked into the maelstrom that was The Rusty Bucket.

"What in the literal fuck—"

Myrna's House

He couldn't believe this was still going on.

The alien infestation movie (turns out, it was called *Planets Clash* and was some of the most heavy-handed 50s-era anti-Communist propaganda he had ever seen) had ended and he was a solid hour into one about a fifteen-story-tall lizard that came out of the jungles of Mexico to ravage a small Texas burgh, and his parents were still bumping uglies upstairs. Loudly. Vehemently. Disgustingly.

Having maxed out the volume on the television long ago, Clayton had since turned on the surround sound and cranked it up as high as it would go as well. Most of the noise was drowned out now, but the incessant thump of the bed legs on the floor (*how are they even doing that*, he thought) could not be ignored.

In desperation he had gone into the kitchen and taken his dad's "secret" bottle of Kentucky Gentleman bourbon out from the depths of the canned goods cupboard and was drinking it straight from the plastic gallon jug. It didn't make the noises go away, but it did make him care somewhat less. In fact, though he had never really believed in the old "hair of the dog" thing, he was starting to feel pretty good, other than the severe psychological trauma.

Suddenly, his pants tingled.

This concerned him deeply. All he had felt up until now was a queasy disapproval and an enormous irritation. He knew there were people out there in the world who were perfectly all right with the idea that their parents had sex, but he was emphatically not one of them. Sure, they had obviously done it once, but as far as Clay was concerned, his conception was the single time they had ever touched each other in that way, and even then they probably approached it with a businesslike efficiency.

So why was he feeling this buzz in his crotch all of the sudden? There was no way in hell this was beginning to turn him on. No. Way. In. Hell. He had tried early on to pretend that it was two other people upstairs banging each other stupid, two people he could accept as being sexually active. The Parkers, maybe. Allison Parker was a pretty decent-looking lady. If she was not fully a MILF, she was definitely MILF-adjacent. He'd tried to imagine the Parkers in his parents' bed, humping energetically. And every single time, the image was ruined by a shout of "yeah, Myrna, take it all!" Was he losing his mind then? Was this sudden tingle in his groin an early manifestation of some sort of Stockholm syndrome?

It came again, and he realized, with no small amount of chagrin, that his cell phone was vibrating in his pocket.

He fished it out and read the display before flipping it open.

"Jerry, you would not *believe* the shit that is going down upstairs right now."

Jerry said something, but he couldn't make it out.

"What? Dude, are you at the Bucket? It's noisy as fuck over there."

More muffled words from the phone, then he suddenly had an epiphany. "Hang on, Jer. I'm gonna turn down the TV."

He set the phone down on the coffee table and picked up the separate remotes that controlled the television and the surround sound, muting each in turn. Without the screams of Texas ingénues beset by giant lizards, he was assaulted by the full force of bangs, squeaks and groans from the top of the stairs. He was somewhat relieved, though, to notice that his father had taken a break from yelling disturbing internet-porn-quality phrases.

He shuddered and picked the phone back up.

"Can you hear this shit? Ralph and Myrna are goin' buck nasty up there!"

"Clay, can you hear me? *Clay!*"

"Yeah, yeah, I hear you. Sorry, I had to turn the TV up to Who concert levels to drown out the sound of my parents. What's up?"

"Clay, shit is going down at the Bucket. Like…seriously, I can't even describe the level of what-the-fuckery here."

"Seriously? Like what?"

"No time to explain. Me and Tara gotta get out of here, and I rode my bike and her tires got slashed. You need to get your ass over here. *Now*."

"Who the hell is Tara? Dude, are you calling me to pick you up with a hookup? So not classy. Especially when you hear what I'm going through over here right now."

"She's not a fuckin' hookup, Clay, and we are in real and serious danger! Please, I need you to get in Myrna's car and get your fat, hairy ass over here."

"Fine, fine. I'll be there in ten. Keep your damn panties on. Or take 'Tara's' panties off." He snickered. Jerry did not. He knew this was a bad sign.

"Just get here. I don't know how much longer I can keep the doors held shut."

"Keep the doors...Jerry, what the fuck is going on?"

"*Goddammit, Clayton, get in the fucking car and get over he—*"

The phone cut out.

Worried, Clay pulled on his shoes, picked his wallet and keys up off of the hall table and walked to the foot of the stairs. He winced at the continued cacophony.

"Uh, dad?" he yelled up tentatively. "Mom? I'm gonna take your car for a minute. Jerry needs a ride from the Bucket. Are you cool with that?"

"Yes...yes, oh god yes...take it...fucking take it..."

"Cool, thank y—"

"Take it deep, baby. Take all Daddy's got for you, you dirty little thing."

Clay rushed for the door, desperately hoping to get out on the lawn before the vomit made its way up.

Main Street

In his rush to help his best friend and also to escape the horrifying noise of his parents' noisy (and, apparently, rather kinky) lovemaking, Clayton nevertheless took the time to eject the Hank Williams CD from the stereo of his mother's car and replace it with his patented "Speeding Ticket Mix", which consisted largely of the kind of heinous, grumbling heavy metal music that's little more than someone dragging their vocal chords over a bed of hot coals and broken glass, accompanied by double kick-drums that were so far forward in the mix that they were practically in the listener's lap.

The right song for the right situation was his motto, and as such he kept a flip folder full of various mixes designed for different situations. He had, for instance, a "Makin' Moves Mix" for his increasingly infrequent special times with the ladies, which was filled with slightly slower death metal with somewhat less distorted vocals and lacked any songs about fucking the dead or pickaxe murders, and a "Celebration Mix" for life's little victories that had death metal with more-than-usually distorted vocals and featured a far greater abundance of necrophilia and pickaxe murders. He fancied himself something of a soundtracker of life.

With the proper tunes in place, he carefully buckled his seatbelt and tore off toward the Rusty Bucket with all the haste he could safely muster. He was, by his own admission, more than a little drunk, and had been so pretty much all day. But the straight, empty rural routes that headed out of town allowed him to get up to a rollicking forty-nine miles per hour. He wasn't worried about a DUI—everyone knew that Steve Barley, the city's one and only police officer, never worked nights. It was an unspoken rule in Fulton: if you wanted to drive drunk, at least have the decency to do it after ten when most of the people were off the roads. So off he modestly sped.

At the blinking red stoplight downtown, he shot a quick look up and down Harrison and spotted a car a few dozen feet away. He was pretty sure he'd make the light first, so he slowed down to about five miles per hour and rolled on through, what the locals affectionately called a "California stop" though none of them had ever been to California nor, as far as they knew, met anyone who had. He hit the accelerator five feet into the intersection then slammed on the brakes when a shadow-shrouded form shambled out in front of the car. In the intermittent red glow he could definitely tell that it was a person, that it was completely nude, and that it was sporting a pretty rockin' hard-on.

Perplexed and more than a little drunkenly fascinated, he threw the car in park and got out.

"Hey dickwad, watch where you're going! I almost ran you over. And put some fuckin' clothes on, you perver—*Martin*?!"

Martin, who had continued shuffling across the street as though nothing had happened, stopped and looked curiously at Clayton, who immediately averted his eyes.

"What the fuck, man? Cover up that broadsword of yours, would you?"

Martin just stared.

"Is that…is that blood on your chest? And your face? And hands, and…Martin, you alright?"

Now Martin was turning slowly, his eyes fixed on Clay's.

"Martin, man, seriously. Don't go pointin' your wang at me like that, it ain't polite. You're freaking me out a little, dude."

He looked around for help and realized that the car he had seen before didn't appear to have moved an inch, though the lights were on and he could hear the motor humming softly.

"Hey Martin," he said, extending his arms, palms out toward the undertaker, "why don't you just stay right there? I'm gonna go ask that guy over there if he's got a spare jacket for you, ok? Just…just stay right there, alright? Martin? *STAY!*"

Martin, perplexed, stopped in his tracks.

"Good…uh, good boy. Good Martin. Just hang on a minute and I'll get you somethin' to cover up with." He backed away from Martin toward the other car. "Look, I know how it is. You're home gettin' really stoned—I mean, I can only imagine that you'd have to smoke a shit-ton of weed to survive in your profession—and then you, I don't know, run outta porno tapes to watch?"

He was getting close to the car now, and Martin hadn't moved, just followed him with his eyes, a confused look on his face. "So out you go into the streets to find some more porno, right? Because there's a huge abundance of porn stores here in downtown Fulton Flats, and—"

His foot came down with a dull crunch and squish. *Funny for there to be a mud puddle in the middle of the street now*, he thought. *It hasn't rained in—*

He looked down at his shoe, which had sunk a few inches into what he could only guess used to be someone's ribcage. Most of the bones had been broken off, sucked dry of their marrow, and discarded to the side, but there was enough of a jagged remnant to be able to recognize the architecture of the human torso. The squish had definitely come from the massive puddle of blood and shredded tissue pooling beneath the carcass. In his increasing state of shock, Clay was reminded of a sloppy joe sandwich.

He looked slowly up.

Martin had begun walking toward him again.

"Uh, Martin…do you know what's goin' on here? Is this…do you know this guy?"

Martin ambled closer, his arms limp at his sides, his face a mask of fury and hunger. He leaned slightly forward as though fighting against a mild headwind. Clay shook his foot free of the pile of bones and meat and inched away. It took him a few steps before he realized that he was moving in the opposite direction of his car.

He looked around desperately, wishing, not for the first time, that there was some goddamned life on the streets in this town at night. He moved laterally, hoping to get far enough to Martin's side that he could get around him and make a dash for the car, but Martin simply changed direction as well and kept approaching; slowly, steadily.

Realizing that the street was too narrow to make a real break around his pursuer, Clay continued to back away. He nearly tripped on the curb, but through the miracle of drunken physics managed to regain his feet before he crashed down to the pavement. The short lag, though, allowed Martin to get even closer. He was within ten feet of Clayton now, and had brought his arms up, reaching.

"Hey Martin, come on now. Let's talk, ok? Tell me what's going on. I can help you."

No reaction.

"Did you kill that guy? I'm sure it was an accident, right?"

Nothing.

"Hey, you want me to help you get rid of the body? I mean, I got a quick errand to do here, but as soon as I get back I'd be more than happy. Anyone who drives a hybrid car basically had it comin' to him, anyway, am I right?"

Martin was only five or six feet away now. Clay looked over his shoulder and noticed that he was nearing the end of the block. He thought about the movies he'd been burying himself in all evening. There was definitely some sort of Romero-esque nightmare scenario going on here, and there was one thing that he knew about zombies: you could outrun them. Formulating a quick plan, he pointed down Harrison Street behind Martin.

"Holy shit, dude, is that the brains delivery truck?"

Martin turned away for a second, and Clay took off running. He figured if he could get Martin to follow him around the block, staying just ahead of the slowly lumbering undertaker, he could safely make it back to his car.

He got just out of sight around the corner and stopped, not wanting Martin to fall too far behind him lest he just turn around and walk back to the car himself. Catching his breath—even a run of a few yards is hard work when you're drunk and pathetically out of shape—he waited to catch sight of his pursuer before his next sprint. The plan, he thought, smiling to himself, was a solid one. Then Martin came wheeling around the side of the Ace Hardware, flat-out running. Clay hightailed it.

"Martin, seriously," he shouted over his shoulder, "what the fuck did I ever do to you? You want my clothes? Here." He pulled off the t-shirt he was wearing over a long-sleeved undershirt and threw it behind him. "Take it. It's my favorite, but you obviously need it more than I do."

Martin didn't even flinch as the shirt tangled in his feet and sent him sprawling to the cement face first. Clay kept running for another dozen feet—just to be safe—then stopped and looked back.

As Martin stood, Clay gasped. The skin on Martin's cheeks, nose and forehead was torn from the fall, and blood was beginning to well up in the tatters and weep down his jaw. He seemed utterly unfazed. He got back to his feet, the flesh of his palms and knees as ripped up as his face, and continued the chase.

"Fuck me," Clay screamed as he took off again.

Luckily for Clay, the parsing of land downtown had changed very little since Fulton was a small pioneer farming village, so the block was relatively small. He whipped around the second corner, slowing down only to topple an aluminum trash can that had been left on the curb despite the fact that everyone knew that Tuesday was trash day. Though the tactic always seemed to work in the movies, in reality the can simply fell ineffectually to the ground with a clatter and rolled back and forth, completely failing to insert itself into Martin's path.

As he wheeled around another corner and saw the car door standing open in front of him, Clayton could hear Martin's pounding footsteps coming closer.

In a rush of adrenaline and unadulterated panic he pushed for an extra ounce of speed, pulled slightly ahead, and dove into the car head-first, quickly torquing himself around to pull the door closed behind him.

Martin ran full-force into the car, his tattered and bleeding face pressed against the window, then ricocheted back and plopped down on his ass. Clay sat in the driver's seat panting, his lungs and legs burning from the exertion of the most running he'd done since that hated day in junior high school when they were forced to run the mile. The window, fogged from the heat of his breath and smeared with Martin's blood, was completely opaque. He hit the toggle to roll it down a few inches and saw Martin slowly get to his feet, his nose now crushed and sitting nearly perpendicular to the rest of his head. He stuck his lips up to the opening.

"What the fuck, Martin? Are you methed out?"

Martin stood and shambled over to the car. Clay barely managed to get his face away before Martin's fingers were reaching in. He managed to get in up to the wrist before Clay hit the switch to roll up the window, pinning him in place.

"Dude, knock it off. I'm gonna roll down the window now. Pull your hands out and I'll go find you some help as soon as I can, ok?"

Martin said nothing, which Clay took as assent. He rolled the window down just far enough for Martin to free himself. Martin, instead, reached further in. Clay quickly rolled the window back up, stopping him halfway up his forearms.

"Fuck! Seriously, stop it!" Clay looked down. "I'm not fucking around, Martin. I will drive off like this. Just try me, bro. I'll do it."

Martin didn't budge.

"Alright, cocksucker, you asked for it." Clay dropped the car into drive and eased his foot off of the brake. The car rolled slowly forward. Martin, looking more confused and angry, trotted to keep up. When he'd gone about half a block, Clay rolled the window down slightly again, expecting Martin to fall away. Instead, Martin got both of his arms in up to the elbows and managed to grab Clayton's ear.

"Fucker!"

Clay leaned away from the window and stepped on the gas. He got up to about ten miles per hour and Martin began to falter. He rolled the window down again, but Martin managed to grasp onto the frame of the door with one hand while continuing to reach in with the other.

He rolled the window back up, leaned even further to the right, and gunned it. Martin was pulled off his feet immediately and dragged behind the car. The asphalt acted like a cheese grater on the tops of Martin's feet, leaving a trail of blood and skin behind, but his face registered no pain; only anger, and that strange hunger he'd displayed at the funeral. His fingers wriggled as he tried desperately to get a hold on Clayton's face.

Clay slammed on the brakes. Martin's body, still anchored to the car by his arms pinned in the window, made a wide arc and slammed into the windshield. He turned his face to stare in at Clay with unabashed hatred.

"Yeah, that wasn't one of my best ideas, was it?" Clay hit the gas again and Martin rolled up over the roof of the car with a crunch that Clay could only assume was his shoulders dislocating. He flopped briefly then fell over the side, his knees now taking the brunt of the damage on the road.

"Fuck fuck fuck fuck fuck fuck fuck fuck fuck fuck fuck," Clay muttered. "Dammit, Martin, let go. Jesus, you're ground chuck out there."

He took one hand off of the wheel to fish his cell phone out of his pants pocket and press it up against the window. "I have a phone. I'll call 911 the moment you let go of my fucking car. Deal?" He clumsily hit the numbers and hovered his thumb over the "call" button. "See? I'll get you help, I promise. But you gotta let go, dude. Alright?"

He slowed the car down to let Martin get to what was left of his feet again, then tapped the toggle to open the window a hair, but only earned Martin another quarter of an inch into the cabin, which he used to snatch the phone out of Clay's hand and crush it in his fist.

"You dick! You owe me ninety bucks for that!" Clay slammed the gas and the car jumped. He tore down Main as fast as he could, slaloming, trying to shake Martin free. But it was fruitless; even if his arms weren't wedged into the window, Martin had made it quite clear that he was not interested in help or ending the continuing shredding of his lower extremities.

As he approached the edge of town, Clay spotted what he thought was his last salvation. He straightened out the wheel and pulled toward the left side of the road, accelerating to a speed that was, frankly, reckless even on a deserted rural route. He took a deep breath, waited for the optimal moment, then rolled down his window slightly just as Martin's head collided with the signpost on the side of the road. There was a crunch and a spurt of blood, and the arms disappeared.

Clayton closed the window and drove on without slowing down, looking in the rear-view mirror to make sure that he wasn't being chased. He was safe. Martin's inert body lay at the foot of the large, carved wooden sign that read:

Welcome to Fulton Flats
A friendly place to live.

The Rusty Bucket

Clay pulled into the Bucket's parking lot to find Jerry and a thin brunette woman he'd never seen before with their backs pressed against the door. He pulled up close, brazenly ignoring the fire lane parking rules, and rolled down the passenger-side window.

"Jerry, you would not believe what just happened to me."

"Dude, I bet you a bottle of Everclear my story is better."

"You're on, let's hear it."

"Get your ass up here and help me first. We can discuss as we drive away from this place as fast as we can."

Clay put the car in Park and hopped out.

"What's the deal? And who's your lady-friend?" He spared a moment to leer. Not really his type in general, a little bookish and kinda skinny, but she'd certainly do.

Still bracing himself against the door, which seemed to be thumping outward at irregular intervals, Jerry inclined his head toward Tara. "Clayton Barre, this is Tara Sokoloff. She just moved here a couple months ago from Omaha."

Clay nodded approvingly.

"Tara, Clay. He's my best friend."

Tara touched a finger to her forehead.

"Now that we're all old hands, can you please put your hefty ass against this door? Those fuckers are gonna break through any minute now if we don't do something."

"What fuckers?" Clay said, nudging Tara aside to wedge himself in between them. "What's going on here?"

"Tara can explain it best, she saw the whole thing. I just caught the tail end of it."

Clayton looked to Tara and raised an eyebrow.

"They've gone...I don't know how to explain it exactly...they've gone savage in there," she said as a strong slam from inside almost knocked all three from their feet.

With a new-found concern for his safety, Clay narrowed his eyes at her. "'They' who?"

"'They' everyone. Like, the whole clientele of The Rusty Bucket, last I checked. I was the only one in there who seemed not to have lost her goddamned mind."

"Tara came with Joanne Hallstrom," Jerry added helpfully.

"Oh," Clay said with a withering look to Tara. "You're one of Joanne's girls."

"No, I'm not! I barely know her. I met her at the funeral this afternoon and she invited me out to meet new people. She seemed...well, 'nice' isn't really the word I'd use, but..."

"You ain't wrong, lady. Joanne is not what anybody would describe as 'nice'," Clay opined. "'Cold-hearted, soulless hate machine' works a bit better."

"She let me feel her up once in high school," Jerry said. "Did I ever tell you about that, Clay? After gym class behind the basketball courts. She wanted me to vote for her for prom court, I said I couldn't judge her worth by her looks alone. Full over-the-bra grab. Joke was on her, I voted for Cassie. Five times, actually. I cheated that election so fucking hard. I'll never understand how Joanne won. Must've let a lot of dudes squeeze her Charmin."

"Fuck, seriously? She never made *me* that offer!"

"She knew you were gonna vote for Cassie no matter what. No sense throwing good titties after bad, as my grampa used to say."

"Your grampa was a minister. He never said anything like—"

"Guys," Tara broke in, "as fascinating as this is, can we focus for just a moment, please? Remember, we are fighting for our lives here."

"Sorry," Clay said. "I didn't fully appreciate the gravity of the situation here, I guess."

"Yeah, sorry, Tara," Jerry chimed in. "We get caught up sometimes." He elbowed Clayton. "Especially where Joanne Hallstrom's jugs are concerned."

The boys chortled.

"*Focus*," Tara shouted, hip-checking Clay so hard he almost lost his footing.

"Right, sorry. So you came here with Joanne..."

"I came here to meet Joanne. Then she started flipping out,

acting really weird. She had this look in her eye all night, like she wanted to eat my face."

"Holy shit, Jerry, remember Martin's face at the wake? That's exactly what he looked like, too. Which reminds me—"

"One story at a time, Clay. Please. I'm confused enough already. You can tell yours in a minute." Clay shrugged.

"So Joanne's acting weird, and then she starts flirting with the strangest people. Like, guys way below her league."

"Fuck, I knew I shoulda come sooner," Clay said.

"So then she starts disappearing for ten, twenty minutes at a time. With these guys. She was taking them into the bathroom or out behind the bar and, I guess, fucking them."

"*Dammit!*" Clay pounded his fist on the door. It was answered by another racking thump from the other side. The three took a moment to regain their footing.

"Then shit got really weird," Tara continued. "The guys she fucked came back in, and they started hooking up with other women. Like, right inside the bar in front of everyone. Then Joanne…well, she sorta…"

"She ate Maureen Riley, Clay." Clay's eyebrows shot up. "No, not the sexy kind, I mean like put her teeth into Maureen's neck and chewed her skin up. When I got here she was just finishing up chowing down on her tits. Covered in blood. You ever see that movie *Jennifer's Body*? With that hottie from *Transformers* in it? It was like that, dude. Straight-up munchin' on people."

"And then the others started in fighting and fucking and eating each other too," Tara added. "It's like half Roman orgy, half *The Hills Have Eyes* in there. So we hightailed it out. Jerry held the door while I went around back to wedge his bike against the kitchen exit, then we found the tires on my car slashed. I think that's unrelated to the situation inside and very related to the fact that some of Joanne's friends are serious, hardcore cunts."

"But then we didn't have anything to block the front door, so we've been holding it for the last half hour. What took you so long?"

"Long story," Clay said. "I'll tell you on the drive. But why have you been blocking the doors instead of just running for your lives?"

"And let those people get out into the town?" Tara asked. "We have to buy time to warn everyone."

Clay and Jerry looked at each other and shrugged.

"You clearly haven't been here long," Clay said. "I mean, most of the people in this town are dicks, to be honest. A little cannibal holocaust in Fulton Flats might do the human gene pool goo—"

The door exploded from the inside, knocking them down. When Clay looked up he expected to see an army of the walking dead standing in the open doorway, but there was only a single, somewhat petite woman. She was nude to the waist, her small, pert breasts heaving from exertion. She was spattered like a Pollock painting with dried blood and at least three other bodily fluids, one of which Clay could easily identify from the crunchy sweat sock he kept discreetly stashed under the edge of his bed. She was covered in a wide variety of livid bruises, most of them concentrated on her tits, her lips and her face, and had a perfect, glistening bite taken out of her torso just under her ribcage that was languidly dripping mostly-congealed blood.

He pushed himself up to his knees as the woman fell on Jerry, who had landed closest to the door. Jerry yelped and tried to wriggle away, but the woman grabbed him by the belt and dragged him back to her, then began unbuckling him.

"Help," he shouted, then looked down at the woman, falling suddenly silent. Clay watched in utter disbelief as he arched his pelvis in the air to facilitate her taking his pants off.

Clay leaped to his feet and dashed to the door, landing a solid kick to the woman's face. She flew over backward off of Jerry, who glared up at Clay furiously.

"What the fuck, cockblocker?" He landed a solid punch to Clay's hamstring.

"OW!" Clay screamed, kicking Jerry in the ribs somewhat harder than he intended. "Have you lost your fucking mind? Remember what you *just* told me?" He turned back to the door in perfect time to see the woman get up on all fours and crawl toward him, licking her lips. She really was pretty fuckable. He always

liked the little ones—"spinners" the boys liked to call them—and the way she gnashed her teeth he could tell she would be down for a—

"God*DAMN*it!" He shook his head to clear it then aimed another kick to her jaw. She went reeling back again, the lower half of her head seeming to come unhinged with a sharp crack and flopping around of its own accord. He stepped inside to give her another kick to buy Jerry the time to stand. That's when he saw the utter bedlam going on at The Rusty Bucket.

In the center of it all was Joanne Hallstom, completely nude and crimson with coagulating blood. In what could only be described as a scene out of the most fetish-specific porn movie ever made, she was on all fours, surrounded by five men who were taking turns getting behind her and giving her the pipe. The ones who weren't penetrating her or being jerked off by her were busying themselves taking bites out of the other men, who didn't seem to mind or even notice at all. Joanne herself was stripping the flesh off of Jordan Myles' face with her teeth.

Not far from the mass murder gang bang was a burly biker type with his leather pants around his ankles and his face a mashed, pulpy mess, his left hand ending in a ragged stump, being ridden by Kelsey Warren—whose legs appeared to have both broken under the weight of him—while beating a skinny cattle rancher that Clay recognized as Jeff Towers, the current mayor of Fulton Flats, with a beer mug. Towers was trying to crawl away, leaving a wide smear of blood on the linoleum. The biker dealt another solid hit to Towers' head that dropped the smaller man. He lay convulsing on the floor, his hand coming to rest on the almost hilariously enhanced breast of the supine corpse of June Sommers, a morning waitress at The Corner Diner, who was in turn having her meticulously waxed thighs consumed by one of the teachers at Fulton Elementary whose name Clay did not know. The teacher, he noticed, was bare below the waist with what appeared to be a man's arm from the elbow down embedded to the wrist in her vagina.

If he'd had anything left in his stomach after painting his mother's decorative beds with his dinner earlier, he would have expelled it at that moment. Instead, he just convulsed with the most powerful dry heave of his life.

In the far corner of the room was a cowboy-looking guy in a flannel and jeans with the sort of Sam Elliot mustache that shouldn't exist in real life. He had his hands buried inside a doughy man's open chest, pulling out handfuls of gray and pink tissue that Clay couldn't possibly hope to identify. Behind the cowboy a youngish girl in a gingham shirt and short-shorts was screaming. The cowboy looked up from his meal at her and crooked his gore-covered finger. She stopped screaming and looked around as if to say, "who, me?" The cowboy pointed at his crotch. The farmer's daughter bit her lip, took another quick glance around the room, then walked over, unzipped him, and began to suck. The cowboy buried his head back in the fat man's chest and continued eating like a hog at a trough.

Everywhere Clayton looked was insanity. Blood painted the walls and furniture and pooled on the floor in such great quantities that a couple a few feet from the door who were fucking missionary were actually sliding across the room with each thrust, leaving an almost clean trail through the pools of red. He swallowed hard to fight back yet another strong urge to vomit, kicked the half-naked girl crawling toward him in her now-broken and distorted face one more time for good measure, and dashed back outside. Jerry pushed past him into the bar, and Clay grabbed him by the waistband of his boxer shorts and dragged him, protesting, back outside. He threw him into the back seat of the car where Tara was already waiting, tossed his pants in, flipped the child lock, locked the door and slammed it shut behind him.

Jerry tried the handle a few times, then slapped on the window and yelled out at Clay, "Dude, let me out of here. I was totally going to bang that chick! She's a solid seven. That's way better than I should be able to pull. Stop being a dick!"

Clay moved around the back of the car to get into the driver's seat and ran smack into a chubby guy who was standing dead still, staring at him with those now-familiar hungry eyes. He reeled back a step then charged at him, aiming his shoulder at the bigger man's stomach.

Though a brave effort, it was a complete failure and as the man grabbed his waist and dropped him to the ground in a pile-driver that would have made Hulk Hogan blush with envy, Clay cursed all the powers in the universe that movie logic had failed him for the third time that night.

Spinning to get back on his feet, he noticed two women coming up behind the tubby guy. He recognized them as friends of Joanne. The one with most of her shoulder gone and what looked like a tracheotomy made by human teeth was Stacey something-or-other. He didn't know the name of the brunette that immediately began dry-humping the guy's leg, but he'd seen her hanging out at the Bucket a few times. She was looking pretty good.

Fewer open wounds than Stacey, he thought. *I'd tap that.*

Then she bent around, not missing a thrust, and bit a chunk out of Stacey's upper arm. Without so much as flinching, Stacey punched the other girl on the top of her skull so hard that she left a fist-shaped dimple in her scalp, then pulled on her hair, tearing the skin off of her head and opening a hole. She reached three fingers into the opening and the girl's limbs flew out in all directions in a momentary spastic dance. Stacey pulled her fingers back out and luxuriously licked the gray matter from them.

Clay screamed like a schoolgirl.

The guy, momentarily distracted by the leg-humping he was receiving, was suddenly reminded of Clay's presence. He took a step forward, bringing the brunette with him, attached to his hip and now grinding on him more vehemently and erratically than before. She was clearly beginning to lose her fine motor control as Stacey pulled another finger-scoop of brain out of her head and ate it. The convulsing chick wrapped around his leg put enough drag on the man that Clay was able to get up and back away a few steps before realizing that he was headed right back toward the Bucket's front door. He stopped and cursed.

"Guys? Little help here?"

Tara was furiously pulling at the door handle of the car's back seat, but to no avail.

"You locked us in, Einstein," Jerry said with a shrug.

"The child lock doesn't affect the driver's door, dipshit," Clay yelped, inching away from the lurching tangle of ménage-a-trois lumbering toward him.

Tara wriggled over the console between the car's two bucket seats and plopped down behind the wheel. She started to open the door, took one look at the enormous guy mere steps away from Clay now, and realized that there was absolutely nothing she could do against that much hungry-hungry human. She closed the door, dropped the car into drive, and pulled away.

"You bitch," Clay screamed after her. "That's my mom's car! Come back here!"

"What are you doing?" asked Jerry. "We can't just leave him there!"

"Am I the only person here with half a brain?" Tara muttered. "Well, I mean, I guess I can say conclusively that Bella out there has half a brain…"

With the car no longer in the way, Clay adjusted his trajectory and moved steadily toward the center of the parking lot. The chubby guy, brunette still convulsing on his hip, changed course as well and followed out into more open territory. Clay was just figuring out the best direction to in which to make a run for it when he noticed the car coming back at him. He looked through the windshield at Tara, who gave him a "figure it out, dipshit" face and jerked her head to the side. Clay spent one seemingly endless second completely lost, then realized what she was doing and dove hard to his right, dodging the onrushing plastic bumper by a few short feet.

The car slammed into the pursuing monster, throwing all three of them through the door and back into the bar.

Tara hit the brakes and Clay dashed to the passenger door, jumped in, and screamed, *"DRIVE, DRIVE, DRIVE!"*

Main Street

"Pull over," Clay said. "I have to piss."

"Are you serious?" demanded Tara, her eyebrow arched nearly to her hairline. "There's a pack of flesh-eating maniacs back there that may stop fornicating any minute now and decide to come after us."

"We're far enough away, they won't be able to catch up in the time it takes me to go behind a tree and do my business. Besides, it's a miracle I didn't piss my pants when you almost ran me over."

"And saved your life. Funny how you have forgotten to mention that part each of the seven times you've told this story in the last five minutes."

"Just fucking pull over. I'll be quick. Besides, this way we can switch drivers. If my mom's car is gonna get any more fucked up than it already is, I should be the one responsible."

Tara skidded the car to a graceless halt by the side of the road, crossed her arms, and stared straight ahead. Clay looked at her pleadingly.

"Well, go on!"

"Tara...the child lock."

"Oh shit, right." She got out, walked around to the passenger door and opened it. Clay dashed into the trees, grabbing his crotch the entire way. Tara opened the back door for Jerry, as well.

"Since we're taking the world's most dangerous pit stop, do you need to go, too?"

"No, I'm good," he said after a momentary assessment. "Thanks, though."

"If I have to play mommy, I might as well be the best mommy possible." She flipped the child lock off, closed the door and got into the passenger seat.

"Hey Tara, I have a question for you."

"Shoot."

"How come you're the only one that got out of the Bucket?"

She turned around in the seat to look at him. "What do you mean?"

"Well, I mean…it's just that everyone else in the bar gave in to either fuckin' or killin'. Most of 'em was doing both. But you got out without a scratch. Why do you suppose that is?"

Outside, Clay came running back out of the trees, zipping up his jeans and making a nominal effort to tuck his shirt back in. He opened the door and plopped behind the wheel.

"You know, I hadn't really thought of it," Tara said, buckling her seatbelt.

"It's weird, right?" Jerry asked.

Clay looked from Tara to Jerry. "What's weird?"

"That I got out of the bar without going nuts," Tara said.

"She's the only one," Jerry said. "Everybody else…well, you saw."

"So, what," said Clay, looking to Tara, "you're immune somehow?"

"Well, I didn't say that. I mean, maybe I just got lucky. From what I saw, it looks like whatever was going around in there was passed through sex. Those…ok guys, I'm just going to go ahead and use the word that's got to be on all of our minds right now…those zombies didn't pass their disease on through biting like they do in the movies. The people who got bit just screamed and bled, and sometimes died. It wasn't until they had…" She looked at the two boys, strangers really, and felt uncomfortable for the first time since she'd run into Jerry on her way out of the bar. "…until they had some sort of sexual contact. That was when they freaked out."

The guys both nodded. She felt a little more relaxed.

"You said Joanne was acting weird from the start, right?" Clayton asked.

"Yeah," said Tara. "So she must…she must be patient zero. She hooked up with at least five different guys while we were there, and each of those guys went on to hook up with at least one other girl…"

"And it wasn't just…" Jerry struggled for the word, since they were trying to have an adult conversation here. "…intercourse, neither. I mean, you said you thought Joanne only…" he concentrated for another moment, then gave up on proper terminology; it's hard. "…well, she only gave that one guy a hummer."

"As far as I could tell, yeah. But he might have gone down on her too. I think he picked a pube out of his teeth when he came out of the bathroom. It was the guy who attacked Clay in the parking lot, actually. I mean, I wasn't in there with them or anything, but they weren't gone for long and only her lipstick was messed up when she came out, so…"

"So it's passed through…you know…sex fluids," Clay stammered with a slight blush. "And they put out some sort of…I don't know…horniness hormone or something?" Clay puzzled. "It doesn't make a lot of sense to me."

"I'm not a doctor, but I do edit a lot of science articles," Tara said. "We're just working out theories here, right?"

"Right," said Jerry. Clay nodded.

"So there's something else I noticed." The boys listened intently. "The zombies…" she felt stupid using the word, but didn't have a better alternative at the moment. "They seem to only attack people of their own sex." Clay and Jerry both looked confused. "Boys eat boys, girls eat girls."

"Well sure, that makes sense," said Clay. "If it's passed through sex, you'd want to destroy your competition and procreate with as many partners as possible." Jerry looked at him, astonished. "I watched a thing on Animal Planet last week."

"And the zombies become, like, super attractive to people of the opposite sex when they get infected," Jerry said. "I mean, I felt it myself. When that chick came flying out the door, I wanted her *so bad*. I mean, I thought she was gonna eat my flesh and turn me into some sorta living dead nightmare, and she was way too skinny for me, but I still wanted to plow that ass. Like, *really* wanted to get all up in—"

"We get the point," said Tara.

"Yeah, I felt it, too, now that you mention it," said Clay. "With her, and then again with the two in the parking lot. That's fucked up. Some kind of zombie pheromones." Jerry looked lost again. "They're like scent things you put out that make ladies wanna get with you." He nodded sagely. "Animal Planet, my man. Animal Planet."

"So now we're back to the first question," Jerry said, looking to Tara. "How come you got out without banging anyone?"

"I don't know," she said. "I honestly don't."

"You're sure you didn't sneak off to the ladies' room yourself?" Clay asked. The boys inched back away from her. "Be honest, lady."

"If I had, don't you think you two hornballs would be all over me like funny on a monkey right now?"

They considered a moment, then sheepishly nodded.

"I mean, if we're being honest, I would definitely give you a spin," said Jerry. Tara shot him a glare sharp enough to cut diamonds. "Just bein' honest. It might be some kinda early symptom."

"Sure," Clay said thoughtfully, bringing Tara's glare onto himself, "I mean, Tara, I'm definitely moderately attracted to you. Come clean: did you get it on at all in there? Maybe you just got a mild case. Like, did you give some dude a handjob? Maybe that would make you, you know, *less* infected or somethin'."

"I didn't touch anyone, you assholes," Tara said, narrowing her eyes. "Did it ever occur to you that maybe I'm just kind of attractive? Jesus, way to make a woman feel good. No wonder everyone in town hates you."

"We just wanna be sure," said Jerry. "No offense meant. It's all of our lives on the line here, you know."

"Well, I swear on whatever you want me to swear on that I didn't so much as touch anyone in there. The only thing I—" She realized she was running her finger over Joanne's panties, which she must have stuffed into her pocket at some point during her escape. "Nope, nothing. I'm clean, I swear it."

"And you weren't, like, drawn to anyone while you were

there?" Jerry asked. "You didn't feel like letting some dude fluff your pillows or anything?"

"No. Honestly, there was nobody in there I had any desire to fuck at all. I can't explain it," she said, though an idea was definitely beginning to form in her mind.

"And nobody attacked you, either?" said Clay. "Think hard, did anyone even try?"

She scoured her memory. "No, nobody really made any move toward me in there. I mean, I got out pretty quickly, but I was only a few feet away from Joanne when she went off the shit cliff and started eating her friend." She thought for a moment, then added, "She looked up at me when I made a sound, but it was like...well, it was kinda like she couldn't see me or something. She just looked right through me."

"So you're immune," said Clay. "That's good to know, right? That's something we can use. Now if we can only figure out why we might be able to save other people."

Tara inhaled sharply, opened her mouth, then thought better of it and stopped, hoping the boys hadn't noticed she was about to speak. The three were silent for a moment, the boys lost in thought and Tara doing her best to look like she wasn't thinking at all. Finally Jerry, stroking his chin like a third-rate community theater actor's portrayal of Sherlock Holmes, spoke up.

"It must be because you're from Omaha. Something in the water there that makes you immune, maybe? Or, like, living near all those cows?"

Tara shook her head. "I have a confession to make, guys." She bit her lip. *Give them a little information, then you won't feel so bad about the big omission.* "I'm not from Omaha." The boys both suddenly got very interested. She demurred, and then gathered her courage to finish out the admission. "I'm from San Francisco. Born and raised. I've actually never been to Omaha."

Jerry and Clay were perplexed. "Then why on earth would you ever tell people you were from there?" Jerry asked.

"Because every time I told them I was from San Fran I got an earful about how wicked a city it is, and I was sick of people looking at me like I was born in Gomorrah." This seemed to satisfy them.

"You know, you don't have a Nebraska accent, anyway," Clay said. "We shoulda known."

"I'm sorry I lied to you, but…well, you know…I didn't want my cover blown."

"No, it's cool," said Jerry. "I understand. You deserve your privacy."

"Anything else you're not telling us?" Clay joked.

Tara's head raced. "No," she said, a little too quickly. "Nothing I can think of."

"Hey Clay," said Jerry, "what was it you were gonna tell me before? When you first got to the Bucket?"

"Oh hell," Clay said, perking up, "I completely forgot! It's not quite as crazy as what happened to you two, but it does make a lot more sense now."

He told them about Martin attacking him naked in the middle of the intersection downtown and about the running car and the remains of what he could only assume was its driver. They listened intently, Jerry occasionally interrupting with a "…and he was still *naked*?" When he finished the story, he looked triumphantly at Jerry.

"I guess we're gonna have to split that bottle of Everclear, man," Jerry said. "Because that was just about exactly as fucked up as my story."

Tara looked deep in thought.

"What's with the forehead wrinkles?" Clay asked.

"I'm just trying to piece things together here. Like…" she paused to gather her thoughts. "Well, if Martin's gone all zombie too, that means Joanne's not necessarily Patient Zero, right? There might be someone else in town who started this. Unless at some point Martin and Joanne…"

The boys looked at each other and shrugged.

"It's possible, I guess," Clay said. "They don't seem to be too discriminatin' once they zombie out. And Martin had that look in his eye at the funeral, right, Jer?" Jerry nodded. "It was the same look I seen on him when he attacked me. The same look you musta seen on Joanne."

He stopped for a second, his eyebrows knit. "Now that I think of it, I'm pretty sure Joanne was in the visitation line not too far behind us. I couldn't say whether she had the look or not at that point —we was pretty wasted, and the whole goddamned room wanted to kick us in the pants." He lowered his eyes a bit at the memory. He was ready to admit now, several hours later, that they had perhaps not exhibited model behavior earlier that day.

"When were you all at the funeral home?"

"'Round noon, I reckon," Jerry answered.

"I was there a little before two, and I caught Joanne on her way out. If she was behind you in line she spent an awful long time there."

Jerry shrugged. "So she was visitin' with people, maybe?"

"I guess that's one explanation," said Tara. Her expression made it clear that it was not the explanation that she thought correct.

"So what if Martin is Patient Zero?" Jerry chimed in helpfully. "Maybe him and Joanne got it on at…" The realization of what he was about to say hit him and his eyes opened into near-perfect circles. "Martin and Joanne musta got it on at the funeral." He shuddered. "Freaky."

They all took a moment to process this new information. Nobody in the car was particularly comfortable thinking about it. Each, in their own silent way, worked out the logistics, and none of them came up with a scenario that didn't make them fairly nauseous.

They sat in silence and pondered. After a few moments passed, a new thought hit Tara that she did not like at all.

"Guys, if Martin passed the zombie virus whatever thing on to Joanne, where did he get it from?"

There was another moment of silence while they all mentally danced around the conclusion that was becoming more and more obvious. At length, Tara spoke up again, in a voice barely above a whisper.

"What killed Cassie Yearwood?" Jerry and Clay looked to one another, neither willing to be the one that said it out loud. "Guys?"

"Some strange disease she picked up in Barbados, far as any of us knows," said Clay at last. "Some kinda bug bite or something, I think."

"Leg herpes," Jerry said. Tara gawked at him. "I mean, that's what the guy who works at Dr. Jerrit's office called it. I don't know that it was really herpes, but…"

Clay stared blankly at Jerry. "Hey Jer, I…" He swallowed hard. "I hate to say it, but…"

"Dude, please. I know where you're about to go and I really *really* wish you wouldn't."

They stared at each other silently, nodding in slow motion. Jerry chewed on his bottom lip mercilessly. Clay wrung his hands.

"*WHAT?!*" Tara exploded. The boys jumped. "Where are you going? Clue me in here."

"Well," Jerry said, "after the wake me and Clay were having a few beers in the park—you know, just to relax a little after we…anyway, we were talking, and…" His face twisted into a look in which Tara could distinctly read grief, disgust and disbelief.

"We were saying how good Cassie looked," Clay picked up. "Like, way too good to be dead. I think I mentioned that I would have given it to her right there in her coffin. And when Jerry went up to pay his respects, he—"

"*DUDE!*"

"Jer, she deserves to know. She's been honest with us." Tara cleared her throat awkwardly.

"I gave Cassie a kiss. That's all."

"You practically sucked her lips clean off her face, more like. And you were straight up coppin' a feel, as I remember it."

"Yeah, so I got a little lost in my grief. Give me a fuckin' break."

"And what was it you told me Tim Worth said about Cassie? Something about just before she died?"

A sickly realization dawned on Jerry's face. "That she was actin' all weird just before she passed. Sayin' some wild shit. The way he tells it, she was comin' on to ol' Dr. Jerrit somethin' fierce."

There was another long moment of awkward silence, then Clay reached between the seats and put his hand on Jerry's shoulder.

"My friend, you clearly were not the only one who had designs on Cassie's corpse."

Tara looked from Clay to Jerry and back. It was painfully clear that neither of them had any intention of going forward with the conversation.

Not sure that she wanted to know the answer, but determined to get to the bottom of things, Tara took a deep breath and asked, "Did Martin have a chance to see Cassie before she died?"

Clay shook his head. "No, the only people that saw her still alive were her parents and Dr. Jerrit. Which means that Martin…"

"He must have…" Jerry trailed off.

Tara waited a moment, but both the boys had sunk into silence. "He fucked her dead body."

Clay and Jerry simultaneously opened their doors and vomited.

"Sorry, but someone had to say it."

"No," Clay said, wiping his mouth, "Nobody ever had to say that."

"She was our friend," said Jerry, then leaned out the car and puked again. He sat back up, tears running down his cheeks from the violence with which he expelled the contents of his stomach. "I was perfectly fine with not hearing that."

"Sorry," Tara said, "but now it's out. Whatever this is came to town with Cassie. And then Martin—" The boys glared at her. Jerry hovered near the door, just in case. "Martin did what he did. Then he gave it to Joanne, who gave it to half the male population of this town."

"And while we sit here playing Encyclopedia Brown, that mob of horny, flesh-hungry maniacs might be bearin' down on us," Clay said. "We need to figure out our next move."

"We should go see Dr. Jerrit," Jerry offered. "He might know what's going on. He treated Cass before she died, and examined her body."

"Yeah, that's a good plan," Clay said. He turned around and bucked his seat belt. "Let's start there. He lives pretty close to my folks' place." He started the car and pulled away from the shoulder while Tara and Jerry buckled in. They drove in silence for a few minutes until the high-beam headlights picked up a silhouette walking down the side of the road, staggering awkwardly and dragging one leg behind it.

"Oh fuck," said Clay. "It can't be..."

"What?" said Tara.

"We're only about a quarter mile from city limits."

"...and?"

"And the sign that I smashed Martin's skull into going sixty miles an hour."

There was a gasp of recognition from both Tara and Jerry.

"You don't think that's..." said Jerry.

"I ain't taking the chance," said Clay. He hit the gas pedal and picked the car up to an insane speed.

"What the fuck are you doing?" Tara screamed.

"I'm gonna find out how much punishment those things can take. We already know they're strong, and I smashed Martin's head in once, so they're pretty durable."

The car was up to seventy-nine miles per hour by the time they could identify Martin for sure. The top of his head was nearly perfectly flat with shards of bone sticking out in all directions like a wreath of flowers. Tara just had time to gasp before the car plowed into him, clipping him in the pelvis and sending him tumbling over the roof head over foot. In a fraction of a second he somersaulted the entire length of the vehicle and crashed to the pavement behind.

Clay pulled back on the lever by his right hand to spray the windshield with soapy fluid and wipe the blood away. Then he slammed on the brakes and pulled the wheel hard to the left. The car spun around exactly the way it would have for James Bond. Clay smiled, pleased that movies had finally done him some good.

Then he gunned the engine and headed back.

Martin had just managed to get himself up on his hands. Everything below his chest was a mangled, shapeless mess. Clay slammed the gas again. This time, Martin took the radiator grille straight to the face. The car shook as the tires on the driver's side ran over what solid mass was left to his body. Clay slowed and turned around again, this time driving right up to the now seemingly lifeless form in the middle of Rural Route 1455. He put the car in park and the trio got out.

"Looks pretty dead to me," said Jerry, poking Martin with his foot.

Tara gingerly leaned down and examined the mashed remains of his head. "Yeah, I'd say he's definitely done. So they can be killed."

"Great," said Clay. "I just have to smash everyone at the Bucket's skull in then run them over a few times. That should only take a few days."

"Oh god," Tara said, realization washing over her. "If Martin wasn't at the Bucket, that means there might be more of them ahead of us."

"What?" said Jerry, now full-force kicking Martin where his ribs once were.

"Well, Martin could have…I mean, he could have fucked someone else here in town, right? We were working on the assumption that all the zombies were coming in behind us from the Bucket, but there might be more already here."

"But we killed Martin, right?" asked Jerry.

Tara shrugged then nodded, clearly not following.

"Well when you kill the head zombie, ain't the other zombies supposed to go back to being human again?"

"Vampires," said Tara.

"Huh?"

"You're thinking of vampires. Kill the head vampire and the rest turn back. I don't think there's a way to turn zombies back human. Though, these don't seem to be typical movie zombies. For one thing, they're not dead."

"Anyway, it don't seem likely there's more in town," Jerry said. "This time of night, the Bucket's the only place with people in it. Even the Corner Diner's closed by now, right Clay?" He turned his attention to Clayton and found him pale and completely slack-faced. "Clay? What's wrong?"

"The Diner…"

"…is closed, right?"

"Yeah," he drawled. "Mom closed tonight." He walked back to the car in a daze. "We gotta go. Now."

Tara stood up. "What's the—"

"*Get in the car.*"

Myrna's House

Clay could have sworn that he locked the door when he left, but it swung open the moment he put his hand on it. He peeked his head tentatively inside and looked around. The lights were out and it was quiet. He walked inside and hit the lights in the entryway. Jerry followed silently.

"I don't get it, Clay," Tara said, closing the door behind her. "Why are we here?"

"Because of the other part of my story that I forgot to tell you about. Just give me a minute, ok? It's probably nothing, but I wanna be sure." He inched to the bottom of the stairs and crooked his neck, listening. No sound came down from above. "Well, at least they're done."

"Who's done with what?" said Jerry. He had instinctively walked into the living room and flopped himself down on the couch and was reaching for the remote control.

"Mom got home from work late tonight. And when she got in, she didn't say a word, just gave me a weird look and went upstairs. Then…" He shivered at the memory. He tried to tell the tale, but his mouth refused to form the words that his brain was having such a difficult time putting together. Finally he managed to stammer out a few sentences. "Then she went upstairs. And after that, I guess…well I'll just say that her and dad was bein' awfully loud up there."

"Loud?" asked Tara, beginning to understand.

"Like, headboard-slamming-against-the-wall loud. By the time I left I was pretty sure the chandelier in the dining room was gonna fall out the ceiling. I heard words coming out of my father's mouth that would make the filthiest sailor blush."

"Damn," Jerry smiled. "Go Ralph!" Tara and Clay both turned to stare at him. "What? Can't a man congratulate another man on his performance?"

"First, not when it's my dad, you sick fuck," Clay said with venom. "Second, don't that M.O. sound at all familiar to you? A woman walks in with a funny look in her eye then disappears to have—" he choked on the words, due equally to fear and disgust. "To have loud, sloppy, athletic sex. Ring any bells?"

Jerry's smile melted. "Oh shit, dude…I'm sorry, I didn't think about…" He jumped up from the couch. "If your parents might be zombed out, what the hell are we doin' here unarmed?"

"I already had to listen to my folks doin' the nasty tonight," Clayton said. "I don't think I can handle having to murder 'em in cold blood too. I just wanna be sure. Can you chill out here for a minute? I'm just gonna run up, make sure they're safely asleep in bed and not eatin' the neighbors' faces, then be right back so we can go visit the doctor. Is that an ok plan?"

Jerry nodded, his nerves obviously jangled now.

"Do you want me to go with you?" Tara asked. "You know, for moral support or whatever?"

Clay shook his head. "It's bad enough that one of us has to risk seein' them naked. I wouldn't wish that on my worst enemy."

Tara nodded solemnly. Clay began ascending slowly, one step at a time.

When he was out of sight, Tara looked over to Jerry. "I'll stay here and keep an eye out. You go to the kitchen and find us some weapons."

Jerry took a step toward the hallway then stopped.

"Wait, why are we splitting up? Ain't you never seen a horror movie?"

Tara waved him off impatiently. "We're not splitting up. You're going, like, fifteen feet away from me."

"Into a dark room where we can't see each other. I know how this ends."

Tara rolled her eyes. "I was sending you because you've been in this house before and will probably have a better idea where to find a few big knives than I would. But if you're too chickenshit to go, then you stay here and watch while I go to the kitchen."

Jerry weighed his options for a moment, then resolve settled on his face. "You're right," he said, taking a step toward the bottom of the stairs, "you should go look for weapons. I'll stay here. By the front door. So I can run like a little bitch if anything happens."

Tara hesitated a moment, but when it became clear that Jerry was not, in fact, being facetious, she stormed off down the hall, shooting dirty looks over her shoulder at Jerry and grumbling a string of exquisite and disturbing obscenities under her breath.

When she got into the kitchen she flipped on the light and started rummaging around the counter for anything they could use to combat Clay's parents, should it come to that. There was a knife block by the sink, but it only contained five flimsy steak knives shoved into slots made for much more substantial cutting tools. She opened the drawers systematically, looking for one that contained silverware, but found only Scotch tape, twine, forks and spoons and various other functionally useless items.

In a fit of desperation she opened up the dishwasher, where she found a single large kitchen knife. With a sigh of relief she pulled it out. It was crusted with what she decided was dried meatloaf. She tested the edge and found it rather dull.

"Don't these hicks know you don't put knives in the dishwasher?" she muttered. "They lose their edge when you do." She tucked it into her belt anyway, just to be safe, and continued to toss the kitchen for weapons.

Back at the foot of the stairs, Jerry was getting impatient. He was not a coward, he thought, and had proved that by heroically holding the door closed at the Bucket instead of just turning tail at the first sight of trouble. But he wasn't a fool, either. He knew how situations like this worked. He was a lovable, affable doofus. Since there were no black guys in Fulton Flats and Joanne—the slut—was already infected, he was the next in line to die. And splitting up like this never, *never* turned out well.

He shifted his weight back and forth on his feet and alternated looking up the stairs for Clay and down the hall for Tara, neither of whom seemed in any hurry to get back to him. He inched back toward the front door and double-checked that it was unlocked.

Then, in a Boy Scout-like fit of preparedness, he turned the doorknob and pulled the door open just a titch, enough to keep the bolt from setting into the hole in the frame. That way, when trouble inevitably reared its ugly, blood-soaked head, he could fling the door open without a thought and head for the hills.

He nearly jumped out of his skin when he heard footsteps on the stairs and quickly spun around to find Clay coming down.

"What'd you see?" he asked. Clay was pale and shaking.

"Worst case scenario," he said, reaching the bottom of the stairs. Jerry put his hand back on the doorknob.

"They're eating the neighbors," he whispered.

"No, they're laying on top of the sheets naked." Clay's torso spasmed with a quick dry-heave. "But they seem to be sleeping, so that's good."

"So what took you so long? Please don't tell me you were standing in the door staring at your naked parents."

"No, asshole," Clay said with a soft but dead sincere push to Jerry's shoulder. "After I checked in on them I went into my room to get this." He pulled up the hem of his undershirt to reveal a pistol stuffed into the waist of his jeans.

"Holy shit, Clay, you're a genius!"

"I know, right? I totally forgot I had it."

Tara walked in from the kitchen. "What's the verdict?"

"Nekkid and exhausted," Jerry said with a smirk. "And Clay's got himself a piece. What did you find?"

"Just this dull knife," she said, pulling it out from her belt, "and this wicked-looking barbecue fork." She displayed the fork in her other hand, its long, sharp tines pointed at Jerry's face. She turned to Clayton. "You got a gun?"

Clay beamed and held out the pistol to show her. Tara nodded approvingly. "Do you have any extra ammo?" she asked.

"Of course, I ain't no dummy," Clay said and fished in his pants pockets, pulling out a small Ziplock bag filled with tiny black spheres.

"What the hell is that, birdshot?" Tara asked, leaning in to examine the bag.

"BBs," Clay said, snatching it away. "Must be eighty or ninety rounds here."

"BBs," Tara drawled. "So you're gonna, what, irritate the zombies to death?"

Clay's smile faded. "It's better than a dull knife and a long fork. Are we defending ourselves here or grilling?"

"At least these will break the skin," Tara growled. "Here, let me show you." She jabbed the fork at Clay, who dove back and bumped into Jerry, knocking him against the door.

"What the fuck?" said Jerry to Clay.

"What the fuck?" said Clay to Tara.

"What the fuck?" said Tara, looking up the stairs with her eyes wide.

Coming down one step at a time, her footfalls muffled by the taupe carpet on the runners, was Myrna. She was completely naked, and her mouth hung slackly open. She had her eyes set unwaveringly on Jerry.

"Oh shit, ma, sorry if we woke you up," said Clay. "We was just headin' out. Look, you and dad need to stay in for a while and make sure all the doors and windows are locked, there's some crazy—"

Myrna reached the bottom of the stairs, planted a hand on Clay's shoulder, and threw him aside hard enough to send him tumbling to the floor in the living room. Jerry screamed and grabbed the door, but when he pulled on the knob, proud of his forethought, his hand flew off and whizzed behind him, smacking Myrna in the face.

As she wrapped her arms around him he realized with a great, biding fury that Clay had knocked the door shut when he bumped into him.

He braced himself for the feeling of teeth sinking into his neck, but instead Myrna hugged him tight, her floppy breasts pressing into his lower back and her hands running over his chest. He could feel her breath on the back of his neck. *It's Clay's mom*, he thought frantically. *Myrna is not one of those hot "best friend's mom" types you see in the pornos. She's a* mom *mom. She's over sixty years old. I can feel her tits on my lower back. MY LOWER*

BACK. She's almost as tall as me…

All his mantras were in vain, however. Even while he fought back the urge to heave for the third time in half an hour he found himself unable to push her away, and as her hands slid down to fumble with his belt he discovered he was staring to grow some wood.

Clay picked himself up off of the floor, shook his head to clear it, then glanced over to the door to find his nude mother grinding on his best friend like a discount stripper. He looked to Tara for help, but she was frozen in place, her barbecue tools held out in front of herself defensively.

He staggered to his feet and, still wobbly from the force of Myrna's shove, hobbled over to try to pry her off of Jerry. He got behind her and hesitated. There was absolutely no way to do what he needed to without at least getting another eyeful of her, and the prospect of that was only marginally better than letting her devour Jerry.

He reached out tentatively and, wincing, wrapped his arms around her waist, his hands sinking into the soft, clammy skin of her belly. He took a deep breath to steel himself and caught the tangy, slightly coppery scent of the old "alone time" sock he kept under his bed. He gagged and turned away, unable to let go but equally unable to deal with the concept of his mother covered in splooge.

As he gasped for breath he caught a glimpse up the stairs and saw his dad flying down, two steps at a time, his face a mask of pure, unadulterated starvation.

Suddenly motivated, Clayton released his hands and tumbled to the side, narrowly avoiding Ralph's oncoming open maw, which whizzed past his right ear and lodged itself in Myrna's shoulder, catching both parents by surprise. Myrna whirled around, momentarily forgetting her prize, and bared her teeth at Ralph, who inched back, chewing on his mouthful of shoulder with a look of distaste. He turned and spat the chunk of skin and muscle on the carpet.

"Interesting," Tara said, now training the fork on Ralph and the knife on Myrna.

"Guys," whimpered Jerry. "Please...help...me..."

Myrna took a step toward Ralph. Then, quick as thought, she grabbed his arm and took a chunk out of his bicep. She chewed it experimentally, grimaced, and spat it back in his face. Then she turned back to Jerry, who had just managed to get himself turned around enough to watch with a mixture of disgust, horror and frat boy lust. His belt was dangling from the loops in his jeans and half the buttons on his fly were undone.

Clayton, in a moment of heroic disregard for his own safety that mere seconds ago he would have thought himself incapable of, pulled the BB gun from his waist, leveled it Myrna, cocked it to the side like Tupac Shakur, and unleashed a volley of pellets to bounce off of her face, leaving welts that almost instantly covered the entire side of her head.

Swollen and misshapen and looking for all the world like a Batman villain, she turned on him and took two slow, lumbering steps in his direction, then stopped, confused. Her head swiveled from Clay to Jerry and back for a moment, as though she were watching an extremely slow tennis match. Then she grunted and turned back to Jerry.

"Interesting," said Tara as Myrna pinned Jerry to the door with her pelvis and began to lick his collarbone while Ralph dove at Clayton, his wounded arm leaving a trail of blood across the otherwise pristine carpet.

"Fucking *help us*," Clay screamed as he rolled out of the way of Ralph's pounce and fired the remaining BBs wildly, shattering a lamp and three small porcelain statuettes depicting children playing various games with Jesus.

"Clay, do you really want me to stab your parents?" Tara shouted. "Think about this for a moment."

Clay, now lying on his back with his feet on Ralph's chest, trying desperately to push Ralph's open mouth away from his throat in a twisted parody of the airplane game that his stoic father never indulged him in as a child, did not have to think very hard. "I love my dad, but seriously: cut this fucker."

Tara screwed her mouth into a twist, gave a curt nod, and fell on Ralph, the knife held in front of her, putting all of her hundred and ten pounds into the attack. Ralph grunted and turned, looking right through Tara as though she didn't exist, then shivered for a moment and rolled off of Clay. Tara smelled shit.

"I think I got him," she said as she helped Clay up. "His bowels released. People do that when they die."

Clay cleared his throat. "That, uh…that wasn't him."

Tara took a step away.

"Guys," Jerry grunted. "Please…"

They both turned to the door to see Myrna on her knees, tugging Jerry's jeans down. Clay took another deep breath and rushed her, throwing his shoulder against her ribcage and knocking her free of Jerry's pants. He pinned her to the floor, his knees on her shoulders and started slapping her wildly across the face.

"Wake up, mom! This ain't you! Stop trying to seduce my best friend!"

Myrna only looked up at him, the confusion returning to her face. And then, without warning, there was a barbecue fork sticking out of her eye.

"Goddammit, Tara, stop stabbing my parents!"

"They're not your parents anymore, Clay!" Tara screamed, tears beginning to run down her face. "They want to kill you and fuck Jerry. Would your parents want to do that?"

Clay looked from Tara to the convulsing husk that used to be his mother. "Well, killing Jerry was never entirely off the table…"

"They've turned, Clay."

"Maybe there's some way to cure them. Maybe we can—"

Before he could finish his sentence, Ralph, the knife swaying luridly where it emerged from his back, flung himself onto Jerry, who had collapsed in a heap on the floor. Tara leapt over Clay, put her foot on Ralph's spine and, with a great effort, pulled the blade free. Ralph turned to look at her, again showing no recognition that she was actually in the room with him.

"Interesting," Tara said, then took the momentary opening and plunged the knife down at his face. It hit the bone of his jaw and ricocheted off, flaying a good portion of his cheek. He looked utterly confused now and started flailing his arms as though warding off a cloud of gnats he couldn't quite see, the motion causing the flap of skin that was once the left side of his face to flop like a fish in the bottom of a canoe.

Tara, just as confused as Ralph seemed to be, brought the knife up and slammed it down again, this time, by pure luck, tearing through the cartilage of his nose and lodging it into his brain. Ralph's eyes widened for a second then narrowed. He continued to windmill his arms, and Tara leaned on the knife's handle, angling the blade up further into his brain. His right arm instantly stopped moving and dropped dead to the floor. She shifted her weight and his left arm followed suit. One more twisting push, accompanied by a quiet crunch, and Ralph jerked once and lie still.

Tara nodded. "Interesting."

"I hate to break up your train of thought," groaned Jerry, "but do you mind getting him off of me?"

Tara stood and bent over Ralph's now-still body, placed her foot on his sternum and pulled the knife free of his head. It popped out with a wet, sucking sound, the part nearest the hilt ringed with blood and the rest sandpapered with small grey flecks of tissue where the dried bits of meatloaf had grated against his brain. Then she hooked a foot under him and lifted with all of her might, rolling the body over and freeing Jerry.

"You just stabbed my dad in the brain," Clayton said, his eyes distant. "I mean, you stabbed the fuck out of him."

"Not your dad," Tara repeated. "The zombie that used to be your dad."

"You keep using that word," Clay said, "but I don't think it fits. I mean, I've seen *Day of the Dead* about a hundred times, and zombies don't act like Ron Jeremy one minute and Jeffrey Dahmer the next. They pretty much Dahmer-out full-time. Plus, zombies are the walking dead. These…whatever the hell they are…they ain't dead yet, right?"

Tara thought for a moment. "Well, when you come up with a better name for it, you just let me know, ok?"

"Guys, I hate to break up your discussion yet again," Jerry interrupted, pulling his pants back up and buckling his belt, "but we've still got one sex-zombie-whatever-thing to deal with here."

"He's right," Tara said. "Finish her, Clay."

Clay looked at Tara, then down at his mom.

"I can't do it. No matter how naked and stabbed in the eye she might be, she's still my mom."

"Clay, she's definitely infected," Jerry said, getting to his feet. "She was giving me serious pants tingles. Your mom sure as shit never did that for me before."

Clay managed to croak out an "Ew" then slumped back. As soon as Myrna felt his weight shift she twisted to the side and threw him off then got up on all fours and crawled over Ralph's body toward Jerry.

"Fuck, not again!" Jerry screamed.

Tara threw herself between them, but Myrna simply ran into her as though she was invisible.

"Interesting," Tara grunted as Myrna's head knocked the wind out of her.

Clay, in a daze, walked over and straddled Myrna's back, grabbed the handle of the fork sticking out of her eye, and pulled up on it as hard as he could, jerking her head back like a Pez dispenser. Myrna shook violently and crashed to the ground, losing control of her limbs.

Clay twisted and jerked the fork like a butter churn, a single tear rolling down his cheek. After a few agonizing moments Myrna stopped moving. He stood and, without a word, walked over to the couch and sunk down into it.

"Interes—" Tara began.

"What is so fucking interesting?" Jerry shrieked. "I swear, Doctor Science, you better have some pretty fascinating theories going on here."

"Well, we've learned a few things," Tara said, twisting the fork. Myrna's leg jumped. "First of all, you have to obliterate their brains to stop them. They don't seem to feel any pain, and the zombism…" She shot a look to Clay who appeared more or less catatonic. "Sorry, the sickness that looks an awful lot like zombism to me—gives them above-average strength as well."

"What I think is weird," Jerry said, still slumped against the door, "is that neither one of them seemed to notice you at all. Come to think of it, those three in the parking lot at the Bucket didn't either, and that chick who came busting through the door of the bar practically walked over you to get to me."

"Yeah, uh…" Tara stammered. "I have a couple of theories about that, too."

"How come I was startin' to get all worked up over Myrna but Clay wasn't? And how come you didn't get all twitterpated over Ralph?"

"Well, we already figured out that these things release some sort of pheromone, right? So I guess it doesn't work on people that aren't potential breeding partners."

Jerry took a moment to process this information. "So since Clay is—was—Myrna's son, her fur gnomes didn't work on him?"

"Yeah, I think so. Just a theory, but still it makes a certain amount of sense. The sickness passes through intercourse, right? So why would it bother with bad breeding partners?"

"So how come you're immune to this?"

Tara took a long, slow breath then stood up, walked into the living room and sat on Ralph's cherished recliner.

"Because I'm not a potential breeding partner."

"The fuck do you mean? You got a vag, right? As far as I'm concerned that makes you a potential breeding partner."

"I wasn't entirely upfront with you before," she said, staring at the floor. There was a long silence, then Jerry came in and sat down on the couch to stare at her. Even Clay seemed to be coming out of his stupor.

She steeled herself. "You asked me if there wasn't anyone at the Bucket I wanted to sleep with and I told you there wasn't. That's not entirely true." She slipped her hand into her pants pocket and ran her fingers over the satin underwear still wadded inside. "I kinda went there precisely because I wanted to sleep with someone…" She fell quiet, still staring at the floor.

"Well who the shit was it?" Clay said, coming slowly back to life. "What's so shameful about a secret crush?"

Tara looked up from her feet and locked her eyes on Clay's.

"Do I really have to say it? Haven't we solved enough mysteries tonight? I'm pretty sure if you think about it for a few seconds you'll figure it out yours-"

"*Holy shit, she's a lesbo!*" shouted Jerry, beaming. "I get it now!"

"A for logic, F for vocabulary," muttered Tara.

Clay's face suddenly lit up. "Oh sure, I see it now. Dad's pheromones didn't work on you 'cause you're not a breeding partner. You're a carpet muncher."

"And sex pheromones only work on members of the opposite sex, so your mom's didn't, either." She decided to let the slur slide for the moment, but made a mental note to come back to it later. "It's weird that neither of them seemed to notice me at all, though. At a guess, I'd say they sense people more by smell than by any other sense. Since I don't smell like a man and I don't smell like a straight woman, I'm more or less invisible to them."

"Interesting," Clay and Jerry agreed. Clay stood and, without a word, headed for the stairs.

"Where are you going?" asked Jerry.

"To change my underwear. We need to go pay Doc Jerrit a visit." He got halfway up the steps then stopped. "Get those barbecue tools free of my parents' brains. We may need them."

Myrna's Car

Clay was silent for most of the drive, downcast and contemplative. Jerry and Tara had kept talk to a minimum out of respect, but something was nagging at the back of Jerry's mind and he couldn't keep it to himself anymore.

"Clay, man, I'm sorry to have to bring this up, but how d'you suspect your mom got infected?"

Clay kept his eyes locked on the road and didn't so much as acknowledge that Jerry had spoken, much less answer. Jerry waited patiently for a moment, but his curiosity got the best of him.

"It's just, she had to get it from someone, right? Do you think she and Martin—"

Clayton slammed on the brakes and came to a screeching stop in the middle of Garfield Terrace. Tara jerked forward in her seat with a yelp. Jerry very nearly hit his forehead on the dashboard.

"I just scooped out my mother's brains with a giant fork, Jerry," Clay said through a clenched jaw, never diverting his eyes from the road ahead of him. "Do you think I could maybe go a few more minutes before I have to think about my mom having sex with a zombified Martin Lutz? Just a moment or two, please. I beg you."

The three sat in silence. A deer popped out from behind one of the houses and cautiously made its way across the perfectly manicured lawn, then edged out into the street and stared into the car's windshield. Clay locked eyes with it and the two shared a brief sense of communal bewilderment.

Where's your mom, little deer? Clay thought. *Did some hunter shoot her? I just shot my mom. In the face. Like, thirty times. Because she was trying to seduce my best friend and turn him into a zombie.*

He laid his forehead down on the steering wheel and wept. The deer bolted and disappeared back into the blackness. The car started to slowly roll forward.

"Clay," Tara said softly. "The brakes, Clay. Please put your foot back down on the brakes."

The car came to another jolting stop. Jerry, tentatively, put his arm around Clay's shoulder.

"I'm sorry, buddy. I just got into mystery-solving mode. Here…" He opened up the glove box, rummaged around for a moment and pulled out a small packet of tissues wrapped in flimsy plastic. If there was one thing for which Myrna could be counted on, it was to always have a Kleenex on hand.

He pulled one out and waved it next to Clay's head like a small flag of surrender.

"Blow yer nose, champ. No sense gettin' the steering wheel all snotty."

Clay picked up his head and glared at Jerry, but took the tissue and blew.

"What are we going to do?" asked Tara after a long moment. Her voice was heavy with the despair that was beginning to settle over all three of them. She was beginning to deeply regret leaving San Francisco. "I mean, we're going to go consult with the doc, and that's great and all, but what are we going to *do*? I've never been much for horror movies. How do zombie flicks end? How do you solve this kind of problem?"

The boys thought. Clay began absentmindedly wringing his hands, the tissue still clenched inside. After a moment he realized he was smearing snot all over himself, grimaced, wiped his hands on his pants, took a deep breath and turned around to look at Tara in the back seat.

"You don't 'solve' a zombie invasion. Mostly the movies end with an escape."

"Well, that sucks," said Tara. "You mean we just have to get out of town and hope it doesn't spread?"

Jerry nodded. "That's pretty much how it goes in the movies, yeah. Except…"

"Except what," Tara asked.

"Well, the original zombie movie, *Night of the Living Dead,* doesn't end with an escape, really."

Tara smiled. "So there's hope?" The boys looked at each other without saying a word. "Wait, how does *Night of the Living Dead* end?"

"The only survivor gets shot by the cops for being black," Clay said.

There was a depressed silence.

"Well, at least we're all white," said Jerry helpfully. It was greeted with even more silence.

"Jerry, maybe we should go check in on your parents," Tara suggested.

"My parents is dead already. Went when I was a kid. Only family I got left is my grandma, and honestly I'm not too worried about her. She's older'n dirt and tough as leather. Don't reckon anybody'd wanna fuck *or* eat her."

There was another long silence then. The three each chose a window and stared out it. Nothing moved in the dead and deserted wasteland that was Fulton Flats after dark. Even the smoke from the encroaching forest fire seemed suspended in time, a dingy grey ceiling over their heads. The shadows of the hills surrounding town loomed huge in the dark. Clay could feel them towering around him, almost bearing down on the car where the three sat.

Despite its name, Fulton Flats was actually a valley, surrounded on all sides by the foothills of the Bitterroot Mountains. Charles Fulton, the leader of the wagon train that had gotten lost on its way to Oregon and decided to settle in the valley, was notoriously short-sighted and legendarily stubborn, qualities that marked the population of the town he founded ever after. Though several members of his party, including his own wife and children, tried to explain to him that they were in a valley and he simply couldn't make out the hills in the distance, he insisted that they were in the famous prairies of Wyoming.

Later, upon actually taking a long enough walk to bring him to the base of the hills, Fulton insisted that the land was flat between those hills, so the name was still valid. It was precisely that geographical isolation and utter refusal to acknowledge reality that made Fulton Flats the solipsistic, time-warped backwater that it was. Clay had always thought of those hills as the prison walls that kept him out of the bigger, better world outside. And he had never felt them as keenly as he did sitting there in the car, snot hardening on his pants and tears drying on his cheeks.

Tara felt a familiar tickle in her ribs, the feeling she always got before she had to embark on one of her massive life changes. She'd felt it when she first came out to her parents, though she knew they'd be supportive. She thought of that moment as the official beginning of a new life: you're not *really* gay until you break the news to your parents. And so she'd sat at the dinner table, her palms sweating and her chest feeling like it was full of wriggling caterpillars.

Her folks had laughed when she said it and rolled their eyes. "Good lord, Tara, are you only just now figuring that out?" her mom had asked. They were so proud of her for being brave, though, and they broke out a bottle of champagne they'd been saving for a special occasion and toasted her grand revelations, letting her drink two full glasses even though she was only fifteen.

She'd felt the same tingle when she broke up with Betsy, her only real long-term relationship. She felt it when she decided that her breakup with Betsy was affecting her a lot more than she expected and that she would have to move away from home and head to this strange little backwater where she knew she wouldn't be welcomed for who she was in order to escape the constant, crushing heartache.

It always meant the same thing, that tingle.

It meant "run".

"Guys," she said, her voice crackling. She cleared her throat. Jerry and Clay continued staring out their respective windows. "Tell me about her, will you?"

"Who?" Jerry asked, his eyes glued to something out in the dark that she couldn't see.

"Cassie. I'm just curious. I mean, this is kinda all her fault, isn't it?"

Jerry's head whipped around like a shot, his face contorted

with grief and fury.

"Don't you fuckin' dare try to pin this on her."

Tara blushed. "I don't mean that she did it on purpose or anything, but this thing got here because of her, right? I just think it's interesting. Fulton Flats' perfect little darling inadvertently brought about its downfall."

"She wasn't perfect," Clay said, still staring out her window. "That was what made her so great. Everyone thought the sun shined out Cassie's ass, but she fucked up just like the rest of us. She got drunk and stupid with me and Jerry all the time. Once we bought this bottle of some kinda cinnamon booze, something real cheap and rot-gut, and we was passin' it around in the churchyard over at the Methodist. Cassie was tellin' us this story about somethin' or other, and she was gettin' all emphatic the way you do when you're drunk as hell on a fall night. That bottle shot right outta her hand, broke one of the big windows on the back side of the church. She couldn't stop laughing the rest of the night."

He turned to Jerry and they shared a smile. "Me and Jer took the fall on that one. Not that anyone would have believed that perfect Cassie Yearwood coulda gotten drunk and broke a window. I think she always felt bad about that, lettin' us be blamed."

"Not like it did our reputations any harm," Jerry laughed. "We was already out of high school by then, I don't think anyone in this town could have possibly thought less of us by that point. I spent three months workin' weekends baling hay at Pritchert's to pay my half of that window."

Clay smiled. "I did chores for Myrna for a year and a half. Good times."

"So she wasn't the saint everyone made her out to be?" Asked Tara.

"Oh lord no," Clay said. "She was human, just like everyone else. She was just a ridiculously sweet, incredibly smart, painfully good-lookin' human. That's why she liked us, we were the only people in town she could let her hair down with. Everybody in Fulton Flats needed Cassie to be the perfect angel, but me and Jer, we just wanted her to be herself. I mean, fuck, who are we to judge, right?"

Tara smiled to herself. She had worried about revealing herself to them for nothing. Backwater hicks they may be, but these boys—aside from some seriously offensive terminology that she knew she was going to have to beat out of them—were far and away the least judgmental people she had met since moving to Idaho. Against all odds, she was beginning to like them.

"Guys, why are we doing this?" she asked. "I mean, why go to the doctor's house? What do we hope to accomplish here? We should get out. We should get as far from this place as possible right now."

The boys turned in slow motion to face her with looks of horrified disbelief.

"I hate to sound insensitive, but your parents are gone, Clay. Everyone in town thinks you guys are fuckups, you've said so yourselves. Cassie was the only person around here who gave a fuck about you. Why stay? Why even try?"

"I still have my grandma," Jerry said sheepishly. "She's worth tryin' to save, I suppose. Nice enough lady."

"If you ignore the 1870s-era racism," Tara muttered under her breath.

"This is our home, Tara," Clay said. "And we…we can't just leave it, can we? We have to…I don't know…try to save it or something, right? Isn't that how it works?"

"It just doesn't make sense to me, I guess. I mean, I live here, too, but if it comes down to the choice between saving Fulton Flats from a zombie apocalypse and getting myself to safety…" Tara held her hands out as if physically weighing the options, then raised her right hand abruptly while her left fell into her lap, the middle finger sticking out and angled up toward Clay's face, "…fuck Fulton Flats. Fuck it right in its eye."

The tension was broken, and Clay chuckled quietly. "Look, here's the thing: if we bug out now, we're just proving everyone right. Every single person in this town thinks me and Jerry are fuckups. I, at least, want to put a little effort into proving them wrong."

"Plus," Jerry said, coming out of his reverie, "there's only one road goes through this town to the outside world. The fire's gonna make it awful hard to get out one direction, and the Bucket's the other direction."

Tara groaned. "Fuck. I honestly hadn't thought of that."

"So," Clay said, dropping the car into gear, "to the doctor's house, then?"

Tara nodded resignedly. Clay drove the remaining few blocks to Dr. Jerrit's house, pulled into the driveway and shut the car off.

"I don't know what the plan is from here," he said to nobody in particular. "Maybe the doctor can help. Maybe he can't. Maybe we're all going to die tonight, or be turned into one of them…them things. But I can say one thing for goddamned sure." He pulled the BB gun from his waist, held it up in front of him, and pulled the slide back, loading a pellet into the chamber. "I ain't going down without a fight."

"Hell yeah!" Jerry yelled.

"You do know that gun did fuck-all last time you used it, right?" said Tara.

Clay smiled, oblivious to her critique. "Ain't going down without a fight…"

Dr. Jerrit's House

They stood at the door, not entirely sure how to proceed. It was well after three in the morning, and though Dr. Jerrit was known for being available for house calls at all hours to take care of any ailment, he was also well known for not liking people to come to *his* house. He was a firm believer in drawing a line between his personal and professional lives, and that line was the sidewalk in front of his two-story colonial. Arranged like bowling pins with Clayton at the front (he was the most familiar, as his parents had been in a bridge club with the doctor since before Clay was born), they fidgeted nervously. Clay reached out his hand toward the doorbell, hesitated, then brought it back down to his side.

"It's just weird, is all," he said. "The doc doesn't really appreciate having people show up on his doorstep in the best of circumstances, he certainly ain't gonna take too kindly to us wakin' him up in the middle of the night."

"I think these are pretty extenuating circumstances," said Tara, growing increasingly irritated. She had not yet met Jerrit, and as such was not particularly susceptible to his legendary isolationism. She reached past Clay to ring the bell, but Clay instinctively swatted her hand away.

"Don't you dare," he said. "If someone's gonna ring that bell, it best be me." He stretched out his finger, brought it within half an inch of the lighted button, then let it drop to his side again. "Dammit, he is *not* gonna like this."

"Clay, this is, like, probably the most important thing we ever dealt with, he's gonna understand," said Jerry, who was none too keen to wake the doctor himself. He swallowed. "I think."

Clay closed his eyes, took a deep breath, and jabbed his finger at the doorbell. He missed by several inches. Cursing under his breath, he waggled the hand for a moment to clear the pain then tried again, this time with eyes wide open.

The sound of the bell inside might as well have been a shotgun blast on the silent lane. All three of them flinched, but there was no sign of movement in the house.

They waited for a long, tense moment then rang again. This time a light came on on the second story. The boys tensed visibly, and even Tara was growing increasingly uncomfortable. They heard clomping footsteps come down the stairs, then Dr. Jerrit's disheveled face appeared between the curtains in the door. He glared at them, held up his wrist and pointed to where his watch would have sat had he been wearing it, then raised an eyebrow and pursed his lips as if to say "you do know what time it is, right?"

Clay started to speak, but his voice broke and he cut off with a squeak. The three stood for a second, fumbling with their hands, until finally Tara pushed forward and put her face a few inches from the door and shouted "Sorry to wake you, but it's extremely important."

The doctor raised his hand again, extending his thumb and pinky and pressing it to the side of his face.

"There wasn't time to call," Tara said, a little louder than before. "I swear, doctor, this is a crisis and we need your help. We wouldn't have bothered you otherwise."

"Lower your voice, girl, I can hear you just fine," the doctor said, his voice muffled by the closed door but still entirely audible and clear enough to make out the depth of his irritation. "My wife is trying to get back to sleep, and I would love to do the same."

"Please, doc, you got to let us in," said Clay. "I'm real sorry for this, but you know I wouldn't do a damn fool thing like come to your house in the wee hours if it wasn't important."

"I can't think of a single damn fool thing you wouldn't do, Clayton," the doctor said sourly. Then he relented. "What's the problem?"

The three looked to one another, and Tara finally spoke up. "We'd rather not discuss it out here." Jerrit cocked his head and twisted his mouth in a look of disbelief. "It has to do with Cassie Yearwood. We think whatever killed her is spreading through the town." His face softened just a bit as he weighed whether or not this was a prank in incredibly poor taste. "Please, just let us in.

Lives are in danger here. Our lives, and yours and your wife's, too."

"And who are you, young lady?"

"I'm Tara Sokoloff. I'm new in town."

"And you knew Cassie?"

"No, but I-"

"Doctor," Jerry said, looking nervously around, "Tara and me were at the Bucket tonight and—"

"So you're drunk. That explains a lot," the doctor huffed and turned his back, heading for the stairs.

"No," Jerry cried, louder than he intended. Jerrit stopped, but stayed with his back to the door. "We're not...well, I'm definitely not drunk anymore. Look, people's goin' crazy and we think it's to do with Cassie's sickness. Please, we need your help."

Jerrit turned slowly and looked them over, giving each one a thorough glaring inspection through the three small, leaded panes of the door, then unlocked it and pulled it open. "If I find out this is some kind of prank, I swear to Jesus I'll have your parents over here so fast your heads will spin."

"That's gonna be pretty damned difficult," Clay said. Jerrit gave him a curious look, then stepped aside and let them into the house.

"Have a seat," he said, gesturing to the couch. Clay and Jerry balked, but Tara pushed between them and settled herself in, leaning against the couch's arm.

"If you're just gonna stand there, why did you get me out of bed?" Jerrit said with a glare at Clay and Jerry. The boys flinched and set themselves down. The doctor took the recliner facing the couch. There was a long, awkward silence in which none of the three youngsters dared open their mouths.

"Well," the doctor growled, "out with it. What's going on?"

"It's a bit hard to explain," Tara said when it became obvious that the boys weren't going to speak up. "I know this is a delicate question, and maybe even a little unethical, but we really need to know—what did Cassie die of?"

Jerrit chewed his tongue a moment, studying Tara as if he had just dissected her. "Why would you ask a question like that, young lady? Are you some kind of doctor?" He put the slightest emphasis on the word "you", clearly indicating how unlikely he found it that a young woman—especially one who would be running around town in the middle of the night with two such known reprobates—could possibly be a medical professional.

"No, I'm a technical writer. I…" She faltered. Until this moment she had been the science expert of the group, and she was not entirely ready to cede her authority to someone who was undoubtedly better informed in the subject than she. "I edit a lot of medical and scientific articles, and…well, here's the deal: there's something going around the population here in Fulton Flats. Some sort of disease that…so this is going to sound ridiculous, but…you see…" She tapped her foot nervously. "It kinda turns people into zombies. Sorta."

Jerrit stared at her, his glare shooting daggers. His words were slow, deliberate, and made of pure ice. "You woke me up in the middle of the night to tell me a story about zombies attacking this town? Are you out of your fucking minds?"

"That's just what we been calling 'em," Clay said. "We know there's no such thing as zombies, we ain't kids anymore." Jerrit switched his gaze and Clay demurred.

"Doc, folks is goin' nuts," Jerry chimed in. "They're tearin' each other apart and eatin' each other and…well…they're…they're doin' it like crazy…"

Jerrit slowly swept his eyes over to Jerry, who fell silent. "'Doin' it,'? Doing what?"

"Intercourse," Tara said, trying her best to sound scientific. "They're having sexual intercourse."

"People do that, you know. You're a *technical writer*," he said with an audible sneer, "you should be aware of this."

"No…I mean, yes, I know that, but…well, they're fornicating in the streets, doctor. They're attacking everyone they come into contact with. They mate with the opposite sex and feed on the same sex. I've deduced that it's something to do with pheromones." She beamed, proud of her thoroughly intellectual explanation.

The doctor sat in silence for a long time, passing his gaze from one of the three to the other. At length he settled on Clay.

"Clayton, you know your folks and I go way back, so I'm willing to forget this ever happened if you kids get out of here right now and never, ever try to pull something so hare-brained over on me or anyone else again."

Clay met his stare. "Doctor Jerrit, my parents are part of the reason I'm here. They're dead." He gestured to his companions. "We had to kill them because they were attacking us. You know me, doc. I may have done a lot of shitty things in my time, but I would not joke about something like that. I love my…"

He choked a bit, cleared his throat and carried on. "I love my parents, but I had to mash my mom's brain with a fork to keep her from literally screwing Jerry to death."

Jerrit stared into Clay's eyes and saw the tears beginning to form. It took a few seconds, but his suspicion at last began to crack and his innate bedside manner took over.

"So your folks are…"

"They're dead, doc. Both of them. Believe me, we had no choice."

The doctor looked at Tara. "What's this about pheromones?"

"Well, as I said, they seem to be sexually aggressive toward potential mating partners and violently aggressive toward those of the same sex who they see as, I guess, rivals?"

"Meals, more like," Jerry chimed in.

"True," Tara said with a nod. "They're expressing a tendency to cannibalism. I think they're sensing us by smell. I theorize that the disease is transmitted sexually, maybe through some virus in the…" she struggled for the correct phrase. "…the sex fluids?"

"Through semen and vaginal secretions? There are certainly a number of infections passed that way."

"Right, so we think that's how it's spreading, which would explain why their behavior toward other people is so different based on whether they're potentially sexually available or not."

"And you witnessed this first-hand?"

"Repeatedly," said Jerry, shivering, "and in great detail."

"I see."

"Also," Tara continued, "the infected seem to have increased strength and resilience. And they become...well, it's hard to explain precisely, but they become intensely attractive to members of the opposite sex, both the infected and uninfected alike. I think that also has something to do with pheromones."

The doctor nodded. "Makes sense. And what makes you think this is related to Cassie?"

Clay spoke up. "We think Martin Lutz was the..." He turned to Tara. "What did you call it?"

"Patient zero," she said.

"Right, patient zero. We're pretty sure he banged Joanne Hallstrom during the funeral and gave it to her, then Joanne went and screwed half the men at the Bucket. Martin attacked me downtown earlier tonight, and I found another body there. Well, part of a body. It was pretty well ate up. Then Joanne took a bite out of Maureen Riley at the bar, and it all went tits up after that, if you'll excuse the phrase."

Jerry snickered quietly. "'Tits up', that's good."

"When I got home, my folks attacked us. I guess...well, it pains me to say it, but I guess Martin must'a gotten to mom while she was closin' up the Diner. Then she...you know, she...she gave it to dad in a wifely manner..."

"I still don't see how this comes back to Cassie," Jerrit said.

"Well, she came down with some sort of tropical infection that killed her," said Tara. "It just made the most sense."

"So if Martin is patient zero," Dr. Jerrit said, now lost in thought, "you think he must have contracted the disease while he was preparing Cassie for the funeral. Obviously I'm not sick, and I was conducting the autopsy with Martin, so you think he..." He shuddered. "He's such a nice boy, I can't imagine..."

"He *was* a nice boy," Jerry said. "Now he's a corpse layin' out on the highway with its brains bashed in."

"The corpse of a maniac who tried to eat me," Clay said, somewhat defensively.

"I don't know precisely what killed Cassie," the doctor said at length. "She had some sort of infection that caused a fever she couldn't possibly have survived, though she held out through it far longer than she should have. She was raving, delirious." His eyes became distant. "I didn't tell anyone outside my office the specifics because I had a great deal of respect for Cassie and her reputation, but I felt like she was...well, she was coming on to me pretty seriously in her last moments. I chalked it up to the fever. There are certain sicknesses, cancer among them, which drastically increase the libido right before the patient dies. I didn't want to go spreading stories about the poor girl."

Tara swelled with pride. "So we were right? Cassie was the one who brought this on us?"

"It would seem so."

"Was it the leg thing?" Jerry said. "The bug bite, I mean?"

The doctor shook his head slowly. "I sincerely don't know. During the autopsy we discovered some...let's say some irregularities in her uterus. It was covered with growths of a type I have never seen before. It's possible that she..." He cleared his throat, obviously reluctant to go on. "She may have contracted some manner of sexually transmitted disease on her vacation. Or, from the looks of things inside her uterus, possibly an amalgamation of several different STDs. I don't mean to cast aspersions about her, we all know Cassie was a good girl and smart, but sometimes when a young person strikes out on their own for the first time..."

The boys were dumbstruck. It had never occurred to either of them for a second that Cassie might have hooked up on her vacation. It was just not in her character.

"But why did it kill Cassie and not Martin?" Tara asked, breaking the silence.

"I beg your pardon?" Doctor Jerrit said, coming back from his reverie to focus on her.

"The disease, infection, whatever it is, it killed Cassie. But it didn't kill Martin, it turned him into a zombie."

"Well, it's possible that the—for the sake of discussion, let's say virus—mutated somehow. Possibly because of the introduction of a secondary infection."

"The bug bite," Jerry said. "Mosquitoes carry things, don't they? Remember when we had that outbreak of West Nile ten, fifteen years ago? That was caused by mosquitoes, right? Maybe the mosquito bite had one bug, and it mixed with the sex bug and turned into the zombie virus!"

There was a stunned silence as everyone in the room realized that Jerry might, for the first time in his life, have come up with a reasonable answer.

"Well," Dr. Jerrit said, "we need to contact the CDC immediately."

"Didn't you call them when Cassie came down ill?" asked Tara.

Jerrit lowered his eyes. "No, I'm ashamed to say I didn't."

"Why on earth not?"

"Where are you from, miss?"

"Omaha," said Jerry and Clay simultaneously.

"San Francisco," Tara said.

The doctor nodded. "You haven't spent much time here yet, so I understand why you might not comprehend this, but we're a tiny, conservative town in the middle of nowhere. Fulton Flats is about as Tea Party a place as exists on this earth. Folks like us, we have an inherent distrust of the government, especially an agency like the CDC who has a tendency to take over when they can and run a place into the ground. I didn't want to cause a fuss, and it seemed like whatever did poor Cassie in was limited to her, so I saw no need to bring the feds down on our peaceful home."

He looked into Tara's eyes. "In hindsight, it might not have been the most prudent decision but I made it and I will live with the consequences."

There was a long silence in which everyone looked at their respective hands. It was broken by Jerrit's wife, who peeked her head around the door frame and said, "Ed, what's going on?" All four jumped at the sound of her voice.

"Evelyn, good, you're up. There's been a medical emergency

and we need to get moving right away. Can you head upstairs, get dressed, and bring me down my red suitcase and house call bag?"

"Oh my, what is it?"

"I'll explain in the car, my sweet. Please, just do as I say." Evelyn nodded and disappeared.

"What's the next move, doc?" asked Clay. "Do you need to examine my parents? Or I could take you back out to where we left Martin."

"You said there was a horde of these infected people at the Rusty Bucket?"

"Yeah," said Jerry.

"And how long ago did you leave there?"

Jerry looked at Clay, then at Tara. "Oh, an hour and a half, I'd guess. Maybe two."

"So if they started walking when you left, they're likely back in town by now, or getting awfully close."

"Yeah, I reckon so. And maybe more already in town, owing to Martin and the Barres having been here the whole time."

The doctor nodded. "There's very little time, then. We must get moving. If you'll excuse me, I need to go get dressed." He stood and ran his fingers through his gray, tousled hair. "I trust you can see yourselves out."

Tara and the boys stood. "Where should we meet you?" she said. "Clay's house?"

"Oh, lord, no," said Jerrit, heading toward the stairs. "It would be foolish to get involved in an autopsy in the middle of the kind of war zone this town is about to turn into."

"So what's the plan?"

"I'm taking my wife and getting the hell out of here, and I suggest you do the same."

"But, doc," Clay said, perplexed, "we can't just pull up stakes and leave."

"Why on earth not?" asked Jerrit.

"This is our home!" cried Jerry.

"This place is a shithole. I have given my entire life for Fulton Flats, and I refuse to die here. I'll call the CDC from the car. With luck, they'll be here in a few hours. Maybe nobody else will get infected or eaten in that time. Now go on, get yourselves clear of here before the shit hits the fan."

"But the fire," Clay said. "And the other direction is the Bucket, and—"

"I will take my chances on the road, Clayton. They're bound to be much better than my chances staying here."

"Doctor," Tara said, flabbergasted, "you can't be serious."

"Young lady, you seem very nice and you're obviously smart. I don't know how you got involved with these two miscreants, but that's your own business. I've spent the last sixty-three years keeping this town healthy. They can work this one out without me."

"But you're a doctor! Didn't you take an oath?"

Jerrit stopped on his way up the stairs, turned to his left and pulled a framed diploma off of his wall, and threw it at Tara's feet. The glass shattered.

"I'm retiring."

Myrna's Car

It took all of Tara's willpower not to say "I told you so."

"Well, what the hell do we do now?" Clay moaned. They'd pulled out of Dr. Jerrit's driveway and gone around the corner after he convinced them that he really wasn't joking by bundling his wife into the family Lincoln and taking off in the direction of Boise.

"We're so fucked," said Jerry. "I mean, like, deeply, passionately fucked."

Tara was still in shock. "I can't believe he just buggered off like that. It was his fault this didn't get reported to the CDC in the first place…"

"Tara, seriously, get your head in the game," Clay said. "We can't be worried about that now. He said he'd call them when he got safely out of town, and there's no reason to not to believe him. So let's concentrate on our next move."

"No reason not to believe him?" Tara practically shouted. "Clay, he clearly demonstrated that he doesn't give a rat's ass about this town or anyone in it. If he called the CDC now he'd be exposing his guilt. Why would he put his own neck on the chopping block for a town he's not willing to help save?"

That shut the boys up for a minute.

"Well, we could call them ourselves," Jerry said after a moment. "Anybody got the number?"

Tara rolled her eyes. "Sure, I always carry it with me. Let me see…" She lifted up off the seat and reached under herself. "Must be up my ass here somewhere…"

"If only y'all had some sorta device that could connect us to the internet," said Clay with a smirk. "Perhaps something you carried around in your pockets all the time..."

There was a moment of stunned silence. At no point in the entire night had any of them thought for even a moment about the fact that they all carried cellular phones as capable of looking up information wirelessly as they were of placing a call to, say, the local police department. Jerry immediately fished in his pocket, and Tara in her purse, and they pulled out their devices.

"Where's your phone, Clay?" Jerry asked.

"That prick Martin smashed it. You got signal?"

"Dead," said Jerry.

"Roaming," said Tara.

"Roaming? That's great," Clay said. "That means you still have battery."

"Less than five percent, it says. But I'm roaming. Do you have any idea what the data to look up a phone number is gonna cost me?"

"And you faulted Dr. Jerrit for saving his own life," said Clay.

"Fine, fine. Hang on." She danced her fingers around the screen for a moment, then sat and stared. "You know, the problem with living out in bumblefuck is you only get three Gs, and it's like they held an intensive round of interviews to find the world's slowest Gs to give you." Another moment passed. "Come on, come on…" At last, her eyes lit up. "Ok, got it. Dialing now…" There was a moment of breathless anticipation while the burbling sound of the phone dialing through filled the car, then was suddenly and brutally choked off. "…aaaaaaaaaaaand the phone just died."

"Fuck," said Jerry. "Teach us to be out all night without a charger."

Clay pounded the steering wheel with his fist. "God *damn* it! What are we going to do?"

"Look, let's just go back to my place," Tara said. "It's on the opposite end of town from the Bucket so it might buy us some time. I can plug in my phone and call for help. And we can make our plans from there. Does that sound good?"

Jerry nodded, defeated. Clay opened his door and stepped out of the car.

"What are you doing?" asked Tara. He leaned back in.

"You know where you live, and I'm exhausted. You drive."

Tara hopped out and they switched seats, and Tara drove to her place in silence.

Tara's House

She paused a moment before opening the door.

"You have to excuse the state of this house," she said. "I haven't had anyone over since I got to town and, you know, it's a bit of a mess at the moment. If I'd known I was going to have company tonight…"

"We seen a few messes in our time," said Jerry. "Do you really think this is the time to come over all shy about your living arrangements?"

Tara shrugged and pushed the door open. The first thing the boys saw was a stack of pizza boxes as tall as they were sitting just inside the foyer.

"Damn," said Clay. "How does such a little thing like you put away so much garbage food?" Tara blushed. "I'd tell you I was in love, but I know I ain't got the right equipment for you." She gave him an affectionate shove and walked into the living room.

"It's going to take ten minutes or so for the phone to charge up enough to use it."

"Even if it's plugged in?" asked Jerry.

"Korean technology," she said with a shrug. She set the phone down on a table in the corner and attached the charger cable. "Can I get you boys something to drink while we wait? I have a few beers in the fridge."

"What kind?" said Clay suspiciously. "I mean, no offense, but you *are* from Frisco. They drink all manner of fruity beer out there, I hear." He cleared his throat. "If you'll pardon the expression."

"First, anyone who has ever been within a hundred miles of the place can tell you that we hate it when people call it 'Frisco'. The gold rush is over. Second, it's Sam Adams. That's the fruitiest beer you can get in this backwater wasteland."

Jerry winced. "I prefer my beer don't taste like much of anything," he said.

"Your loss," said Tara. "Clay?"

"Sure, I'm game. I never had an expensive beer like that before."

Tara crooked an eyebrow.

"Oh hell, I'll take one too," said Jerry. "Probably can't even taste it at this point, I'm so exhausted."

Tara disappeared into the kitchen, glad that the boys were staying in the living room instead of witnessing the utter chaos that reigned in there, and returned with the beers. "I hope bottles is ok. I uh…I don't have any clean glasses at the moment." The boys nodded and she distributed the drinks, took a seat, and raised her bottle. "To our next move."

The boys raised theirs toward hers, nobody willing to put in the effort to actually stand up and toast. They drank. Jerry and Clay downed about half of their respective beers in a single pull. Tara finished hers entirely and gave an enthusiastic and appreciative belch when the bottle left her lips.

"Pardon me," she said with a sheepish grin. The boys laughed. She jokingly tossed the empty bottle over her shoulder and it landed with a dull thunk on the carpeted floor to another, softer laugh.

They sat for a moment in silence and, as the excitement of the long day overcame them and the rush of adrenaline they'd all been coasting on for the past several hours receded, fell asleep one by one.

When Tara opened her eyes the sun was streaming in through the open window in the living room. She blinked and twisted, trying to work out the kink in her back. *Why am I sleeping in the living room?* she thought. *No wonder I had such fucked up dreams last night.*

She sat up, stretched, and let out a tiny yelp when she noticed the two young men snuggled up together on her couch, both snoring softly. A wave of despair hit her when she realized that it wasn't a dream, after all. Then she was struck by a momentary beam of joy. As quietly as she could, she stood up and tiptoed over to the corner table where her phone lay fully charged. She picked it up and unplugged it, activated the camera, and tiptoed across the room to stand over the boys and take a picture. The flash caused

Clay's eyes to flutter open.

"What in the holy hell are you—"

"If the world doesn't end today," Tara said, "this is *so* going on Facebook." Clay turned his head and noticed Jerry leaning on his shoulder, his arms wrapped around Clay's waist. He jumped up, waking Jerry. "Woah, dude, we…we were just…you know, it was cold in here and…"

Tara laughed until tears streamed down her face. "My friend, I am the last person on earth to criticize you for your forbidden love." She launched into another peal of laughter as Clay's face turned scarlet. Jerry stretched out across the couch and fell right back in to snoring.

"Quit messing around," Clay said. "Your phone works, so call the CDC."

Tara, wiping away the tears streaming down her face, flipped back to her phone's browser, did a quick Google search, and dialed the Centers for Disease Control. After waiting some time on hold, she finally got hold of a live human being and began to explain their predicament. The operator promptly hung up on her. Tara stood slackjawed.

"They think we're perpetrating a hoax," she said. "Apparently, there's been a huge uptick in zombie apocalypses since the CDC released joke guidelines on how to deal with one."

"Ok, so call 911," said Clay.

"Good idea." She dialed and put the phone to her ear. "Hello? Hi, we have a serious problem here and I'm hoping you guys can help. There's been a widespread disease outbreak, and we can't get a hold of emergency services to…Fulton Flats, Iowa…Yes…Yes, well I tried calling…ok, great. Thank you." She put her hand over the microphone. "She's connecting me to emergency services."

There was a pause. "Hello? Oh, you have got to be kidding. No, sorry, it's just that I called you guys like two minutes ago and your operator hung up on me. Yeah, sure, not your fault. Yes, I can hold." She rolled her eyes. "They forwarded me back to the CDC. Can you fucking bel—Oh, hi. Yes, I need to report an outbreak of an unknown disease. Symptoms? Well, it's going to sound funny but please hear me out. The victims become extremely aggressive and cannibalistic toward members of their gender and fornicate wildly with members of the opposite gender... Yes, I guess you could call them sex zombies if you really had to put a name on it, but...hello? *Fuck!*" She threw the phone down on the couch. "Any other ideas?"

"We could call the sheriff. He's probably on duty by now," Clay suggested.

"Don't suppose you know the number, do you? I really don't want to take my chances with 911 again."

"Just look it up online. Fulton Flats PD has an AOL-era website, but the number hasn't changed."

Still angry at her phone, Tara retrieved her laptop from the bedroom and fired it up. She ran a search on "Fulton Flats Police Department" and got a single return, something she had never seen before on Google. "This really is the ass end of the earth, isn't it?" she grumbled as she clicked the link and was greeted by a page with a baby-blue background and a clip art picture of a cartoon policeman in shades directing traffic. The top of the page blinked the headline "FLUTON FLATS POLIC ON-LINE".

"Oh dear god," she groaned. "There's even a hit counter on the bottom. The page has only been viewed 253 times."

"Not a lot of reason to look at the police website here," Clay said. "Most people use the yellow pages if they need a cat saved from a tree." Tara sighed heavily then walked over to the phone, picked it up from between the couch cushions where it had settled itself, and dialed. After two solid minutes of ringing, she tossed it back.

"No answer. Not even voicemail."

"Oh, they never had voicemail. Again, not a lot of call for police around here. Mostly Steve just writes parking tickets for the farmer's market on Saturday mornings and goes on the occasional house visit when some asshole hits his wife hard enough to compel her to call in a complaint."

"So what's plan D?"

"I think the first thing we oughtta do is take a look outside and see if civilization's crumbled yet," Clay said, moving to the window. He knuckled aside the drape and peered out at the street.

"What's it look like?"

"Quiet," he said, looking from one end of the street to the other. "Not a soul in sight. I guess that's a good sign. Isn't it?"

"Well, my street hardly ever gets any traffic anyway. Hell, no street in this town gets much traffic. But I guess no hordes of zombies roaming around is good news."

Clay let the curtain go. "So what do you think?"

"We were only out for a few hours. Even if the group from the Bucket made it into town, there's no way they could have infected the whole place by now, right? And we didn't see anyone else last night, so it's a fair assumption that Martin and your parents were the only ones here."

Clay's face sank at the mention of his parents.

"Well, there was somethin' weird about that," he said. "When we got to the house last night the door was open. I know I locked it when I left. So it's possible that mom and dad…well, I guess they could have gone out for a…for a bit of a night on the town, if you get my drift."

"Zombie swinger party with the neighbors?"

"I'd really rather you didn't put it like that."

"Sorry. But that does mean there could be a lot more of them than we originally thought. Still, it does look pretty deserted out there."

"So what's the move, boss?"

"Why do I have to be the boss?"

"Your house, your rules."

Tara wrinkled her nose. "I think I want to take a shower and clean the cigarette stink from the bar off of me. Change my clothes. Then I guess we venture out into the world to see what's going on."

"Why don't we just hole up here? Wait to see if the doc actually called in the threat or not?"

"You saw the stack of pizza boxes in the hallway. They don't even wait for me to place an order anymore, the delivery guy just shows up every third day around seven o'clock. I don't keep food in the house, Clay. At the very least we need to go out and stock up. A weapon more powerful than a fork or a BB gun would probably come in handy ,too."

"Well, the car's running on fumes so we're gonna have to stop and get gas, too. Maybe we can get some food at the Speedway downtown. Only gas in fifty miles of here. But first, maybe we should drop by the police station. It's on the way there, and it couldn't hurt to check it out. You know, just make sure everything's cool down there."

"Sounds like a plan," Tara said. "Ok, I'm gonna go wash up." She didn't move. "I uh...I have a sorta delicate question to ask you."

"Shoot."

"Can I trust you?"

"What do you mean? 'Course you can trust me."

"I know I can trust you in general, but...well, here's the thing...the bathroom door doesn't lock, and I know everyone's been all riled up at some point or another in the last twelve hours, so...can I trust you, or do I have to kick you two out and lock the door until I'm done?"

Clay feigned indignation. "Madame, how dare you make such vile insinuations against my character? I am a gentleman, through and through." He smiled. "Besides, you're too skinny for me. I like 'em nice and curvy." He raised an eyebrow playfully.

"It's a wonder nobody's married you up yet, Clayton Barre," she said and turned to head off to the bedroom to collect new clothes. As she walked away she did her best Jessica Rabbit impersonation, swinging her hips with each step. Clay whistled and cat-called. As she disappeared into the back of the house Jerry came to.

"What the fuck you bein' so noisy about," he said, rubbing the sleep from his eyes.

Clay turned around. "Tara said she's gonna run a shower for you. Give it a few minutes to get nice and warm and head on back."

Myrna's Car

"You're a prick," Tara said. "You know that, right? You're a class-A industrial grade dickbag. You'd better hope you don't get attacked again, because from here on out, if I see anyone humping your leg or taking a bite out of it, I'm going to just sit there and chuckle." She crossed and uncrossed her arms. "Prick."

Clay hadn't stopped laughing for the past twenty minutes. Jerry had been completely silent and unable to make eye contact with Tara. He had also punched Clay's shoulder so hard that a bruise in the perfect shape of his fist was beginning to darken Clay's skin.

In Clay's estimation, it was totally worth it.

They were rolling slowly down Tara's street toward the gas station, taking their time to fully scout out every intersection before they proceeded. So far, there wasn't a single sign of another human being to be found. The smoke was beginning to roll in in earnest now, coming down off of the hills surrounding town in oily blue billows that looked like spoiled skim milk running down the sides of a sink. A haze had settled on the town, and everything smelled like campfire. If he squinted, Clay could see an orange glow on the tops of the furthest-away hills, way down south toward Stockton and west toward Washington State. He half-wondered if getting out of town wasn't a good idea, after all.

"I'm really super sorry, Tara," Jerry said, speaking up in her presence for the first time that day. "Clay told me that—"

"I know damned well what Clay told you," she said then made a concerted effort to bore holes in Clay's forehead with her eyes. "Clay is a prick," she said to his face, then turned and gave Jerry a huge, fake smile. "It's not your fault."

"I know it's not, but I still feel kinda...well, I'm just really sorry is all. I swear, I wasn't looking. I think I only saw your titties for, like, half a second. That's all. And I'll forget all about how they look if you want me to."

Tara grumbled, shot another icy glare at Clay, took off her seatbelt, turned around to face the back seat and lifted her shirt up to her neck.

"Here, now you've gotten a legitimate look," she said, her voice slightly muffled by the thick cotton of the blouse she was wearing. "And you got it on my terms." She righted her clothing and sat back down. "Feel better?"

Jerry just stared straight ahead, completely at sea. "I…I guess so?"

"No fair," yelled Clay. "I'm driving! I didn't get to see!"

"And you never will," said Tara. "Because you're a prick."

They drove on to the police station in silence.

Fulton Flats Police Headquarters

It was an absurdly small building, the kind you'd expect to find Andy Griffith sitting in, whittling a stick and drinking coffee while Otis sleeps off a drunk in the solitary cell. The front was rough wood paneling painted brown, with a series of dark-tinted windows set high in the wall. From the outside, Tara estimated that it was one, maybe two rooms. It was sandwiched between an empty storefront and a store that sold country-style knick-knacks and various other touristy items.

She was amazed that a store like that could possibly stay in business in a town that, as far as she could tell, had never seen a tourist. The police station identified itself with a Fraternal Order of Police sticker under the bar on the door and an ancient-looking slab of wood across the top of the building with the words "Fulton Flats Police Department" cut into it with a router. On the curb was a pair of signposts a car-length apart reading "Police Parking Only".

And, oddly, the door was hanging open.

They drove past slowly, all three angling to try to see through the crack in the door. It appeared to be dark inside, but they couldn't discern any movement.

"What do you think?" asked Clay. "Should we get out and have a look?"

"I don't know," Jerry replied, a slight whimper in his voice giving away the barely-suppressed terror he'd been fighting to hide since they first rolled into the completely deserted downtown area. "What if Steve's in there and he's infected?"

"What if he's in there and he needs our help?" Clay retorted.

"How much help could we possibly be?" said Tara. "Are you going to save the policeman with your BB gun?" She snickered. "Prick."

"Well, we'll never know if we don't go in, will we?"

"Fine, pull over then," Tara said. "But be sure you don't block the designated police parking. It'd serve you right to get the car towed in the middle of the zombie apocalypse."

Clay parked the car and the three of them cautiously stepped out, keeping a sharp eye up and down the block. Downtown was still and quiet, not so much as a breeze stirring the haze. They surrounded the door, Clay with his gun pointed through the opening, Tara brandishing her knife and Jerry wielding the barbecue fork. Clay took a deep breath and cautiously put the ball of his foot up against the door.

"You ready, guys?" he whispered. Tara and Jerry both nodded solemnly.

Clay gave the door a push and stumbled inside, far less gracefully than he had intended to. It was dark, and impossible to make anything out. Tara and Jerry spread out in opposite directions along the wall, feeling for the light switch.

"Aha!" grunted Jerry triumphantly as the fluorescents came flickering to life.

They took in the scene. It was indeed, as Tara had surmised, a single room. Against one wall was a row of bars split into two cells, both of which were empty. Opposite the cells was a desk piled high with paperwork. A seventies-vintage television set perched on one corner of the desk. There were two doors in the back wall. One was hung with a "Restroom" sign, the other with "Authorized Personnel Only".

And in the middle of the floor was a pool of nearly black, coagulating blood strewn with shreds of cloth and skin, in the center of which was an arm sheathed in the navy blue sleeve of a policeman's uniform.

"Oh shit…" said Clay. "Shit shit shit shit shit shit shit."

"Oh god, Clay, you think that's Steve's arm?" asked Jerry.

"Who the hell else would it be?" said Clay, agitated. "Looks like they got him."

"It's worse than we thought," said Tara. "They're definitely in town. So why haven't we seen anyone yet?"

"Maybe they're afraid of the daylight," said Jerry. "Ain't zombies supposed to get killed by the sun?"

"Vampires," said Tara.

"Huh?"

"Vampires are killed by the sun. Zombies don't give two shits about whether it's day or night."

"You sure about that? I seem to remember all those zombie movies taking place at night."

"You think *Day of the Dead* took place at night, nitwit?" asked Clay.

Jerry thought for a moment. "Well no, when you put it that way it just seems silly, doesn't it?"

"So where are they?" mused Tara. "And what are we going to do about it?"

Clay pointed toward the back wall. "What do you suppose is in that closet?" he asked.

"The toilets, Clay," said Jerry.

"It's probably a supply closet," said Tara, shaking her head.

"Wanna see if we can get it open?" asked Clay.

"Be my guest," Tara said, bowing with a flourish.

Clay searched around the room for something hard with which to break in the door. After a few minutes the best he could come up with was the rolling chair that sat behind the desk. He picked it up, turned it over, and slammed the wheel struts against the wooden door. The struts, being cheap Wal-Mart plastic, broke off, sending the little plastic wheels flying through the air. He cursed and gave it another whack, cracking off more of the structure of the chair but leaving the door unharmed.

"Hey Clay, do you think—" started Jerry.

"Hush, Jer, I'm trying to work here." He spun the chair bottom around to bring a fresh set of struts to the front then swung as hard as he could. The new struts shattered as well, raining little fragments of hard plastic down on Tara and Jerry.

"Easy there, cowboy," said Tara. "You're gonna put someone's eye out with those flying shards."

"I can feel it starting to give," said Clay. "A few more hits and I should have it."

He took another swing, smashing the struts down to stubs. He reached around and rotated again, bringing the last remaining strut to the front.

"Clay, seriously, you haven't tried—"

"Jerry, man, give me a minute to work here, ok? This is tiring and I need to concentrate. Only one leg left on this chair. Gotta make it count." He took a few practice swings, aiming for the small divot that his previous strikes had left. Then he wound up and, with a battle cry that would have done William Wallace proud, smashed the chair against the door one final time. Black plastic exploded in every direction. The wheel caromed off of the door and flew into one of the empty cells. The door did not budge.

"Fuck me," he screamed, whirling around like a shot-putter and flinging the chair at the windows on the front of the building, where it bounced harmlessly off, leaving the Plexiglas wobbling.

"Dude, chill out," said Jerry. "Just—"

"*Shut the fuck up, Jer,*" Clay growled, then whirled on the desk, picked up the television and ran back toward the door, hefting it over his shoulder, cocking back his arm to throw it. Just as he released, the television hit the end of its power cord, which was still plugged into a surge protector strip under the desk.

As Clay hurtled clumsily forward, the momentum of his interrupted throw pushing him face-first into the door, the television dropped to the tiled floor, the screen shattering and spewing glass. Clay knocked his forehead into the door hard and fell backwards to the ground, landing on his ass with a thud.

Jerry, shaking his head, stepped over Clay's prone form and turned the doorknob. The door opened with a creak.

"Grandma always said, 'try the easiest way first'," he proclaimed as he walked into the supply closet. Tara burst into hysterical laughter and followed, giving Clay a slightly-harder-than-playful kick in the ribs as she passed him.

"Prick."

The closet, it turned out, was a treasure trove for the aspiring survivalist. Though Fulton Flats had only one policeman and practically no crime, the NRA-friendly attitude of the town had compelled its citizens to vote for levies for new police equipment every few years. With no pressing need to institute updated computer systems or advanced technology of any sort, the department (which is to say Sheriff Stephen Barley) had simply stockpiled increasingly outrageous and unnecessary guns.

Hanging on the wall were a staggering variety of handguns, assault rifles and shotguns, and a shelf in the corner held box upon box of ammunition for each. A shelf on the opposite wall was piled with road flares, flashlights and electrical devices whose purpose Tara could not begin to fathom. Perplexingly, there was a compliment of ten high-powered walkie-talkies sitting on the floor in their chargers. Steve had bought them three years ago in a rare flash of forward-thinking: occasionally one of the town's children wandered off into the woods and search parties had to be formed to retrieve them. He hadn't yet had a chance to use them and, it would seem, never would.

"Jack-fucking-pot," said Jerry, in awe. "There's enough firepower here to kill every motherfucker in this town fifty times over!" He jumped up and down giddily. "Zombified motherfuckers only, of course," he added when he noticed the way Tara was looking at him.

"Are you experienced with guns?" she asked.

"Never shot one in my whole life. You?"

"I'm from San Francisco. If you even think about a gun there eight cops appear to drag you down to the station and lock you away for life."

Jerry was aghast. "How do they know what you're thinking?"

Tara spent an entire half-second debating whether or not it was animal cruelty to fuck with Jerry. She decided that in extremis, such cruelty was excused. "Oh, the SFPD has had mind-readers since that guy offed our mayor and Harvey Milk in the seventies."

"Amazing," Jerry said with an appreciative shake of the head. "They really are progressive out west."

"Sweet mother of Rambo," said Clay as he walked into the room, rubbing the expanding lump on his forehead. "It's like militia Christmas in here."

"Clay, do you have any training with guns?" asked Tara.

"Training? Sweetheart, out here you don't train with guns. You shoot guns. Usually at animals or IRS agents."

"Great, so you've shot guns? At...at animals, I hope?"

"Oh hell no, I never touched a real gun in my life. Mom wouldn't let dad keep them around the house. I spent a fair amount of time knockin' over soda cans with the BB gun though, and I got all the shooting practice I could ever want on *Call of Duty*."

Tara's shoulders slumped. "So we've got endless guns and no training. That's...that's just fucking..."

"Can't be that hard to pick up," said Jerry, pulling an AR-15 assault rifle off the wall and pointing at the barrel. "This end goes toward what you want to die. Done and done." He slung the strap over his shoulder and stuffed a few handguns into his belt. "Shit, I feel like Arnold Schwarzenegger." He pointed the rifle at Clay. "Remember when I said I'd kill you last? *I lied!*" He squeezed the trigger and the gun jumped, three bullets slamming into the wall just over Clay's right shoulder.

"Motherfucker!" Clay screamed, dropping to the floor in a heap.

"Oh shit, Clay! Sorry. I didn't think it was loaded!"

"You coulda killed me, you asshole!"

"And that, my friends, is why I'm so worried about training," Tara said, putting her fingers in her ears to stop the ringing.

Jerry carefully set the safety on the rifle and let it fall back over his shoulder, extending a hand to help Clay up from the ground.

"Let's not load up too heavily on guns. I don't think shooting 'every zombified motherfucker in town' is going to help. And it doesn't do us any good to be slowed down by carrying a hundred and fifty pounds of guns."

Clay, tucking a hand cannon the size of a deli salami into his belt, called over his shoulder "The only thing that can stop a bad guy with a gun is a good guy with a gun."

"But...but the bad guys here don't have guns, they're—"

"You can take my machine gun when you pry it from my cold,

dead hands," said Jerry, his face set without a hint of irony.

Tara sighed. "Fine, keep the machine gun. But put at least two of those pistols back. You won't be able to walk with your belt full like that."

"If you've never shot before, Tara, you should probably have a shotgun," Clay said. "Don't need to be too precise with those, and they've got a lot of stopping power."

"I thought you didn't have any training," Tara said, impressed.

"*Call of Duty*, man. *Call of Duty*."

Tara found a shotgun with a pistol grip that she felt comfortable with and slung it over her shoulder. Jerry offered her a surprisingly dainty pistol, which earned him a withering glare, then handed her one of the mid-sized .9mm semi-automatic pistols. Clay pulled down a shotgun for himself, and slung a small sub-machine gun over his shoulder for good measure. They then proceeded to take half an hour matching bullets to guns to make sure they had the proper ammo.

"We should take these walkies, too," Jerry said, rifling around the other supplies. "In case we get separated."

"Good idea," said Tara. "Any idea what this other stuff is?"

Jerry picked up a taser and placed the electrodes against his forehead. "This might be one of them mind-readers the San Fran cops got."

Clay's eyes lit up. "Hey, I think you're right. Push that button on top and see if you can hear what you're thinking."

"*NO!*" shouted Tara, running to Jerry and knocking the device out of his hand. She turned on Clay, planting her fists on her hips. "Prick!"

"You gotta admit, he was just *beggin'* for it!"

Tara leveled a finger in Clay's face. "No more fucking around, ok? We might be fighting for our lives any minute, and I want to know I can trust you. And that Jerry's not going to be unconscious because you felt the need to pull some dickwitted redneck prank. Ok, Clay? Can you agree to that?"

Clay rolled his eyes. "Fine, *mom*."

Jerry picked up a handful of road flares from the shelf and put them in his pocket.

"What do you need those for, Jer?"

"No idea. But better to have them and not need them than to need them and not have them, right?"

"Guess so," said Tara. She gave the boys a look-over. "Ok, are we all stocked up now?" They each had at least two guns secreted about their persons. They also each carried a satchel pack with extra ammo, a walkie-talkie and an enormous police-grade flashlight.

"Locked and loaded," Jerry yelled, raising the AR-15. Clay instinctively hit the floor.

"Hey, look what I found," he said, pulling a cardboard box out from the bottom shelf of the unit he had fallen next to. He dipped his hand inside, then held it out toward Tara, a compact gas mask dangling from his fingers.

"What do we need gas masks for?" asked Jerry. "We're fighting zombies, not skunks."

"Pheromones," Clay said.

Tara nodded appreciatively. "If we can't smell them…"

"…we won't want to pork them," Clay finished for her.

"Good eye," said Tara. "And surprisingly good thinking. I'm proud of you, Clayton. In honor of your find, I'm not going to call you a prick for the next twenty minutes."

"I'll try to live up to your praise."

"Good. Now, let's go fuel up," said Tara, and the left the supply closet.

As they carefully stepped past the mess on the floor, Clay stopped and walked back to the desk.

"What are you doing?" asked Tara.

"Well, I thought I'd leave a note. You know, just in case Steve ain't dead."

He pulled a pen from a coffee cup on the corner of the desk opposite where the television had sat and scribbled on a notepad emblazoned with the logo for a company in Spokane: "Kobest Industries – for all your plumbing supply needs!"

Dear Officer Barley,

If you don't know yet, all hell's broke loose in town. We borrowed some guns and other stuff to protect ourselves. We swear we'll give it back when everything is back to normal. If you need us, use the walkies. We each have one.

I really hope you're not dead, it would be a big help to have a cop on our side.

Thanks,
Clay Barre

He put the coffee cup on the corner of the note to hold it down, and tiptoed past the arm on the floor and out the door.

Speedway

As far as they could tell, the streets were still entirely empty. It was only a short two blocks from the police station to the Speedway, but there was absolutely no sign of life to be found. There was no attendant at the gas station so Tara, being the only one with a credit card and therefore the only one able to activate the pump, was left to fill the gas tank while Jerry and Clay went inside for supplies. She brought her shotgun with her—just for safety's sake, of course—and glanced around nervously the entire time she stood at the pump. When the car was fully gassed up, she went inside to join the boys shopping for supplies.

"We're making a pile on the counter," said Jerry when she opened the door. "Find what you need and add it in."

Tara's shoulders sagged when she saw the heap of Hostess treats, beer cans and Doritos next to the cash register. "Shouldn't we look for...I don't know...something a little healthier?"

"We been to your apartment," said Jerry. "No offense, but it didn't look like you ever cared much for healthy food."

"Well, we're in survival mode now," Tara countered. "We need...you know...vitamins. And stuff. Beta keratin. We're fighting for our lives."

"You ever find a salad bar at a Speedway?" asked Clay, dropping three unopened boxes of Twix bars on the counter. "It's a convenience store, not a grocery store. If you're so worried about eatin' right, we can drive to Boise and knock over the Whole Foods. In the meantime..." He walked away to peruse the magazine rack, pulling out everything that had an opaque plastic cover hiding it from children.

"We should consider some medical stuff, too," said Tara, wandering toward the small rack of first-aid supplies. She picked up a bottle of antacids, a few Ace bandages and a box of Band-Aids.

"Not sure how much good the Band-Aids are gonna do us,"

said Clay. "I mean, it's not like these things are givin' us paper cuts."

"Well, they're certainly going to be more useful than that issue of *Juggs* you just looted. Isn't sex sorta the enemy at the moment?"

"Speak for yourself, missy. The one person on earth I know it's safe to have sex with right now is me. I ain't gonna deprive myself of the joy of my lovin' touch just because the world might be ending."

Tara rolled her eyes and brought the bandages and medicine to the counter. She walked around to the teller's spot to find a bag to pack their scavengings in, but found nothing.

"Hey guys, there are no plastic bags here. How are we gonna get all this stuff out to the car?"

Jerry joined her, his arms bulging with Vitamin Water, and began to set the bottles on the counter one at a time. "Did you look under the register? That's where Bethany always gets 'em from when I come in on my shopping trips."

"You mean your 'ogle Bethany Williams' trips," said Clay thought a mouthful of Funyons.

"She might be in her late fifties, but I'd still turn her out," said Jerry.

"I looked everywhere," said Tara. "There are no bags here." She looked nervously out the window at the car. "I guess I'll have to go out and get one of the ammo satchels from the back seat."

"Good plan," said Jerry, and went back to the cooler for more beverages.

Tara threw a Hostess Sno-Ball at the back of his head. "Just because I like pussy doesn't mean I wouldn't appreciate a little chivalry every once in a while."

"And just because I like pussy don't mean I owe you anything," said Jerry, stacking Bud Lime six-packs on the floor.

"I showed you my tits!"

"I'd be willing to go out there for a flash," said Clay.

Tara's eyebrows lowered. She opened her mouth to say something scathing, then turned and silently stalked out to the car.

She looked up and down the street, found it clear, and bent

down into the back seat to empty one of the supply bags, arranging its contents carefully on the seat. Realizing that one bag wasn't going to be remotely enough to hold the ever-growing mountain of looted junk food on the counter inside, she popped the trunk and rifled through Myrna's collected detritus, hoping against hope for a few reusable canvas shopping bags. She was disappointed—but not surprised—not to find any.

She stood up and slammed the trunk, then turned around to find herself face-to-face with a middle-aged man stripped to the waist, his mouth smeared with blood and his right arm ending in a fringe of torn skin and the gnawed stub of a bone just below the elbow. She screamed, and he seemed to notice her for the first time. He reached out an arm to her experimentally, the way one would when walking to the bathroom in the dark in the middle of the night. She urgently but quietly scrambled backward onto the trunk and then the roof of the car.

The man took a tentative step forward and ran into the rear bumper. He looked down, puzzled, and then back up to where he thought Tara might be. In that brief moment, she had leveled the barrel of her shotgun at his face. His eyes met hers with a look of confusion, and she pulled the trigger. His skull exploded, raining blood and bits of bone on the asphalt behind him. His body dropped in a heap. Tara screamed her lungs out, hopped off the roof of the car, and ran inside.

"Did you get the bag?" asked Jerry, emerging from the beer cooler.

"Did I get the—what the fuck, did you not hear the shotgun blast?"

"We figured you were taking practice shots at something," said Clay.

"*In a gas station?!*"

"I looked out, didn't see nothin' but you on the roof of the car, and I made my assumptions."

"One of them was this far from my face," Tara screamed, holding her hand a few inches from her nose.

"Oh fuck," said Jerry. "You ok?"

Tara tried to slow her breathing. "Yeah, I'm fine. He didn't seem to notice I was there at all until I screamed. I guess I really am invisible to them." She set the empty satchel on the counter. "Twenty-five years in, being a lesbian is finally starting to pay off."

"You could have avoided all of this with a little flash," said Clay. "But *noooooooo*. You'd rather go risk death. See what self-respect gets you?"

"Let's get this shit packed up and get out of here," Tara said. "That guy came out of nowhere. I'm worried there might be more hanging around." She started stuffing the bandages into the bag, then sifting through the pile of food to find the least awful stuff.

Clay walked over to the window. "Oh shit," he said, pulling his pistol out of his belt. "When you're right, Tara, you are way too right."

Tara looked up from the bag to see no fewer than fifteen more people stumbling in under the awning of the gas station. The first three men to arrive at the car were already consuming what was left of the man she'd so recently decapitated. "Fuck! Quick, block the door!"

Clay looked around for something to push in front of the double doors leading into the convenience store. He decided that neither the waist-tall bucket of cold drinks nor the wire rack of free employment magazines sitting right next to the entryway was enough of a barrier, so he found a set of jumper cables on the shelf that contained emergency auto supplies and air fresheners and ran them through the door handles, tying them off to secure the doors.

"This isn't going to hold too long," he said. "What do we do?"

Tara thought frantically as she watched the zombies outside mill around. A woman with one breast hanging out of her bathrobe and the other missing entirely looked in through the giant plate glass window that was the entire front of the store and, seemingly noticing the moving bodies inside, came closer. She smacked face-on into the window like a bird on a patio door, stumbled back a step, and pressed her face experimentally against the glass. Clay, his breath coming ragged now, raised his pistol and aimed it at her face.

"*NO!*" screamed Tara, and Clay stopped to look at her,

puzzled. "You'll break the glass. It's holding them back for the moment. We need a better plan."

"Well, think fast. More of 'em are figuring out we're in here."

He was right. Another woman had come up behind the first and began to chew on her shoulder while gazing into the store, her eyes fixed on Clay. There were a number of men drawing up to the window as well.

"Jerry," Tara said, holding perfectly still, "you're closest to the back. Go see if there's another door. But move as slowly as you can."

Jerry slowly turned around to face the employee door to the back room of the store and, going up on tiptoes, inched gingerly toward it. Immediately, all zombie eyes were on him. They watched intently, their faces pressed to the glass, until he disappeared. Tara tried to steady her breathing. There was a man with his jawbone completely exposed not three feet away from her, smearing his blood on the glass as he looked back and forth, searching out signs of movement inside.

"Jesus, this is just like *Jurassic Park*," Clay whispered out of the side of his mouth. "Where the fuck is Jerry?"

"Calm and easy, Clay," Tara said. "They can't smell you though the glass. As long as we're still they don't seem to know we're in here."

Just then, Jerry came crashing through the door. "There's a back entrance," he yelled, waving his arms. Every zombie eye immediately turned to him. "Oh shit," he grunted, and ducked behind a shelf of cracker boxes.

"Great distraction, Jer," said Clay. "Ok, I'm gonna slowly make my way back there now. Let's go one at a time." He backed up carefully, never taking his eyes off of the hungry beasts outside. They seemed not to notice him, still stuck on the spot where Jerry had disappeared.

Halfway to the door, he backed into a stack of Monster energy drinks, knocking them to the floor with a loud and protracted clatter. A number of the cans broke open, spraying their lightly-carbonated fluid around the store. The creatures immediately locked their eyes on him. One of the men began pounding on the window, making it shake in almost hypnotic waves.

"Run!" shouted Tara. Jerry and Clay picked themselves up off of the floor and the three made a mad dash into the back room, slamming the door closed behind them. Clay pulled a metal shelf with extra stock over to block the door and they leaned against the shelf panting.

"Let's get outta here," Jerry said.

"What if there's more out there in the back?" said Clay.

"I checked. The alley's clear."

"How long is it gonna take for them to figure out where we went?"

"Well, they don't seem too smart," said Tara. "Still, they might get curious and walk around back on their own. We should make a run for it while they're still interested in the store." As if to punctuate her point, there was a loud crash on the other side of the door. She took a step toward the back door then turned around. The boys were frozen in place. "They're going to break through that window any minute now. We need to run."

"We can't just leave the car here. We're sitting ducks without it," said Clay.

"Fuck, you're right," said Jerry. "Someone's gonna have to go after the car."

There was a moment of silence, during which Tara realized both the boys were looking at her.

"Fuck you! I'm not going back out there! I already put my skinny ass on the line for you two mopes once. It's someone else's turn."

"They can't smell you," said Clay. "If you take it easy you can get out there, get in the car and bring it around back here before they even know you're there."

"He's right, Tara," said Jerry. "You're the only one who can do it."

"We could just go out there guns blazing," Tara said, desperately grasping at straws. "Cut our way through to the car."

"All the spare ammo's in the back seat," Clay said, "and the gas masks. Me and Jerry go out into that mess, we're horny schoolboys in ten seconds flat. Hungry Man dinners in twenty."

"Plus, I think it was your gunshot that drew them," said Jerry. "It's safest for all of us if you go get the car."

Tara looked from Jerry to Clay, then down at her watch. "It's been twenty-seven minutes, so I am now free to call you both pricks." She threw her best death-laser glare at each of them in turn, but it had no effect. She sighed. "Fine. *Fine.* But I swear, if I get infected out there I'm leading them right back to you assholes." She pulled the clip out of her shotgun. "Clay, give me one of the shells from your gun. If I'm going out there, I'm going with a full load."

He pulled the clip from his gun and handed it to her. "Just swap me." They slapped their clips in and Tara walked over to the door and cracked it open just enough to see outside.

"Coast looks clear," she said, and opened it far enough to slip out. "Here goes nothing."

She walked out into the alley behind the station and cautiously made her way to the end of the building, peering around the corner. She saw a few more stragglers coming down the street toward the gas station, but they were far enough away that they didn't seem to notice her. She inched along the side of the store, pressed against the wall with her shotgun raised, until she reached the next corner.

To her relief, most of the zombies had gathered around the now buckling window, leaving the car more or less free.

She took a deep, slow breath, set her jaw, and started slowly walking out into the fray, her watchful gaze darting between the group at the window and the incoming stragglers headed almost straight for her. The larger mob was pounding on the plate glass, which was shaking violently. She could see the beginnings of spider cracks forming around the edges. She moved slowly and fluidly on, doing her best to be invisible.

She switched her attention to the incoming zombies and made herself, by sheer force of will, keep walking, even though the first few were directly crossing her path on their way to investigate the mob. They seemed to be completely unaware of her, but her heart raced in her chest to the point where she began to be concerned that they might hear its frantic beating.

She moved steadily on, her feet rolling on contact with the ground to give her the appearance of floating evenly over the cement, a trick she vaguely remembered from her one semester playing the clarinet in her high school marching band. She was entirely focused on a small klatch of three incoming zombies when she felt her sole rolling over something underfoot.

Panicked, unsure whether to freeze and risk detection or keep moving and take her chances as to what she might be stepping on, she stumbled slightly and managed to achieve both. Suddenly, two quick, infinitely loud bell dings rang out, cutting through the bass-drum thud of the zombies pounding on the window like a referee's whistle. She swallowed a scream and froze, dropping her eyes to her feet. She had stepped on the hose that old-fashioned gas stations put out to warn them of the arrival of customers. She rolled her eyes back up to the island of pumps and saw the completely anachronistic phrase "FULL SERVICE" in latex decal letters on the pillar between the pumps.

Go live in the boonies, I thought. It'll be nice and peaceful, I thought. Escape all those bad memories of home, I thought. Take my mind off of Betsy, I thought.

She shot a glance over to the mob at the window, who were standing stock still, looking around in all directions like a pack of prairie dogs.

Who the fuck still offers full-service gas? This is just God's revenge for my atheism.

She looked over to the incoming group, who were also searching for the source of the noise. They seemed to ascribe it to the convenience store and started walking again, picking up their pace slightly.

Tara slowed her breathing as much as she could, afraid to make even the tiniest move. She could feel the sweat beginning to roll down her forehead and gather in her eyebrows, preparing to run down over her eyes.

Betrayed by my own body, she thought.

The mobile group was passing within a few feet of her now, still not appearing to recognize her presence but seeming to be on heightened alert nonetheless. They cast their gazes about them as they moved toward the bigger group, scanning the area in case they were wrong about where the sounds had come from. She had to bite her tongue and hold her breath to keep from screaming as an elderly man with his chest torn open to the ribs walked within half a foot of her. He shuffled along with his pants and dingy briefs tangled around his ankles. The flabby skin on his thighs swayed as he walked, and he was sporting an erection that, to Tara's mind, looked like nothing so much as a caveman's club in one of the old Hanna-Barbara cartoons she used to watch on basic cable when she was a kid. The warm, coppery scent of blood filled her nostrils as he passed and she nearly gagged.

When he was directly in front of her, his boner thankfully gone from her field of vision, the thumping on the window began again with a vengeance. Tara, startled by the sudden noise, nearly jumped out of her skin but panic or self-preservation or the intervention of some benevolent deity took hold almost immediately and she managed to contain her terror to a clenching of her jaw and a minor twitch in her arm.

Slowly rolling her eyes from side to side, she determined that she had not given away her presence, as the group of zombies that was passing her had only increased their speed even more, heading toward the store.

She stayed frozen, sweat pouring down into her eyes and pooling between her breasts, until the roving group joined the others. A quick scan showed no more zombies headed toward her, so she took another step forward and, cursing herself, froze anew when lifting her foot from the hose caused the bell to ring out again. Same as before, the mob at the window stopped what they were doing and looked around, but the pause only lasted a second this time. Tara silently thanked the powers that be for the placement of the bell inside the store and, as the pounding on the window resumed, power-walked to the car.

She got to the island and pressed against the pump, placing it between herself and the ravenous mob, buying herself a moment to catch her breath. She hadn't gotten a clear count, but she guessed there were somewhere in the neighborhood of twenty to twenty-five zombies pounding on the window. What really struck her in the gut, strangely, was seeing two young girls in the group, neither looking much older than thirteen or fourteen years old. She shuddered when she realized the only way they could have been infected. Quite incongruously, and utterly against her will, she was reminded of an article she'd edited for some medical journal or other a few weeks previous, which was about kids—especially girls, and especially in rural areas that consumed a lot of beef— reaching sexual maturity at a younger age due to the frankly absurd abundance of hormones given to cows.

If I survive this, I am going full-on angry lesbian vegan, she thought.

She slowly walked around the rear of the car to the driver's door and opened it as quietly as she could. She eased herself into the seat and put the keys into the ignition, wincing at the chime that sounded to remind her that her door was open. None of the zombies seemed to notice, though, so she pulled it softly shut and steeled herself to turn the key.

She took one last glance over at the group and a thought struck her. So far their whole plan, insomuch as it was a plan at all, had been reconnaissance. When they found themselves trapped, the plan shifted to escape. But none of them had really thought about an end-game. What were they hoping to accomplish by staying in Fulton Flats instead of fleeing on the heels of Dr. Jerrit? Were they trying to save the town? Or stop the threat from spreading out into surrounding towns and, theoretically, off into the world at large? Whatever the goal, she realized, killing zombies was a means to the end. And here she was, presented with a perfect, though insanely risky, opportunity to do away with a couple dozen of them in one fell swoop.

She looked at the group, then back at the open street. *I could just leave,* she thought. *I've got nothing invested in this pisspot town. I could just start the car and get the fuck out of here right now. Those two idiots are a drag on me anyway.*

She looked longingly at the two-lane road stretching off to the horizon, tracing it with her eyes until it disappeared into the burning hills in the distance. Despite herself, she knew she couldn't go without the boys. Crass though they were, she had grown to like them.

Fuck it, she thought. *We're all gonna die some time. I might as well take a lot of flesh-eating motherfuckers with me.*

She took the keys out of the ignition and left them on the passenger seat then slowly, slowly pushed on the car door, her breath catching as it creaked open. She stood, leaving the door hanging wide, and marching band roll-walked her way to the island nearest the mob. The window was showing serious signs of distress now from their incessant pounding. She crept to a pump directly behind the mob and slowly, gingerly pulled her Visa card out of the jeans pocket she'd stowed it in after filling the gas tank. She held her breath and swiped the card, hoping this was not one of those automated gas pumps that beeps when you bring it to life or press a key.

To her relief, the screen silently switched over to asking her if she wanted a receipt. She smiled and pushed the button for "no", confident that there would be record enough of this transaction if all went as she planned. She carefully lifted the nozzle from the pump and pressed the button for the high-grade 92-octane Premium gasoline. She watched intently as the counters reset themselves to zero and the screen flashed "BEGIN FUELING".

She squeezed the trigger carefully, suddenly worried that there might be some sort of mechanism to prevent exactly what she was planning to do, something that required the nozzle be safely inserted into a gas tank before fuel was dispensed. She smiled when a spurt of sickly green-yellow gasoline splashed onto the ground, splattering up onto her shoes and the cuffs of her jeans.

She checked to see if the zombies had noticed the sound of her experiment, but their fists slamming against the plate glass window drowned out all other noise for them. She took another deep breath for courage and instantly regretted it as she gagged on the strong chemical stench of the gas. Then she dragged the hose as far from the pump as it would go – a paltry few feet – aimed it at the far end of the parking lot, and squeezed.

The gas arced a respectable ten feet, nearly reaching the sidewalk. She let a small pool gather, constantly checking over her shoulder to make sure she wasn't noticed. Then she steadily brought the stream back toward herself, leaving a trail of fuel leading back to the pump. She discovered that she had to work extremely slowly, as the station's pavement was the kind designed to soak up minor gas and oil spills. When she was satisfied at the standing river of gasoline leading away from the island, she coated the pump itself for good measure.

Just as she was tracing a trail of gas to the next adjacent pump, a thunderous crash came from the storefront. The window had finally buckled under the pressure of the crowd pounding on it and shattered with the force of a small explosion, throwing shards of glass in every direction. The zombies at the front of the mob were hit the worst, splinters shredding the flesh from their arms, heads and torsos and lodging in the soft tissue of their cheeks and chins and arms like icicles growing parallel to the ground.

There was a second of stunned stillness then, with a chorus of groans that Tara guessed was the zombie equivalent of a soccer mob's roar, they started climbing through the opening, hands that were already julienned from the flying glass now being impaled on shards sticking up from the bottom of the frame. Those in back, who were the least injured by the breakage, began climbing over those in front of them to get inside.

The whole mess reminded Tara of those YouTube videos one saw every year of insane herds of sale-maddened shoppers mauling each other when Wal-Mart opened their doors on Black Friday. Without thinking, she turned the nozzle on the writhing, struggling mass of bodies and began to soak them. Those on the outer edge, who had no hope of getting in until the way was clearer, turned to see where this choking rain was coming from. The familiar look of confusion crossed the faces of a handful of men on the edge of the crowd, and they turned to follow the stream of gasoline back to its source.

In an effort to confuse them, she turned the stream away from them and began coating other pumps with gas. It worked better than she'd expected: three of the four men headed her way turned and walked toward where the fluid was splashing down, rather than the source of the stream.

Enjoying the game now, she switched directions and aimed

her stream at the metal discs that covered the access tubes to the fuel reserves below the station, the tiny manhole covers that were always removed and had a large, fluted plastic hose put in them when the station was being stocked up from one of those silver tanker trucks. The three headed off in the new direction, stumbling over each other and knocking one man to the ground. The guy behind him walked blindly over his outstretched arm, eliciting a sick crunch. The one on the ground took no notice and attempted to push himself up with his hands, his right arm crumpling beneath his weight and sending him face-first back into the pavement.

Tara chuckled for a second, set the latch on the gas pump that lets you keep fueling while you go inside to buy cigarettes, carefully placed the nozzle down on the ground, and turned back to the car to discover the fourth man stumbling around perplexed. She threw her hand up to her mouth to stop herself from screaming and, catching the movement out of the corner of his eye, the man turned and walked tentatively toward her.

Without thinking, Tara resorted to the age-old advice she'd received in so many women's self-defense classes and landed a savage kick between his legs. The monster dropped as though the ground had fallen out beneath him, letting loose with a screeching wail of pain unlike anything Tara had ever heard. It writhed on the ground for a moment, wrapping itself up into a tight ball, then stopped moving. She gave him another experimental kick to the face, feeling the thin bone around his eyes crunch and his nose snap, but he remained perfectly still. She noticed he seemed to have stopped breathing.

"Interesting," she whispered, then shot a quick glance over her shoulder to see that the remaining three had been drawn by the shriek and were headed back toward her.

"Fuck," she muttered under her breath, then ran back to the car, slid into the driver's seat, and started it up. The sound of the engine turning over caused most of the larger mob of zombies, who were in the process of pushing each other through the shattered window and into the convenience store, to stop and look back in her direction, and a few more turned to wander toward her, their looks of confusion deepening. She dropped the car into drive and peeled out, leaving black tire tracks for the first few feet. She pulled out onto the street and whipped the car about, skidding around the corner toward the alleyway, honking the horn the moment she was behind the station.

Clay and Jerry came bursting through the rear door, then fell back against the wall as the car careened down the narrow alleyway. Tara pulled to a stop in front of them and popped the power locks.

"Shotgun!" yelled Jerry, throwing open the passenger door.

"Motherfucker," Clay grumbled.

"Dude, I been sittin' in the back seat all day. It's my turn."

"Fine," Clay said and slid onto the rear bench seat, tossing the bag of food in front of him.

"So I just learned something interesting," said Tara, throwing the car back into gear. "Apparently, their groins are extremely vunerable."

"You wanna put that into English?" Jerry panted, gripping his knees white-knuckled and trying to steady his breath.

"You familiar with the term 'cunt punt'?" Tara asked with a grin.

Clay's face brightened. "You sayin' they go down easier if we kick 'em in the nethers? Holy shit, that's the best news I've heard all day."

"Downside: you have to get close enough to kick them. I think it should definitcly be reserved for last resort circumstances.""You try this out on your way to the car?" Jerry asked.

"Got one of those fucks right in his manbag. He dropped like a brick and died. I swear to fucking god. It was *awesome*. I wish every man had the same reaction."

Clay and Jerry winced.

"Why do you suppose that is?" Asked Clay.

"Beats the hell out of me. That's the source of the infection though, right? So maybe it's more vulnerable? Didn't the doctor say something about a growth in Cassie's uterus?"

"Yeah," Jerry said, noticeably calmer than he had been a mere moment ago. "He said there was somethin' weird in her hoo-ha like he'd never seen before."

"How 'bout we don't talk about Cassie's infected hoo-ha and what grew in it, anymore," Clay winced. "That kinda talk is gonna ruin all my alone-times fantasies probably for the rest of my life. We got a backup plan now, let's just leave it at that."

"Speaking of plans, Clay," Tara said, "get one of those flares out of the ammo bag,"

"Why?"

"Just do it. Trust me, you're gonna love this."

Clay fished through the bag and pulled out one of the red cardboard tubes. "Got it. Now what?"

Tara slammed on the gas and the car leapt forward. "Roll down your window."

"No fucking way. I had a bad experience with a zombie and an open car window."

"Clay, think about what I'm asking you to do: flare. Gas station. Just think about what those two things are going to do when you put them together, and how utterly awesome it's going to be."

Clay pondered for a second as the car rounded the corner of the station and came to a squealing stop. There were still half a dozen or so of the crowd wandering aimlessly around under the awning, trying to figure out who soaked them with gasoline, but the majority were now inside piling up against the door to the back room.

"You mean to blow this gas station up, don't you?" Jerry asked with something like reverent awe in his voice.

"I mean to do exactly that," said Tara, smiling.

"Oh no," said Clay. "Hell no, god no, fuck no. I am not going to be a part of that. Every time I try to do some badass movie shit—every single fuckin' time—it ends up goin' sideways. Chances are, I throw this flare out the window and it just bounces back in and sets us on fire so the creepers out there get a nice char on their man-steaks. I am not ok with this, Tara. Not ok even a little bit."

"Fine, then give the flare to Jerry."

"Oh yeah, dude, I wanna do it! Gimme the flare! I'm set to blow the fuck out of them assholes."

Clay weighed his options. Jerry's success rate in the last twenty-four hours was no better than his own, and he really did want to be responsible for an entire city block in the heart of this dozy little town blowing sky-high.

"Fine, I'll do it. But if we fry, don't say I didn't warn you."

"Ok," said Tara, leaning over the back of the seat to make sure Clay understood the plan precisely, "I'm going to pull down to the corner and turn left, go down about a block and turn around to give myself a good head start. I plan on being up around sixty, sixty-five by the time we pass the gas station. I've soaked that parking lot and most of the things wandering around there. You need to land that flare close enough to the pumps that it catches something I doused. Do you think you can do that?"

Clay nodded solemnly.

"I always had the better throwing arm, Clay," Jerry said, pouting. "Remember, I was gonna go out for quarterback in high school until I learned you had to do exercises every day."

"I got better aim, though," said Clay. "Who always nails you between the eyes when we play deathmatch *Battlefield?*"

"That's a fuckin' video game, dude. This here's real life. I could get the flare closer to the pump 'cause I can throw further."

"That's bullshit and you know it-"

"*Jesus facehumping Christ, I'll throw the fucking thing myself!*" Tara screamed. The boys clammed up. "I can't believe I'm trying to survive the apocalypse with two five-year-olds. Clay, dig back in that bag and pull out a flare for Jerry. You can both blow up the gas station. Are you happy now?"

"Yes ma'am," the boys said in unison. Clay retrieved another flare from the bag and handed it to Jerry over his shoulder.

"Baby!" he sneered into Jerry's ear.

Tara eased the car onto the street and drove down a block and a half, then attempted to turn around. She immediately cursed herself for trying it in the middle of the narrow street instead of at an intersection but, after effecting history's most awkward nine-point turn, managed to get herself facing the right direction.

"Ok boys, pop the tops on those things," she said, then immediately added "outside the windows, please."

The boys lit up the flares and flaming red showers of magnesium fire spewed from the car's windows.

"I feel like we oughtta have some sorta clever catch phrase we yell when we drive by," said Jerry. "Like 'hasta la vista, baby' or something. So them cocksuckers know we mean business."

"How about 'take this, you sex-crazed cannibal fuckpuddles'," Tara suggested helpfully.

The boys considered.

"Probably the best we're gonna get on such short notice," said Jerry. "Fine. On the count of three, Clay. Alright?"

"Alright!" Clay yelled, waving his flare around. "I'm pumped! Let's do this!"

"Here goes nothing," Tara said, and punched the gas. The car lurched forward, accelerating as they raced down the street. It was quickly clear to Tara that there wasn't going to be enough road between her and the gas station to pick up the kind of speed she'd planned on, and she hoped that what she managed would be sufficient to get them far enough away from the explosion.

Half a block from the target, Clay and Jerry nodded to each other and leaned out their respective windows.

"TAKE THIS," they screamed in unison, *"YOU SEX-CRAZED CAN —"*

Realizing simultaneously that their catch phrase was too wordy and they would have missed the target by the time they got it all out, both boys hucked their flares mid-sentence. Clay's fell far short of the pump, but glanced off of the forehead of one of the tween girls, immediately setting her straw-blonde hair ablaze. She tilted her head up momentarily and sniffed at the air as if trying to decide where the smell of burning hair was coming from, then turned and began ambling back toward the store.

Jerry's flare landed almost precisely where Tara's gasoline trail began. The puddle leapt into flame, which travelled swiftly down the river of gas to the pump. As they rocketed down the street, the gas station became obscured from view behind the few other downtown buildings.

Jerry and Clay practically pounced on Tara, shouting in unison, "Turn around! Turn around!"

"Are you out of your fucking minds?" she screamed back, pushing them away. "That explosion is going to level most of downtown!"

"And we're totally gonna miss it," whined Jerry.

Tara took her eyes from the road for a second to glare at them. "You have got to be fucking jo—"

With a crack and a sonorous, resonating boom that shook their guts and rattled the car on its frame, the gas station erupted behind them. The boys looked back to see a ball of orange flame billow out above the building tops, pieces of the metal awning, chunks of asphalt and human limbs flying out in all directions. The windows in all of the surrounding buildings shattered simultaneously, raining glass down on the street in a shimmering diamond coating that reflected the deepening red glow of the spreading fire. Flaming pieces of the station's wooden infrastructure landed on adjacent businesses, setting them ablaze.

"It's possible that this was not the best plan," Tara said, pulling the car to the side of the road when she was satisfied that they were safely out of range.

"Why the hell not?" asked Clay. "We just took out a couple dozen of those fucks in one fell swoop!"

"And at least half of downtown. Does Fulton have its own fire department?"

"Volunteer," said Jerry.

"So it's unlikely that any of those buildings are going to be saved," said Tara.

The boys thought for a moment. "Insurance'll probably cover it?" said Clay, not sounding particularly sure of himself or his conclusions.

"They was ass-ugly, anyway," Jerry added. "Probably for the best."

The three sat and watched in silence as the gas station and all the surrounding buildings burned. Occasionally another bewildered-looking Fultonian would wander around a corner, drawn by the sound of the explosion, and walk directly into the flame, apparently without noticing that they were being cooked. Some then walked away, still aflame, and managed to get several blocks before their roasting muscles gave out, leaving them smoldering piles of squirming flesh in the middle of the road.

"What's our next move?" Tara asked quietly after watching a dottering old woman, engulfed in fire, chase after a boy who looked to be seven or eight, tackle him to the ground and start stripping off his clothes, setting him ablaze in the process.

Clay looked longingly down the road, which stretched out of town into the burning hills. "The forest fires are getting worse. I don't think the highway's gonna be too safe. We need to find somewhere to hide out for a spell. Somewhere we can count on there not being any zombies."

Tara shook her head. "Where? There's no guarantee anymore that there's a single safe place left in this town. I think we'd be better off taking our chances on the road."

"First Methodist," said Jerry. Tara and Clay turned to look at him. "My grandma used to make me go there when I was in high school." He looked at the car's dashboard clock. "It's goin' on noon. That'll be the best time to hide out at the church."

Clay narrowed his eyes. "Why?"

"That's when the Abstinence Club meets."

Fulton Flats First Methodist Church

There is a hackneyed saying about the church being the heart of a community. This was true in a far more literal sense in Fulton Flats, as the huge white (in both color and cultural makeup of its parishioners) Fulton Flats First Methodist Church, which sat at the geographical center of town, was the first permanent building to be constructed when the pioneers who settled the place took a wrong turn on the Oregon Trail, got fed up with the whole idea of going any further west than they already were, and decided to settle in and make the best of a bad situation. The downtown area, which sprung up several decades later, was situated slightly to the south at a respectful distance from the church so as to keep, as Charles Fulton—the city's founder, namesake and longest-serving Methodist deacon—had said once in a sermon on greed, "the money-changers the hell away from the temple". The majority of the residences clustered to the north of the church, making it the de-facto center of the settlement.

First Methodist's steeple was still the tallest structure in town. This was by ordinance, not by coincidence or reverence. In the city's charter it was clearly stated that no building of man could ever stand above the house of god. There had been some bickering as to whether or not this applied to the many farm silos that sat just outside the town's limits, but farmers eventually acquiesced to the populace's demands and kept their silos under five stories tall, mumbling prayers of thanks that the church's architect had decided to create a monument to his god that was towering enough to be seen for miles in the valley that made up Fulton Flats.

The more progressive Fulton Brethren In Christ Church, built in the 1960s by a few rebellious families that were doing their best to modernize religion in Fulton in the wake of the Vatican II councils, was largely shunned by Fultonians and never received enough support to grow out of its small clapboard edifice on the south side of town, almost precisely on the opposite side of downtown from First Methodist. The majority of the town's residents didn't even recognize it as a proper church and looked down on it as an abomination and a gathering of godless hippies. So First Methodist remained, in basically every possible way, the city's heart.

Tara brought Myrna's car to a gentle stop in front of the steps up to the church. The windshield was cracked from an encounter with a rather large logger who happened to be crossing the street at the wrong time. Clay had leaned out the window and made his first attempt to shoot one of the creatures in the crotch, but the moving car had thrown off his already pitiful aim and he had only managed to hit the man in the shin, getting his attention just in time for Tara to plow into him, cursing a blue streak. She had pulled to a stop while Clay and Jerry jumped out and took turns giggling gleefully while kicking him in the stones until he died. The rest of the drive had been comparatively uneventful.

"It's awful quiet here, guys," Tara said uneasily. "Are you sure this is a good idea?"

"It's the best idea," Jerry beamed. "What could possibly be safer than a meeting of the abstinence club? And if things continue to go south," –Clay snickered at the phrase— "we can barricade ourselves in here. The doors are sturdy and old, the windows are high up in the walls and there's a fully stocked kitchen in the basement. Best place in town to wait this thing out."

"Wait it out?" Tara huffed. "You think it's going to just blow over? Like, we'll wake up a few days from now and everyone will have decided to stop being flesh-eating fuckzombies? Because I gotta tell you, Jer, that just doesn't seem too likely to me."

"Well whatever happens, this is a good place to be while we figure out what's next," Clay said, opening his door. "Coast's clear. Let's get while the gettin's good." He leaned out, took a long look up and down the street and, satisfied that there was neither man nor monster in the vicinity, made a dash for the church doors. He stopped at the top of the stairs to wave Tara and Jerry along.

They gathered at the doors, Tara watching the street nervously as the boys pulled out pistols and readied themselves. Then Clay threw the doors open and they glided inside, imitating the orderly movement and absurd hand gestures of every cop show they'd ever watched. The foyer was dark and completely empty, the stacks of service programs and Chick Webb fliers on the counter waiting patiently for a congregation that may never return. Jerry walked to the far wall and flipped the light switch while Tara pulled the doors closed and turned the single deadbolt lock.

"Guys, these doors aren't going to hold against the kind of assault we saw at the gas station," she said. "It's just one flimsy lock. I never thought I'd say this, but I'm really missing urban crime right now."

"We can barricade the doors to the sanctuary if we got to," said Jerry. He gingerly pushed one open and took a look into the church proper. "All clear in there. I guess nobody else thought of th—" He choked off and slowly stepped back, letting the door close as quietly as he could.

"What's the matter?" asked Clay.

"I was wrong. Someone's in there. Third row. Just sittin' there. Gray hair, looks like an older lady."

"Maybe she's just here to pray."

"With all the lights turned off?" Tara asked. "We better get out of here."

"No, it's fine," Jerry said, readying his gun. "If she ain't turned we can help keep her safe. If she is, we just waste her and move on. We definitely got the upper hand here against one single old church lady, don't we?"

Both Clay and Tara wore nakedly skeptical expressions, but neither were particularly thrilled with the idea of going back outside either.

"Ok," Clay said. "We go in both sets of doors. Surround her. That way if she goes after one of us the other one can blast her." Tara snickered. "What's so funny?"

"You want us to trust in your aim, shooting at a running old lady? You couldn't even hit that barn of a dude on the way here! I am definitely going to sit this one out. You boys have fun shooting each other while an old lady force-fucks you. I'll be downstairs checking out the supplies." She turned and, giggling, walked down the stairs.

"You think she's right?" Jerry said, his hands beginning to shake visibly.

"Well I sure as fuck don't trust your aim if you're gonna get all trembly on me. New plan: we flank her like we were gonna, but you go in first. If she's turned, I'll waste her before she can get your pants down. And if she rushes you, sock her in the twat."

"Why do I gotta go first?"

"Because first, you found her and second," Clay held his hand out flat. "I ain't shaking like a goddamned leaf."

Jerry screwed his face up in thought, but couldn't come up with a counter-argument. Instead, he flipped Clay the bird and moved to the door to the sanctuary, inching it open as quietly as he could.

"Jer, wait," Clay said. Jerry pulled his head back into the foyer. "Gas masks. Might help if she's turned."

"Good thinkin'"

The boys reached into their bags and pulled out the small masks, stretching the straps over the backs of their heads and pulling them tight.

"Ha, we look like Darth Vader," Jerry laughed, his voice muffled by the mask. "Clayton, I am your father."

Clay's head sagged visibly. "Too soon, buddy. Too soon."

Jerry, the weight of what he had just said beginning to sink in, pulled the mask up and reached out for Clay's shoulder.

"I'm so sorry, I didn't think…"

"It's cool, just…you know…maybe a touch more sensitivity in these difficult times?"

"You got it, buddy," Jerry replied. "I'll try to think before I say anything else from here on out. But it's gonna be tough for me. You know I ain't always the brightest bulb in the sign." He brought his mask back down over his face. "Look in your heart, you know it to be true."

Despite himself, Clay chuckled. "Awright, I think we're

ready. Let's go."

Clay moved to the opposite door and slipped inside, then hung back while Jerry crept up. He could see the old woman's form silhouetted by the kaleidoscope light beaming in through the rose window behind the altar. She was definitely small and her hair was short and in neatly kempt curls that spilled out of the back of a kerchief tied under her chin. Jerry got within a few rows of her and stopped, waving for Clay to advance. Clay gripped the gun in both hands and walked down, keeping his weapon trained on the lady.

As he got closer he could begin to pick up the distinct old lady scent of mothballs and ancient perfume. He stopped short of parallel with Jerry then crept backwards into the row of pews, prepared to duck into cover if the woman got frisky.

Jerry looked to Clay for permission to go ahead and, getting a nod, took a deep breath and cleared his throat. He waited a moment, watching for a reaction but getting none, so he tried it again, louder this time. Still, the old woman simply sat, her hands folded in front of her and her eyes closed.

Jerry looked to Clay, who shrugged and made a gesture with his hands that could have been rightly interpreted either as a command to talk or a desire for a hand puppet. Jerry took another deep breath.

"Excuse me, ma'am?"

The woman slowly—very, very slowly—turned her head to look at Jerry.

"Oh sh—" Jerry ran at the woman, arms out, and threw himself at her lap. "Gramma! Thank god you're-"

Gramma stood and took what looked like a defensive posture, one leg slightly behind the other and her knees bent, as though preparing to break a tackle. Jerry pulled up short of his hug and shrunk back, moaning.

"Nooooo…no, Gramma, you can't be-"

She snapped her head around and looked directly at Clay, sensing him for the first time. Faster than either of the boys had ever seen her move, she stepped up on the pew she was standing in front of and tore off at Clay, leaping over the arm rest at the end of the row then clearing a pew in a single jump to land on the one he was hiding behind. Clay promptly abandoned his planned cover and instinctively stepped back, taking the edge of the seat in the back of his knees and crumbling involuntarily into a sitting position.

He raised the gun and aimed it at Jerry's gramma's face, but she knocked it away easily and, with a single impressive but utterly graceless leap, got herself over the pew she was standing on and onto Clay's lap. She tried to plant her mouth on his, but ran into his mask. Puzzled, she pulled back while Clay pushed her gingerly – making a concerted effort not to accidentally touch her breasts – and bucked his hips to try to throw her off. She gripped his shoulders tightly and clung to his leg with her thighs, examining the mask with a doggish look of curiosity.

"No…fuck…no no no…Jerry, get this bitch offa me!"

"She ain't a bitch, Clay, she's my Gramma and…well, ok yeah, she is kinda a bitch, but still-"

"Jerry, just fucking get her—"

With an almost effortless swipe, Gramma tore the mast from Clay's face. She licked his cheek as his pushes became weaker. She was tearing his shirt off before either boy even knew what was happening.

"Oh shit, Clay!" Jerry yelled, then reached back for his gun. He aimed at the woman who was now aggressively licking Clay's nipple. Clay had stopped struggling entirely and was running his hand through her hair, pulling the babushka off. "Clay, you sick fuck, that's my Gramma! Get away from her!"

Clay utterly ignored Jerry and worked his hands down, awkwardly reaching around Gramma's head and arms to undo her powder-blue blouse and peel it back from her loose, pale skin. Somewhere in the back of his head were a thousand different voices screaming at him, telling him that this was wrong, that you don't make out with your best friend's grandmother, that you don't fuck old women at all, and something even further back, even quieter, screaming something about survival, but he utterly ignored them. He had never realized how intoxicating the smell of

Gold Bond powder could be. All he could think about was her withered body and the slack, flabby lips that were making their way down his torso.

He scrabbled with the industrial-strength clasps at the back of her entirely utilitarian and unintentionally ironic Maidenform bra, getting it loose with no small effort and freeing Gramma's small, flaccid breasts. He pawed them eagerly, the gelatinous sacks bulging between his fingers, her shriveled nipples becoming stiff against his palms.

He could hear another voice off in the distance, screaming at him to stop and to "get your filthy fucking hands off of my Gramma", but he paid it no mind either. He gasped as he felt the cold, soft, spongy skin of Gramma's fingers work their way under the waist of his jeans and cup his cock. Then, suddenly, she was gone.

Jerry dragged his Gramma away from Clay, torn between his grief at her having become one of *them* and his disgust at having to clutch fistfuls of her clammy, swagged belly flesh to pull her off of his best friend. She kicked and screamed, her elbows landing against his sides with a force that threatened to knock the breath out of him, but she couldn't get a solid foothold with which to free herself on account of the enormous panties tangled around her ankles.

Clay's mind slowly cleared and, once he realized what had happened, he struggled to reinstate the previous haze in order to wipe the memories of groping Jerry's Gramma's sandbag tits from his consciousness. He looked up and saw Jerry struggling to put her in a full nelson, the fluidity of her flesh making the task difficult. He stood, walked shakily into the aisle, and steadied himself against the backs of the pews.

"Hold her steady, Jer. I just need a second to catch my breath, then I'll end her."

Jerry's face went white. "No fucking way, Clay," he grunted, wrestling with his nearly-stripped grandmother. "You can't kill my gramma! And you can't fuck her, either, Clay. Two rules."

"Jerry, she's gone. Let's give her a dignified death, ok?"

He looked over at the panting creature struggling to get loose of her grandson, her skin swaying in hypnotic swirls instigated by the movement of her torso and her gibbous breasts swinging back and forth like pendulums. "Well, you know, as dignified as she's gonna get at this point."

"No, Clay! No! We ain't puttin' her down."

Clay sighed. "Jerry, we have to. She's dangerous. I know it sucks. Believe me, I do. We killed both my folks yesterday. But it has to be done."

"They might find a cure, Clay! We can keep her locked up safe 'til then. She ain't dangerous now, I got her under contr—"

Gramma swung her hip back into Jerry's pelvis, knocking him off balance and pulling her sensible tan skirt up over her waist, exposing her groin to Clay. It struck Clay that he'd never seen a senior citizen's pubic hair before, and that it was odd that despite the rest of her hair turning a respectable silver, she had a tangled thicket of black below the waist.

He didn't have time to evaluate how much that knowledge nauseated him, though, as Gramma threw her head backward into Jerry's face, mashing his mask into his lower jaw, then immediately flung herself back at Clay. He screamed like a child as they crunched to the ground, Gramma's bony elbow digging in to Clay's solar plexus. His head bounced off the wooden floor with a thunk. He weakly tried to push himself away with his legs, scrambling against the heavily lacquered wooden floor of the aisle, but Gramma scrambled up his torso and spun around, facing his feet. She locked her knees against his sides and went to work unbuckling his belt.

His head swimming with a crippling combination of pain, fear, arousal and mild concussion, Clay reached his fingers up toward the sagging lips of Gramma's cunt. A sudden wave of nausea from his head trauma washed over him, and the sickness compounded on the undercurrent of revulsion at what he was doing, snapping him back momentarily.

He reached for the pistol he kept at his waist, then realized she had knocked it out of his hands. In desperation he torqued his body around, trying to get at whatever weapon was currently grinding itself into his lower back. He burrowed a hand underneath himself and felt a pistol grip sticking out of his waist.

He wrapped his fingers around it just as Gramma managed to pull his pants down around his knees. Her fingers wrapped around his cock again and he almost gave in, but the twinge of queasiness rumbling around his stomach urged him to make her stop. He pulled the pistol out with a triumphant scream, leveled it at the back of her head just as she lowered her mouth to his groin, and squeezed the trigger.

"DIE!" He shouted. The BBs bounced harmlessly off her skull. Gramma stopped and turned back, a quizzical expression on her slack face, then lowered her head back down, taking the head of his prick between her lips.

"*Fuck!*" Clay screamed. Jerry scrambled to his feet and rushed at the old woman, preparing a kick to the head. "No!" Clay shouted. "Don't kick her in the face while she's got my cock in her mouth!"

Jerry pulled up short. "Well what the fuck am I supposed to do?"

As the first rush of ecstasy and terror flooded Clay's brain, he had a flash of inspiration. He grabbed Gramma's hips and pulled her back toward him.

"Clay, stop it," Jerry yelled, covering his eyes. "You are *not* allowed to sixty-nine my Gramma!"

Clay brought the BB gun up and, hands trembling, shoved it into Gramma's twat. He took a deep breath, then immediately reconsidered. This wasn't so bad. Sure, she was old, but she definitely knew what she was doing, and he hadn't had a blowjob in so long, and-

He pulled the trigger, emptying the tiny pellets into Gramma's cervix. She writhed on top him, her screams muffled by her full mouth. Fearing the loss of his genitals, Clay threw his hips to the side, tumbling her off of him and freeing himself from her mouth. Gramma let out an unearthly, grinding noise and vomited what looked like chunks of raw meat and mayonnaise onto the pews. As

Clay stood and pulled his pants back on, she gave one last racking spasm and lay still, blood pooling between her legs.

Jerry took his hands away from his eyes and sighed at the mess, his shoulders slumping.

"What did you do to her, Clay?"

Clayton shrugged. "For some reason—and I swear I wasn't controlling this—I started to imagine it was Tara instead of your grandma. Like, back at the gas station when she was all glistening with sweat and her shirt was sticking to her, outlining her—" He sighed, shook his head and cleared his throat.

"Well, that reminded me of what she said about the things growing on their junk, and how she kicked that dude in the sack and he died. And then I remembered how we done that to that lumberjack on the way here. Figured it would work the same." He looked down at Gramma with half a smile. "Looks like I was right for once." He turned to Jerry, who was staring at him slack-jawed. "Sorry, dude. It was her or me." He zipped his fly and put his arm around Jerry's shoulder. "You gonna be ok?"

"I'll be fine, I guess. But I wouldn't mind a little sensitivity in these difficult times, as the man says. Also,can you do something for me, Clay?"

"Sure, buddy. Anything you need."

"Can you take your arm off my shoulder? It was way too close to my Gramma's pussy for you to be puttin' it all up near my face right now."

Clay sheepishly pulled his arm away and Jerry walked toward the altar, gathering himself. Clay tentatively brought his hand up to his nose and sniffed.

"Well, I smell clean, so I reckon I didn't get any of her juices on me. But keep an eye on me, will ya? If I start to, like, eat you or anything, promise to shoot me in the head right away, ok? I don't wanna be one of them, no matter what."

Jerry nodded wordlessly.

"Promise me, Jer. I'm serious."

"I promise. Now please, can I just have one minute to clear my head from all this?"

Clay nodded. They both sat, each in his own pew, and stared at the altar.

The uncomfortable silence of the moment was broken by Tara crashing through the doors to the sanctuary.

"Hey Tara," Jerry said emptily. "Clay was just talking about you. Right after he shot my Gramma to death." Clay shot him a look that was half a plea for silence and half the threat of a slow, painful death. Tara seemed not to hear them as she began pushing pews against the door.

"Whatcha doin' there, Tara?" Clay asked.

"Block the fucking doors," she said, panting with exertion. "Do it now. No time for questions."

The boys ran up the aisle and helped her, piling as much of the detritus of the church against the two doors as they could. As they worked, Clay hazarded a question.

"So…the abstinence club?"

"They are *so* not practicing what they preach," Tara said as Jerry dragged a wooden podium up from the dais and tossed it atop the pile of pews. "I always thought watching an orgy of sex-crazed Methodist teenagers would be hot. I was so very, very wro—"

She was interrupted by a pounding at the door that was so forceful it knocked all three back on their heels. Tara shot Jerry a look that encompassed the entirety of the malice of Clay's previous look and added the explicit threat of castration. "Some great idea you had there, Jer. Abstinence club, my ass." In the corner of her eye she saw the old woman's corpse laying in its rapidly congealing puddle. "What happened here?"

"Clay killed my gramma, but first he got his tip a little wet."

"*What*? Clay, did you fuck Jerry's zombie grandma?"

"No," Clay stammered, backing away with his hands up. "I got half a hummer off her before I came to my senses and shot her in the cooch."

"You saved his life, Tara," Jerry said with a smirk.

"I did? But I was downstairs with the Young Fuckbuddies club."

"He was fantasizin' about you while Gramma was slobbin' his knob, which made him remember about the deadly crotch shots."

Tara's face froze in an unreadable expression. She slowly slid her gaze from Jerry to Clay, who was still backing away as if she were a particularly hungry and harried badger. "You were what, now?"

"Jerry's just," Clay stammered, "...you know, it's...haha...funny thing, I—"

There was another thunderous crash at the door and the wood of the door frame came shooting at them.

"That door ain't gonna last long," Clay said, regaining his composure. "We gotta get outta here."

"Where?" Tara asked, frantically looking around. "There's no way outside from here." Her eyes landed on a door at the back of the dais. "Where does that go?" She asked, pointing.

"The reverend's office, I think," said Jerry. "Nothin' back there but the steps to the bell tower."

"Well, it's a few more doors we can put between us and them," Clay said.

"Yeah, but then what? We fly away? Getting ourselves trapped up on the bell tower is about the worst thing we can do."

There was a final thud and the door exploded into splinters. Several small, slim arms, each bearing a pink rubber wristband reading "I'm saving myself because I'm Saved" reached through the spaces between the piled junk in front of the door. The mountain of pews, books and candelabra began to sway unsteadily.

"No choice now," Clay said. "Let's get up to the roof and figure out what to do from there." He took off running toward the front of the church.

Tara took a few steps, then turned to see Jerry staring at the body on the ground.

"Come on, Jer. We have to go now."

"I just want one more second with her, if that's ok."

She walked to his side and took his hand. "I'm sorry, Jerry. I know it can't be easy. But we're going to be chin-deep in horny, bloodthirsty high school children in a few minutes, so we really need to—" Her voice caught in her throat as she saw Gramma's face for the first time and, quite against her will, a small chuckle escaped her lips. Jerry peeled his eyes away from the corpse and glared at her.

"Something funny?"

"I'm sorry," Tara said, flushing. "It's just...your grandmother..."

"Yeah?"

Tara bit her lip, trying to suppress another laugh. "I met her at Cassie's funeral. She uh...she said she hoped to see me in church some day. Looks like she got her wish."

Jerry smiled wistfully. "Yeah, that sounds like her." He squeezed Tara's hand. "She was kind of a battleaxe, but I'm gonna miss her somethin'—"

The pile of pews tipped with a crash. Tara and Jerry both looked up just in time to see the lithe, slim form of a teenage girl scramble up the wreckage, her white church blouse drenched in blood, showing the outline of her pink training bra, and her plaid skirt in tatters. She looked directly at Jerry with a ravenous lust generally only seen in heroin-riddled porn stars. She reared back and steadied herself with her hand against the pew she was standing on, then leapt at him.

Unfortunately for her, her pink rubber wristband caught on the ornamental scrolled back of the pew, causing her to do an awkward somersault and land on her back with a sickening snap.

Tara tightened her grip on Jerry's hand and pulled him toward the back door. He gave a little resistance, gazing longingly back at the girl who was frantically tugging, tipping the pew in an effort to free herself. Clay stuck his head out of the office door.

"What's taking you two so lo—*oh shit!* Run!"

Tara gave one last mighty heave and managed to whip Jerry around her so she could push him the rest of the way. She didn't stop when she heard the pew tumble off of the pile, followed by another crunch and a howl of frustration from the girl. Clay ducked back inside as she pushed Jerry through the door. Once they were all in, she took one last peek at the barricade before shutting the door. The girl had managed to tip the heavy pew, which fell onto her midsection, pinning her to the floor. Several ribs jutted from her chest around the edge of the seat, and she wriggled weakly, trying to free herself. A second girl, mousy brown hair pulled into pigtails, had scrambled over the barricade and was chewing the tenderized meat off of the first girl's mangled arm. Blood covered her glasses. Three more girls and a boy—nude and young enough to only have the barest sprouting of hair around his raging erection—were making their way down the pile and into the sanctuary. Tara choked back a gag, flung the door shut and helped Jerry and Clay push a desk, several bookcases and a flimsy, cheap office chair against it.

The Church Office

"I can't be the only one who's noticed that there aren't any windows here," Tara said, slumped against the wall in an attempt to catch her breath.

"There's always the bell tower," Clay said, inclining his head toward a flimsy wooden door at the back of the room.

"And just what the fuck will we do from there?" Tara asked. She was exhausted, drained to the point where she couldn't even muster her usually enthusiastic sarcasm.

Clay didn't raise his eyes from the floor. "Good point. We should just stay here and die."

"Maybe there's a way to climb down from the tower," said Jerry without even a trace of hope in his voice. "Or we could just fuckin' throw ourselves off and see if we grow wings. Whatever. I don't care too much, anymore. I'm sick of runnin'." He curled up in a ball. The scratching noises on the other side of the sanctuary door were joined by the occasional booming thump that shook the furniture piled in front of it.

"Well no matter what we do, this barricade's not gonna hold much longer," Clay said. "Who knew little girls could be so strong?" There was a crash and a chorus of high-pitched screams that sounded like footage of old Beatles concerts. "I think they've managed to draw in some other stragglers from outside. There's definitely a few adult moans mixed in there. I reckon they'll just keep at it 'til they get through. Probably more of 'em on the way too. We're completely f—"

"Shh," Tara hissed, throwing a hand up in front of Clay's mouth and cocking her head to the side. "Do you hear that?"

Clay fell silent and strained his ears. The noise at the door continued unabated, but there was a new, thrumming noise underlining it, a whir like an unbalanced washing machine. "Is that…"

"It's a helicopter!" Tara shouted, jumping to her feet. "Holy shit, guys, we're saved!" She looked at Clay apologetically. "I guess there's some merit to the bell tower, after all."

Clay smiled. "I been on a roll lately," he said. "C'mon, let's go!"

The three filed through the door to the tower and looked up uncertainly at the rickety staircase that led to the top. Though all of the public areas of the church had been refurbished over the years, the interior of the bell tower was still the same sagging wooden mess it had been for more than a century and a half.

"We should find something to block this door off with," Clay said, looking back at the flimsy slab of wood hanging behind them. "In case that horde of little girls breaks through before the chopper can get us."

They all made a cursory search of the base of the tower, but though covered in the dust of ages it was completely free of anything not directly nailed to the wall. With a great effort, they dragged the last few standing bookshelves from the office into the tower, closed the door and barricaded it.

Tara took a deep breath and started slowly up the stairs, testing each one to ensure it would hold her weight before stepping fully onto it. After the first dozen or so she decided that despite its age and general state of disrepair, the staircase must be structurally sound. She picked up her pace. The pulse of the helicopter was growing louder then softer in turns, which she assumed was due to it circling the town. She reached the top of the stairs and pushed open a trap door at the top, climbing up a short ladder into the bell house.

The bell house was open on all sides, affording a breathtaking view of the quaint little town below. The first thing Tara noticed was the near-choking black smoke that cast the town into a haze and threatened to block out the sun entirely. She turned to look south and saw the entirety of downtown Fulton Flats in flames.

"Holy shit," she said, turning to Clay, who was just emerging from the trap door. "We really fucked your hometown up, didn't we?"

Clay lumbered over next to her, panting from the exercise of climbing more stairs than he had in a good, long time. "This shithole was beggin' for it," he said, and grinned. He pointed out toward the east side of town. "There. The chopper. Look, it's circlin' around."

Tara squinted and saw, just barely discernible against the background of black smoke, a black military helicopter making lazy circles over the town.

"We've got to find a way to signal to them," she said, frantically. Jerry pulled himself through the trapdoor.

"You see 'em?"

"Yeah," said Clay, pointing. "Out over Hoffmann's farm. They're coming back our way." He turned to Jerry, his eyes lighting up. "Hey Jer, you got any flares left in your pack?"

Jerry slung the bag around his shoulder and rummaged through, then triumphantly pulled out a brown paper-wrapped tube. "Yup," he said, grinning. "One left. We gonna use it to get their attention?"

"Let's wait until they get closer," Tara said. "I don't want to waste our only flare. I want to make sure they know exactly where we are."

They paced, individually, each too nervous to talk and too excited to stand still. The helicopter made a languid swing over the farmland to the east and slowly worked its way back, apparently searching for something on the ground. Tara squinted, trying to gauge whether or not they could see the creatures milling around. It took a full five minutes, but eventually the chopper swooped over the raging inferno that was downtown and headed toward the church.

"Ok, Jerry, light the flare," Tara said breathlessly, then tuned to him, grabbed his arm and looked him in the face very seriously. "Jerry, of everything you have ever done in your entire life, this is the most important not to fuck up. Do you understand me? Do not, *do not* fuck this up. Light the flare, then wave it over your head." He opened his mouth, but she put a preemptive finger over it. "Don't speak. Talking requires too much of your concentration. Just nod if you understand."

Jerry nodded solemnly and Tara released his arm. He took a long, slow breath to steady himself then pulled the cap off, set it against the end of the flare and looked back at Tara. She gave a single nod of approval, and he struck the cap against the flare's wick, sending it into an immediate shower of sparks that were instantly caught by the wind. Tara screamed and Clay nearly fell through the trap door jumping back from the sudden geyser of fire pointed at him.

"Hold it away from us, dickhead!" Clay screamed, and Jerry immediately turned to face the wind, holding the flare over his head. Clay and Tara moved to the side to shelter themselves behind the corner of the bell tower.

"Remember when I demanded that you not fuck it up, Jerry?" Tara said, her voice icy. "Remember that? Because it was all of seven seconds ago, and clearly you don't have a lot of retention for instructions."

Jerry set his face in a grimace and, without a word, began waving the flare back and forth. The helicopter continued to make its way toward them at its lugubrious pace, not seeming to have noticed the flare.

"Do you think they see us?" asked Clay.

"I don't know," Tara said. "They haven't picked up the pace at all."

"Wave it better, Jer," Clay said.

"Better how?"

"I don't know, just…just make them see it."

Jerry screwed his face up in concentration and began flailing his arms, sending the sparks everywhere in the tiny bell loft. Tara and Clay both scuttled for cover again, but neither lodged a complaint about Jerry's method. Encouraged, Jerry began to jump up and down.

"Hey, fuckers, we're over here!" he shouted. "Come save us. Hey, you see me? Hurry up, goddammit, we got a pack of hungry abstinence-only zombies fixin' to take us out for dinner and a lay."

Swept up in the moment, both Clay and Tara started yelling, too, leaning over the side of the bell loft, waving their arms and screaming. Jerry, encouraged by their support, made increasingly wilder and wilder movements with his arms until, inevitably, he lost his grip on the flare. In sudden silence, and as if in slow motion, it spiraled out of his hand and sailed in a perfect, graceful arc over the roof of the church and into the lawn, where it disappeared into the brittle foliage of a tree. The three stood stock still, in shock and horrified that their last, best hope of being seen had just buried itself so deeply in the branches that only a few meager sparks even managed to fall to the ground.

The helicopter, apparently entirely unaware of the closest thing to a fireworks display that Fulton Flats had ever seen, made a long turn and started heading south, back towards downtown.

Jerry turned slowly to face the others. "I-"

Tara started to interrupt Jerry, but Clay immediately turned to her and shushed her.

"It's ok, buddy. We all make mistakes. I mean, you make a fuck of a lot more than most people, but I guess it's really our fault for trusting you with the single most important thing any of us have ever had to do in our entire lives."

Jerry nodded sadly and turned his back so the others wouldn't see him cry.

"What the fuck was that about?" Tara whispered testily. "I told him…I warned him that he couldn't fuck this up."

Clay stepped closer to her, and for the first time she noticed how big he was, how intimidating he could be when he put his mind to it.

"He's my best friend, and if we're all gonna die here today, I don't want him dyin' with that on his conscience. If you were so worried about it you shoulda lit the goddamned flare yourself."

Tara, taken aback by the sudden change in Clay, could say nothing. She turned and sat on the ledge, watching the chopper retreat into the distance. Clay wandered to the far side of the tower, leaned out over the edge and spat, watching his phlegm drift slowly to the ground below. He sighed, snorted, and spat again. He wondered which would be worse: being eaten and fucked into undeath by the monsters down in the church or splattering himself in the parking lot below. By his reckoning, the jump would be quicker and would at least carry the momentary thrill of freefall before he hit. On the other hand, giving himself up to the zombies would mean he got laid one last time. It was a difficult choice, and he wished he had a quarter to flip to help him decide.

"Hey Tara," he said, turning back to her. She didn't respond. She was staring blankly into the distance, not even watching the helicopter anymore, lost in her own thoughts. "Tara," he said, a bit louder. She took a deep breath and turned to look at him. "I got something to ask you, and I want you to hear me out cuz it's gonna sound a little weird. But just hear me out, ok?"

He waited. She narrowed her eyes, but after a moment she nodded silently.

"We're pretty much definitely gonna die, right?"

She waited for him to go on, but he just looked at her. She nodded again.

"Well, since that's the case and all, I was thinking…I mean, I wonder if we…" He looked away and cleared his throat. When he looked back, she was still staring at him expectantly, her face a mask of calm, chilly indifference. He gathered his courage, but realizing that no matter how much courage he managed to gather he couldn't look her in the eyes, he instead fixed his gaze on her knees.

"You're a…well, you're a woman, after all. And I was wondering. You're awful pretty, in your way, and I was thinking maybe just one time before we die we can-"

"Don't say it," she said, her voice like iron.

"No, now, hear me out. All this…well, this sex goin' on around us and the three of us…ain't it just ironic that we're stayin' alive by not really livin'? I mean, if I have to go down, I wanna just…you know…"

"Don't you fucking say it, Clayton."

"…*go down* one last time, if you get my drift, so…"

"Shut up now and I won't make any attempt to kick your balls into your skull before the zombies get the chance to lay a finger on you."

"…so I was wondering if maybe you and me could do it just once before the end." He looked up, the hesitant expectation in his face a clear indication that he hadn't heard a word she'd said. "I'm real good in bed, I swear. Both the girls I been with said so."

Tara took a deep breath to keep from flinging her entire weight into a punch to his kidney. She steadied herself, licked her lips, opened her mouth to speak, thought better of it, took another deep breath, turned, punched the wall until her knuckles were bloody, turned back to Clay, took a third deep breath, and spoke.

"Why don't you ask Jerry?"

"Huh?" Clay said. Jerry turned at hearing his name, tears streaming down his face, then quickly turned away again.

"Why don't you ask Jerry? He has just as much interest in fucking you as I do, and it would probably be a lot more meaningful, close as you two are."

"I don't under—"

"I'm not here to help you get your rocks off one last time, Clay. I'm not interested in having sex with you, or with Jerry, or with *any* man. I'm a lesbian, Clay. You do know what that means, right? In the real world—as opposed to the porn you've obviously been watching—it means that I'm not attracted to dudes. I don't care for penises. I don't like facial hair. I think balls are gross. I don't want to fuck you, not even if it's my last chance on earth to have a sweaty redneck rub his cock on me."

To his credit, Clay looked rather abashed. To his discredit, he couldn't keep his mouth shut.

"How do you know you don't like it? Maybe you've just never been with the right guy."

Tara closed her eyes. She felt her pulse thudding in her temples.

"Well," she said through clenched teeth, "it looks like I'm fated to die the way I lived: having my sexuality questioned by assholes. Look, Clay, it's not a phase. It's not a passing fancy. It's not a goddamned *choice*. I don't want to have sex with men. It's who I am. And what's more, if I did somehow manage to hit my head and answer my grandmother's prayers by suddenly becoming straight, you are approximately the *last* man I would want to spend my final moments being groped by."

Clay started to respond, somehow managed to think better of it, muttered "sorry" under his breath and sat back on his ledge, dangling his feet out of the bell loft and once again contemplating whether or not to jump. A few more moments of silence followed in which nobody in the bell tower of the Fulton Flats First Methodist Church could bear to look at each other. The helicopter continued its slow, widening circle of downtown, apparently surveying the damage.

"I wonder who they are," Tara said, almost wistfully.

Clay let the comment go unanswered for a moment, unsure of whether he was permitted to speak to her again or not. When it became evident that Jerry was still not going to take part in the conversation, he ventured a "Who?"

"The people in the helicopter. It's hard to make out from here, but it looks like there's some sort of symbol painted on the side. Like maybe a government seal or a TV station logo."

"Way they're hoverin', I'd guess it was the news. Channel 9 out of Boise comes up these parts when something interesting happens, which is pretty much never. But I'd say the whole city bein' on fire and the dead eating the living probably counts as newsworthy."

Tara nodded silently and continued to stare out across the ever-expanding fire. As it crept to the west it threatened to join up with the forest fire creeping down from the hills. She pictured the entire town in flames and, despite herself, couldn't feel too bad about it. Maybe the fire would keep whatever happened here from spreading. Maybe they saved the world by blowing up that gas station. Maybe they'd pin a medal to her corpse.

"Hey Tara, do you have a girlfriend?" Clay asked sheepishly.

She narrowed her eyes and turned her gaze toward him. "And why would you want to know that?"

"Just curious. I mean, I reckon we're about to die here and I thought it'd be nice to at least get to know you a little."

It wasn't quite the apology she had hoped for, but she sensed it was as good as she was going to get.

"Yeah, I have a girlfriend. I mean, I guess I do. Sorta."

"How can you have a 'sorta girlfriend'?"

"I met her on the internet. On one of those hookup sites. Adult Dating Connection, that sort of thing. But she lives in Chicago, so we're not exclusive or anything."

"You ever fly out there to see her?"

Tara clicked her tongue and shook her head, her disapproval obvious. "Of course not. That's how you end up on *Dateline*."

"What made you move to a place like this? I mean, from a big fancy city like San Francisco and all. What in heaven's name could Fulton Flats have that you'd want?"

Tara sighed, her head tipping down to look at the ground beneath the bell tower.

"I moved here precisely because it *isn't* San Francisco. I got tired of the big, crazy city. It wears on you after a while."

"But being as you're...I mean, there ain't a lot of chance for a..." he visibly struggled with the correct nomenclature. "...for a lesbian to meet other...you know...lesbians out here. I mean, you got your girl in Chicago and that's nice and all, but don't you like being around your own kind? Don't you wanna meet other girls and, like, do whatever it is lesbians like to do? Scissor each other and stuff, I guess?"

Tara smirked. "We also sometimes talk."

"You know what I mean."

"Honestly, I moved here to get away from lesbians. Or, really, one particular lesbian." She fell silent and stared off at the helicopter in the distance.

"Bad relationship?" Clay asked.

"My only real long-term girlfriend," she replied, almost mechanically. "Betsy. I was so fucking in love with her. But she...let's just say she was real bad for me. We were together for three years, and even before we dated we ran in all the same circles. Even in a big city like San Francisco it's hard to avoid someone when they're bound up in almost every aspect of your

life. I had to get out, and this a place I knew she'd never find me."
She turned back and looked at Clay. "Funny, I hadn't even been
able to admit that to myself until just now. I ended up in Fulton
Flats because of Betsy Giles. And now I'm up a bell tower waiting
to get devoured by sex zombies. Because of Betsy Giles. What a
cunt."

She fell silent again. Clay decided not to push the issue any
further. He cocked his head for a moment, listening, then walked
over to the trap door and lifted it, poking his head down into the
darkness.

"You hear that?" he asked, straightening back up. "They're at
the door down there. Just starting to hit on it, sounds like."

"Guess it won't be long now," Tara said, still staring at the
chopper in the distance.

"Guess not," Clay replied, closing the trap door and sitting on
it. They fell silent again.

"Hey," Tara said after a moment. "What's that noise?"

"I think the wood of the door is starting to break," Clay said.

"No, not that. I mean that hissing sound. You hear it?"

Clay cocked his head and listened. "Yeah, I do. What you
reckon it is?"

Jerry turned fully around for the first time since he fumbled
the flare. The others had more or less forgotten he was even in the
tower with them. He held out his hand, and in it was the walkie-
talkie from his pack.

"I been listening to the channels," he said, his eyes still red
from recent tears. "Thought whoever's in that 'copter might be on
a walkie too. Ain't heard nothin' so far though."

Tara and Clay were dumbstruck.

"That's…that's a shockingly good idea," Tara said, pulling
her own walkie from her bag. "Clay, you still got yours?"

"No, it's with the rest of my supplies down in the church."

"Well, we'll have to make do with two then," she said,
holding the walkie up to her mouth. "Unknown helicopter, please
come in. We are civilians trapped in the bell tower of the church
just north of your position. Please respond, we are in need of

immediate evacuation."

There was a brief hiss of static as she released the talk button, then silence. They waited, all three staring at the radio. Nothing.

"We have to try every channel. Jerry, that was channel 4. I'll go up, you go down. Repeat that message then wait for twenty or thirty seconds to see if it gets a response. Then move to the next channel down the dial. Got it?"

Jerry nodded, adjusted the channel selector on his walkie to 3 and lifted it to his mouth. "Come in, chopper. We're stuck up the church tower north of you right now, and we sure could use some help. Come back." He released the button and waited.

"Unknown helicopter, please come in," Tara repeated while Jerry waited for a response. "We are three civilians trapped in the tower of the First Methodist Church, just north of where you are now. We are in dire need of help. Please respond."

Jerry switched to channel two and repeated. Waited. Channel one. Tara tried six, then seven. Jerry flipped down to sixteen, the highest channel. They met in the middle with Tara on channel eleven and Jerry on Twelve. They had gotten no response so far. The helicopter continued to circle downtown, seeming to iris in their search radius. Jerry and Tara looked at each other hesitantly.

"Last chance," Jerry said. "Let's do them together, ok? That way I won't be so nervous. I can't handle screwing up one more thing today."

Tara walked over and gave him a quick but sincere hug. "It's not your fault if this doesn't work, Jer. It was a great idea." She took a deep breath. "You ready?"

Jerry nodded. They pushed their talk buttons.

"Come in helicopter," Tara said. "There are three of us stuck in the bell tower of the church north of your position. We need help. There are things down in the church trying to kill us. Please respond."

"Yo, chopper," Jerry said at the same time, his words jumbling over Tara's. "We need help. We're stuck up the tower at the church north from where you're at. There are three of us and if you don't get here soon a buncha monsters are gonna bust down the door and fuck us dead."

They looked at each other and released their talk buttons. There was the usual quick burst of static, then quiet. Moments passed, vast expanses of empty time, eons of silence. Tara set her walkie down on the ledge as she slumped to the floor.

"Well, we tried," she said.

Clay sidled over and sat down next to her, putting his arm around her shoulder just as the first sob shook her frame.

"Goddammit, we were so close," she whimpered through the tears. "Why didn't we leave with Dr. Jerrit?"

"It's ok," Clay said, wiping at the rivulet of water running down her face. "Look, we did our best. And maybe that chopper'll turn around and come this way before they get through the door, you never know."

As if to punctuate the absurdity of the idea, a resounding crash echoed up the inside of the tower.

"Welp, that'll be the first hinge of the door bustin' off," Jerry said. "Look, guys, I didn't wanna say anything, but...well, I got three bullets left in my pistol, and..."

He held the gun out in front of him, laid across his palms like an offering. Clay looked at it with a mixture of horror and relief. It was certainly a better option than either of those he had previously contemplated.

"I don't think I can do anyone else, guys," Jerry continued. He turned the gun in his palm and wrapped his fingers around the grip, tentatively slipping his finger over the trigger. "I wanna be first. My fault we're gonna die anyway, so I might as we-"

He was interrupted by a burst of static.

He froze, the gun pointed at his face, raised halfway to his mouth. He turned his eyes on Tara. She was taking her hands away from her face, where she had lifted them to block out the sight of his suicide. He looked to Clay, who only stared back.

"Did you just hear—"

There was another burst of static, followed by a voice.

"Come in trapped civilians, this is CDC chopper 14. Did you say something was trying to 'fuck you dead'? Please repeat, I'm pretty sure I can't possibly have heard that right."

Jerry didn't even remember dropping the gun. Clay and Tara screamed and scrambled when it hit the ground, but it didn't go off. Jerry reached around his back to where he had clipped the walkie-talkie.

"CDC chopper 14, this is Jerry Stone. Oh thank God you heard us, I was about to blow my brains out here!"

"Jerry, this is Marsh Ganley. Please advise us of your situation."

"Well, you heard right. There's a buncha zombies down there, they're just about to bust through the door and come up here and get us. They wanna fuck us or eat us, dependin' on if they're boys or girls. Pretty sure it's the abstinence club." He paused, looking at the other two, then his eyes grew huge and he hit the talk button again. "Over!"

There was a moment of silence, then Ganley's voice returned. "Jerry, I hate to ask this, but is there someone else there who can explain what's going on?"

Without a word, Tara held her hand out. Jerry sheepishly put the walkie into it.

"Mr. Ganley, this is Tara Sokoloff. There are three of us, we're trapped in the bell tower of the First Methodist Church. We're a couple miles north of where you're circling right now. If you look north, you should see us, the tower is the tallest thing in town."

"Copy, Miss Sokoloff. Can you please explain your situation?"

"As I said, we're trapped in the tower. There are a number of...hostiles, I guess? Let's say hostiles. They're just about to break through the door at the bottom of the stairs here and if they do, we will not survive. We have only three rounds of ammunition to fight them off."

"Copy, Miss Sokoloff. We are preparing to come to your assistance, but before we can, I must ask you a somewhat indelicate question."

Tara scrunched her eyebrows and looked at Clay and Jerry,

waiting for a response that didn't come. After a moment she realized that Ganley was waiting for permission.

"Go ahead, Mr. Ganley."

"Has any member of your group had any sexual contact with another person in the last forty-eight hours?"

Tara laughed. "Funny you should ask."

"No," Ganley replied, "I assure you there is nothing funny about this. I repeat: has anyone in that tower had any sexual contact with anyone else in the past forty-eight hours?"

"Did Dr. Jerrit send you?" Tara asked.

"Yes ma'am, Dr. Jerrit is the one who tipped us off to what was happening in Fulton. Now please, answer the question."

Tara looked at Clay, whose eyes were silently pleading with her. "No, sir, we've all been doing our best to avoid that particular activity for the last day or so."

"Copy, Miss Sokoloff. We are bringing the chopper around to look for your location. If you could give us some sort of visual guide to-"

Ganley cut off. He didn't need to finish his sentence. Just as the chopper swung north to begin looking for the survivors, the tree on the church's lawn burst into flames.

"Well I'll be damned," Clay said. "Jer, you actually managed to fuck something up so bad it came clear back around to being helpful again!"

Jerry smiled.

"Just follow the burning bush, Mr. Ganley," Tara said, bumping Jerry affectionately with her hip. "Follow the burning bush."

Epilogue – The Chopper

Clay watched out the window as the jets streaked across the sky, their payloads falling almost balletically, drifting to earth and hitting with a thud that shook his bones, made him uncomfortably aware of the organs inside his torso that shifted and squirmed with each blast. The entire valley was in flames now. Most of downtown had burned to the ground, and as the helicopter hovered safely north of the glowing embers of Fulton Flats he felt a twinge of guilt at not feeling worse about the destruction of everything he had ever known.

"Tell me again why you're burnin' the whole goddamned place down," he mumbled into the microphone of the headset he, like everyone else in the chopper, wore over his head.

"Containment," said Ganley. He'd turned out to be a grizzled, hard-looking man in his late thirties, the sort of blocky, square-headed stack of muscles that one typically associates with the Marines more than the Centers for Disease Control. But he also turned out to be remarkably kind and had ordered the chopper to hover instead of immediately evacuating so that Clay, Tara and Jerry could watch the firebombing of their town.

"Our recon suggested there were no survivors left in Fulton, and we can't risk the infection spreading outside of town. Thankfully, the outbreak happened in such a tiny, isolated place. As far as we can tell, no infected managed to get out. The forest fire was a big boon in that regard."

"And will no doubt provide you a cover story for what happened here," Tara said, smirking. She'd been raised to be suspicious of the government and its motives, but she was grudgingly glad that the CDC had been called in. *I would have hated to have died in that tower*, she thought. *Sex-positive atheist, killed in a church by an abstinence club...fuck, I'd never get over the irony.*

"Try to imagine what would happen if word of this got out," said Ganley. He seemed almost bored, leaning out the window smoking a hand-rolled cigarette while the city burned. "Americans don't handle dangerous situations well. Remember the complete shit-show this country turned into after 9/11? The anti-Islamic hysteria? The wars we started? Can you even *dream* of the chaos a sex-borne disease like this would cause? Do you want to give Pat Robertson that kind of fodder?"

Tara nodded. She liked Ganley. He was from Berkeley, he had told her, and his views matched hers more than anyone she had spoken to since she moved to Idaho. She was glad that if she had to be rescued by an 80s-era action movie hero government agent, at least he'd turned out to be a raging liberal.

She turned to look at Jerry, who had been silent since he handed the radio off to her. He wasn't watching the bombing like Clay was. Instead, he sat with his hands folded in his lap, looking straight ahead, his eyes fixed somewhere beyond the bulkhead of the helicopter in front of him.

"Jerry, are you ok? You've been awful quiet."

He turned his head to look at her and smiled weakly.

"I'll be fine, I s'pose. It's just…well, that's it, isn't it? That's the end. Never thought I'd get out of Fulton, and here I am watching it go up in smoke. Now I got no choice. Never been more than an hour's drive away from here before. Now I gotta go live somewhere else. Start over." His face crinkled in thought. "Scared, I guess. Just a little scared."

Tara scooted over on the bench and put her arm around his shoulder. "It's a big step, Jer, but I know you can do it. I did it. Left everything and moved here. You can do it, too."

Jerry leaned against her, almost childishly burying himself in her embrace. She adjusted her weight, not expecting such affection.

"Last I heard, San Francisco's still there," he said, his voice muffled in her shoulder. "You can go back. I ain't never gonna see my Gramma again, or have pie in the Corner Diner, or get drunk on the swings in the park. I can't do none of that, 'cause it's all gone. Cassie's gone." He sighed deeply, but no tears appeared on his face.

Tara squeezed him. "You've got me now, buddy. We'll start over together."

Jerry raised his head, and Clay turned away from the burning town to look at her.

"You mean it?" Clay said. "I mean, you still wanna stick with us? Even after how I was such an asshole, and how Jerry nearly got us killed, like, fifteen different times?"

Tara shrugged. "What the fuck else am I gonna do? I guess we're a team now." Jerry beamed. "But as a team, we will have some ground rules, the first of which is that you never, ever hit on me again. Ever. Or I'll tear your fucking balls off and shove them in your eye sockets, which will be empty because I've also torn your eyes out. Do you understand?"

Jerry nodded. Clay smirked.

"Damn girl, you can't go teasin' a boy with sweet words like that, then make him promise not to come on to you."

Tara silently pointed her left hand at Clay's eyes and her right at his crotch. Then she switched them. Clay laughed.

"Yeah, sure, I promise. I hear y'all make good wing-men anyway. That true?"

Tara rolled her eyes. "Yeah, sure, I'm the master at picking up women. That's why I have an internet girlfriend I've never seen in person."

"Should uh...should I just take off my headset for a few minutes?" Ganley groaned. Tara jumped. She had completely forgotten he was on the same channel as them. "I mean, if you guys want a little privacy..."

"No," said Tara. "I think we're about done with the mushy stuff for the moment."

"What are we gonna do, Mr. Ganley? I mean, everything I own is meltin' to slag down there right now," Clay said.

"Well, we're taking you to the CDC office in Boise first. You'll be debriefed there." Jerry and Clay snickered at the word "debriefed", and Tara, deftly leaning across Jerry's lap, managed to hit both of them in their respective foreheads simultaneously. "From there, I honestly don't know. You guys witnessed an outbreak that the government is going to great lengths to hide."

Clay paled. "Holy shit, they're gonna off us, aren't they? They're gonna get all the info out of us they can, then they'll just make us disappear." Flustered, he tried to stand up and hit his head on the low ceiling of the helicopter's passenger compartment.

"I don't think they're too keen on killing any civilians," Ganley said. "You planning on going to the press about this?"

Tara laughed. "I don't think either of these two numbskulls could give a coherent interview anyway."

"Then my guess is they'll resettle you. You can probably go home to San Fran if you want to, Tara. Or start over somewhere new. I can't say anything on an official level—that's way above my pay grade—but I imagine they'll be generous buying your silence here."

Tara closed her eyes. Start over again. Again. *Well, I'm sure as fuck not sequestering myself in a tiny little mountain town this time. Fool me once...*

"I'm just grateful y'all came to save us," Jerry said. He turned his head, looking out over the conflagration for the first time. "And I've always kinda wanted to watch this city burn to the ground."

"It was a real shithole, wasn't it?" Clay said fondly. "A beat-down, no-horse, redneck shithole. I'll be glad to be quit of it."

Jerry untangled himself from Tara and sidestepped over to where Clay was seated, plopping himself down to watch.

"Remember the time we saved our empty beer cans for a year, and you and me and Cassie built a wall out of 'em around Miss Borson's front door in the middle of the night?" he said.

Clay turned to look at Tara. "That dried-up ol' hag was tryin' to turn this into a dry county. A dry fuckin' county. Can you believe that? What the fuck are you supposed to do with your time in a place like this if you can't drink?"

Tara smiled. That old, familiar tickle was setting in inside her ribcage. Starting over. It was what she'd done her whole life. But this time, she was bringing something along: a pair of big, dumb hicks who had never seen a city bigger than Boise. She was going to be a big sister of sorts, a friend and a guide. A mentor. She was going to help them enter the big, bad world.

And, for the foreseeable future, she was going to be celibate as hell.

Acknowledgments

First and foremost, thanks to Sarah Kunchik, who spends an alarming amount of time patiently listening to my story ideas and nodding politely, and who told me it was ok to shoot an old woman in the vagina as long as the plot called for it and there was at least an equal amount of male genital attacks.

Thanks to my beta readers Sarah, Nina McCollum and Keith Wade. Their suggestions were invaluable, and it's always a thrill and a bit of a terror to have new eyes on something you've spent a year living alone with.

Thanks to Paul Anderson for editing this book FOR GREAT JUSTICE, even though he ~~ruthlessly~~ decimated my beautiful and abundant adverbs.

Thanks to Liam Roche, who started this whole mess with nothing more than a title: STZ. I hope it lived up to your expectations.

Thanks to Yoni Wolf of the band Why? for the use of his awesome words in the frontispiece. This is one of my favorite bands on earth, check them out at whywithaquestionmark.com.

And most of all, thanks to Eric Beebe, Stephanie Kania-Beebe and the whole Post Mortem Press family. There is not a better group of people in the publishing business.

This book, like my first, was largely written under the auspices of National Novel Writing Month. Because friendly competition is the best motivator a slack-ass like me can possibly have.

Made in the USA
Charleston, SC
18 April 2015